PENGUIN BOOKS

Monkey Grip

Helen Garner was born in Geelong in 1942. She has
published many works of fiction, including *Postcards
from Surfers*, *Cosmo Cosmolino* and *The Children's Bach*.
Her fiction has won numerous awards. She is also one
of Australia's most respected non-fiction writers, and
received a Walkley Award for journalism in 1993.

Her most recent books are *The First Stone*, *True
Stories*, *My Hard Heart*, *The Feel of Steel* and *Joe Cinque's
Consolation*. In 2006 she won the Melbourne Prize for
Literature. She lives in Melbourne.

GW00371221

MONKEY GRIP

HELEN GARNER

PENGUIN BOOKS

Penguin Group (Australia)
250 Camberwell Road, Camberwell, Victoria 3124, Australia
(a division of Pearson Australia Group Pty Ltd)
Penguin Group (USA) Inc.
375 Hudson Street, New York, New York 10014, USA
Penguin Group (Canada)
90 Eglinton Avenue East, Suite 700, Toronto, Canada ON M4P 2Y3
(a division of Pearson Penguin Canada Inc.)
Penguin Books Ltd
80 Strand, London WC2R 0RL England
Penguin Ireland
25 St Stephen's Green, Dublin 2, Ireland
(a division of Penguin Books Ltd)
Penguin Books India Pvt Ltd
11 Community Centre, Panchsheel Park, New Delhi – 110 017, India
Penguin Group (NZ)
67 Apollo Drive, Rosedale, North Shore 0632, New Zealand
(a division of Pearson New Zealand Ltd)
Penguin Books (South Africa) (Pty) Ltd
24 Sturdee Avenue, Rosebank, Johannesburg 2196, South Africa

Penguin Books Ltd, Registered Offices: 80 Strand, London, WC2R 0RL, England

First published by McPhee Gribble Publishers, 1977
This edition published by Penguin Group (Australia), 2009

1 3 5 7 9 10 8 6 4 2

Text copyright © Helen Garner 1977

The moral right of the author has been asserted

Printed and bound in Australia by McPherson's Printing Group, Maryborough, Victoria

National Library of Australia
Cataloguing-in-Publication data:

Collected Verse

Garner, Helen, 1942–
Monkey grip
ISBN: 978-0143-20271-4
I. Title.
A823.3

Acknowledgment is made to the following:
Judith Wright for permission to quote from her poem 'Train Journey' from *Collected Poems*
published by HarperCollins; the Essex Music Group for the lines from Joni Mitchell's songs 'Barangrill'
and 'Electricity'; Special Rider Music/Sony Music Publishing Australia for the lines from Bob Dylan's
song 'I shall be free No. 10'. The lines from Noel Coward's poem, 'The Boy Actor' from
published by Methuen Publishing Ltd., © The Estate of Noel Coward

penguin.com.au

Contents

Cont...

Acqua Profonda

In the old brown house on the corner, a mile from the middle of the city, we ate bacon for breakfast every morning of our lives. There were never enough chairs for us all to sit up at the meal table; one or two of us always sat on the floor or on the kitchen step, plate on knee. It never occurred to us to teach the children to eat with a knife and fork. It was hunger and all sheer function: the noise, and clashing of plates, and people chewing with their mouths open, and talking, and laughing. Oh, I was happy then. At night our back yard smelt like the country.

It was early summer.

And everything, as it always does, began to heave and change.

It wasn't as if I didn't already have somebody to love. There was Martin, teetering as many were that summer on the dizzy edge of smack, but who was as much a part of our household as any outsider could be. He slept very still in my bed, jumped up with the kids in the early morning, bore with my crankiness and fits of wandering heart. But he went up north for a fortnight and idly, at the turning of the year, I fell in love with our friend Javo, the bludger, just back from getting off dope in Hobart: I looked at his burnt skin and scarred nose and violently blue eyes. We sat together in the theatre, Gracie on my knee. He put his hand to the back of my head. We looked at each other, and would have gone home together without a word being spoken; but on our way out of the theatre we met Martin rushing in, back from Disaster Bay. Decorously, Javo got on his bike and rode home.

Not a matter of decorum, though, with Martin, who said to me shyly, knowing perhaps in his bones that nothing would be the same again,

'I wish I could – you know – *turn you on*.' And he did, and somehow we loved each other: I held his sharp, curly little head very tightly in my arms. We slept peacefully, knowing each other well enough not to need to touch.

1

I woke in the morning and heard at the same moment a rooster crow in a back yard and a clock strike in a house in Woodhead Street. I walked through our house. In the rooms people slept singly in double beds, nothing over them but a sheet, brown faces on still pillows. Gracie and Eve's boy the Roaster sprawled in their bunks. A glass fish tinked at their window.

I put the kettle on to make the coffee, stared out the louvres of the kitchen window at the rough grass and the sky already hot blue.

At the Fitzroy baths, Martin and Javo lolled on the burning concrete. I clowned in the water at the deep end where the sign read ACQUA PROFONDA.

'The others are waiting for me up at Disaster Bay,' said Martin. 'I'm going back today. Why don't youse two come with me?'

'OK,' said Javo, who had nothing else to do, his life being a messy holiday of living off his friends.

'Nora?'

I rolled and rolled in the water, deafening my ears while I thought of, and discarded, all the reasons why I shouldn't go. I popped up, hanging on to the rail, hair streaming on my neck.

'OK. I'll come.'

Javo was looking at me.

So, afterwards, it is possible to see the beginning of things, the point at which you had already plunged in, while at the time you thought you were only testing the water with your toe.

We picked Gracie up from her kinder and left Melbourne that afternoon. By the time we had crossed the border into New South Wales it was well into night. The camp where the others were waiting for the supplies Martin had brought was a mile from the end of the track, round a rocky beach. It was dark and the tide was right in against the rocks. I picked up Gracie, who was too scared to speak, and waded blindly after Martin's voice. I was soon wet to the thighs. Whenever a wave withdrew, invisible crabs clattered round my feet on the spiky rocks. I could dimly see Javo ahead of me with his boots over his shoulder. My ears were full of confusion and the sea thumping. Martin helped me scramble up the last slope,

2

Gracie clinging like a monkey to my back, and in the sudden quiet between waves I saw the gleam of the tent in a small hollow. We stumbled in. The others woke in a mass of rugs and sleeping bags.

'Did you bring anything to eat?' I recognised Lou's voice.

'I couldn't carry it over the rocks,' lied Martin, who had forgotten it in his haste to bring us to the place.

'We expected you yesterday, mate,' complained Lou gently. 'All we've got left is fuckin' flour. Where have you been?'

People were sitting up among the blankets. We got used to the dark.

'I got held up,' said Martin, already having forgotten the problem, and pulling his jeans off ready to sleep on his full stomach.

'You are a little weasel,' Lou sighed. He turned over and went back to sleep.

In a shop window in Merimbula I saw my face reflected and gave myself a fright: my hair was wild and stiff with salt, standing on end all over my head. My face was burnt almost back to paleness and my eyes stared out of dirty skin. I liked myself: I looked strong and healthy.

But Martin was unhappy, and to my shame I was not concerned with kindness.

One morning when the others had gone into Eden to buy food, I squatted on the wet sand between two boulders and rolled sandballs with the children. We rolled and rolled, hypnotised, thrusting the sandballs into the ancient pitted surface of the rocks, singing private songs to ourselves. The sun struck the backs of our necks and shoulders, burnt already brown as leather. We sang and rolled and sang, naked and sweaty. Up on top of the rock sat Lou with his leather-bound *Oxford English Verse*. He declaimed softly to the elements, a small smile of emotion trembling on and off his narrow, mournful face:

'. . . and the huge shipwreck of my own esteem . . .'

I went up and over the dried-out rocks to find my hat, and found instead Javo sprawled on a rug in the springy grass, not

3

naked like the rest of us, but pouring sweat in the fierce sun, his hair matted with it, his skin greasy with coconut oil. I lay down next to him and our hot skins touched. Up close, his face was crooked, wrecked and wild. His eyes were as blue as blue stones or as water coloured by some violent chemical. I put my dry, hot arm across his oiled back. He moved like a boy, hard and gentle by turns. I heard him breathing.

A hundred yards away the children's laughter evaporated into the blue, blue air.

When the ranger came in his long white socks, Selena and Lou had come down with hepatitis, and we broke camp in the afternoon, escaping with the scraps of our dignity and our hastily packed possessions. Javo had never learned to drive, and Lou and Selena were too sick; they propped themselves with pillows in the front seat, white and trying not to complain. Thus it was left to me and Martin to ferry the load down south round the coast highway. At first we were all frantic with temper, jealousy and illness. When it was Martin's turn to drive, I sat in the back with Javo. I held both children on my knee, and told them a long hypnotic story about how they gobbled up the world and then each other. The others listened through the roar of the car, and laughed. Javo sat with his long legs stretched out, touching my knee, sometimes stroking my leg with his bitten fingertips.

In the front the others sang and sang. Selena's sweet voice rose finely, illness momentarily forgotten in the steady movement south as dark fell. Javo croaked,

'Hey – remember *Sixteen Tons*?' He began to sing, 'Some people say a man's made outa mud / A poor man's made outa muscle and blood . . .'

I looked out the window at the moon the shape of a slab of gouda cheese, I smelled the warm grassy air, I felt the bony limbs and soft flesh of the children, I thought, oh, nothing can be as sweet as this: to have two children on my knee and a man beside me and the singing and the summer travelling.

To think this, I needed to forget the unhappiness of Martin who was two feet away from me, driving. And to forget that not

4

one of us would ever have a life that simple, because we were already too far off the track to think about turning back.

That night we forced ourselves past exhaustion and kept going. By the time we reached Melbourne we were beyond speech, too tired to be cordial to each other. I stopped the car outside Gold Street. The sleeping bodies stirred. Lou sat up.

'I see it,' he said, looking at his house, 'but I don't believe it.'

Javo and Martin dropped me and Grace at Delbridge Street. We fell into bed.

This one was going to make me trouble.

Next time I saw him was at Ormond Hall. People lolled against the mirrored walls, or danced, or lay on the floor with their sleeping children safely bundled in nests of discarded clothing. Javo and I spread ourselves on our backs on the floor as on a large double bed. I felt hesitant to touch him, or approach.

But he came back to my house with me, and we lay on my bed and talked and liked each other, and the way it happened was, that we began to stroke each other, and to kiss, and after a long, long time of slow, gentle touching and pausing, and kissing like an idle game that turned serious (he held my head hard with his two hands, we kissed and kissed) I rolled on to him and we fucked ever so gently. 'Wait, oh wait,' he whispered, and I waited, and he started again with the slow and steady rolling under me, his mad crooked face very sweet in front of my eyes; I felt the thin bones in his shoulders, and my heart dissolved to see him change away from abruptness to this kindness.

'At last,' he said, 'I've found someone who fucks soft.'

We slept together three nights in a row. In those three days I drifted pleasantly in a haze while Martin wept and Javo felt guilty.

Three nights in a row was enough to make it too late.

On the fourth morning I went about my business in the house, and came upon him later on the back doorstep. I squatted down beside him in the hot morning sunshine. I pushed my face against his jacket, warm cloth and the smell of his body. He smiled that crooked, reluctant smile, flashing at me sideways with his blue eyes. I went out on my own, leaving him there idle in the yard.

When I came back in the evening he was gone.

It was a clear night, bright high moon, smell of grass on the air.

A person might not be ashamed to wish for love.

I was not aware of having wished. I had fallen asleep, no longer listening for footsteps. At one o'clock in the morning someone pushed open my door quietly, Javo, and sat on my bed and I hugged him round his neck and he held me like anything.

We lay talking for a long time, and dozed and woke and dozed again. The moon moved across the roof. It was hot and still.

'What's happening with Javo, Nora?' enquired our Eve, rolling one of her sneaky fags at our kitchen table. 'You're not – you know – doin' it again, are you?'

I knew what she meant and could not control a grin of guilt. She meant *falling in love*.

'Yeah, I suppose I've done it again.'

'I'll thump you, Nor,' she said, laughing at me kindly. I ran my thumbnail along a groove in the tabletop, feeling abashed but defiant.

'But what can I do to change?' I cried.

'Stop. Stop it. Stop now. You could spend more time on your *own*.'

I can't, I won't. Stop. I thought of his skin and the way I could sense out his skull, and his crazy eyes.

'You know what you're doing, Nor. You're looking at every new one, saying – is this the one?' She squinted at me, breathing out a column of smoke.

'No, that's not what *I'm* doing.'

'Well then, Javo is. I don't want to sound like a mother, but what *future* is there in it?'

We both laughed.

'I'm not all that worried about futures. I don't want to love

6

anyone forever.'

'Look – don't get me wrong, he may be a scoundrel, but I really dig him – apart from anything else, he's a fuckin' *junkie*.'

'He's *not*. He's off it. He got off it in Hobart.'

'Oh, come *on*, Nora.'

We stared at each other across the table. Everything she knew about junkies was written on her face. I knew it too, but at that moment I chose to deny it. I stared at her face, gritting my teeth against the way she loved me. I looked at her thin, long fingers and kept my eyes on them until I heard her sigh. She stood up and picked up the coffee cups and carried them to the sink.

Already too late, too late.

What harsh lives we lead.

I slept alone that night, dreamed deeply, forgot the dreams, woke to a house empty of children. Sunday morning, a cool wind, sun not shining. Eve was right, of course: more time on my own. But there was an image to shake my resolution: Javo lounging on a blue couch, drinking in some flash pub beyond our means, the sun coming through his eyes the colour of blue marbles, blue glass, how his eyes burn in his wrecked face.

He was twenty-three then and maybe, I ignorantly surmised, wouldn't get much older, because of the junk and the dangerous idleness in the bloodstream. I hadn't reckoned with the grit, nor with what would be required of me, nor with what readiness I would give it. Givin' it all away. People like Javo need people like me, steadier, to circle round for a while; and from my centre, held there by children's needs, I stare longingly outwards at his rootlessness.

On Christmas Day we woke together again. Georgie had given me a book by Diane Wakoski, *The Motorcycle Betrayal Poems*. I ready a page or two, quite fast.

'If you're going to read,' said Javo, 'read out loud.'

I did, the one about the big snoring bikie who fell asleep beside her, drunk, and woke not knowing he carried her bullets in his back. I laughed. Lying next to Javo with the book in my hand, I remembered that in some narrow chamber of

7

myself I knew what she was talking about. Love, it's about love.

When he left that morning, he stood in my doorway, looked at me sideways, and said,

'I'm going home. See you when I see you.'

He caught me on the hop. But I was well-disciplined by the orthodoxy, a fast faker. I was sitting at my table. We were ten feet apart, and I grinned at him, neat, sharp and steady.

'Yeah. See you.'

Cut!

I saw him pass my window, though, and a small death occurred. Who am I kidding?

On that dull, still morning, Georgie strode in from Woodhead Street.

'Clive! One of your pigeons got the chopper, mate. A car ran over it.'

Clive buried it in the corner of the tomato bed near the dunny. I came past just as he was dropping the first spadeful of earth on the dead body. I saw its flattened head, its eye closed, its beak open and desperate. The dirt hit the feathers and they gave out a stiff, lively rustling.

Cut off from gritty daily contact with the world, I was floating somewhere else, my time ruled by the children's demands, my ears tuned to the tones of their voices. I slept and woke when they did, served them out of my dream; and lived a short, intense hour of every night in the dark with Javo, living privately in the sleeping house.

He slept on in my bed each morning when I got up to the children. I came back in when they had gone to play, sat at my table to write or read, was aware of him flung across my bed in a running position. I felt dispossessed. I wished he would get up and take cognizance of the world, as I had to every morning. He didn't act, but waited for the tide to lift and carry him.

Not my kind, was that it?

I was afraid of his restlessness, his idleness, his violent

8

changes of mood, his inability to sustain himself. Being with him was sometimes like being with a child: not that he *asked* me, as Grace and the Roaster asked me, to kick things along, to keep it all running; but if I hadn't done it, I would have been at the mercy of his erratic nature – unbalanced, vague, out of sync.

'What about this way I've got of falling in love with people and just as quickly out again?' I asked the I Ching.

'It is not immutable fate . . . that caused the state of corruption,' it replied, 'but rather the abuse of human freedom.'

He sat at my table just out of the shower, wet hair and his blue eyes burning.

'Geez, you're goodlooking,' I remarked over my shoulder as I stood at the sink. His face closed up. His eyes dropped to his bitten hands and cigarette.

'You get excruciated when I say things like that, don't you.'

He nodded.

The bead fly curtain rattled and Clive stepped in from tending his pigeons. He stopped inside the door, grinning at us from under his absurd cloud of henna'd hair.

'Wanna take the kids to the baths?' he said, inadvertantly puncturing the small balloon of awkwardness. Javo sat there smoking while we rounded up Gracie and the Roaster, took their bathers (smelling, like the children themselves, strongly of chlorine) off the line, and disentangled our bikes from the heap outside the kitchen door: my thirty dollar grid, and Clive's blue and silver Coppi racer, which he called his filly. The Roaster rode on Clive's bar, Gracie on my carrier. We bumped over the gutter and on to the softening bitumen.

The kids begin to sing. We roll in unison (me upright and straight-backed with outstretched arms, Clive bent low over his handlebars with the Roaster crouching inside the curve of his body) down the wide road and into the green tunnel, the cave of the Edinburgh Gardens. No-one around, though it is ten o'clock in the morning. The hoses flick silver strings on to

9

the drying grass. The cicadas beat a rhythm that comes in waves, like fainting or your own heartbeat. We sweep round the corner into the Belgium Lane, where the air is peppery with the scent of cut timber and even on this still day the poplars flutter over the ancient grey picket fence; they thrust up their sprouts through the cracking asphalt under our wheels. Between the posts we flash without hesitation and out of the cool we hit the road again and get down to the work of it, pedalling along Napier Street: our speed makes Gracie's legs flail behind me like oars.

'Hang on, hang on!' I shout to Grace, and feel her fingers obediently tighten on my pants as we forge across a gap in the heedless double stream of traffic in Queen's Parade, and coast again (the Coppi ticking soothingly) the last few yards to the racks outside the Fitzroy baths.

Broken glass glitters nastily all along the top of the cream brick walls. We chain our bikes to the rack. The Roaster grabs his towel and springs over the hot concrete to the turnstile. Gracie holds my hand with her hard brown one and we pick our way between the baking bodies to the shallow pool.

The brightness of that expanse of concrete is atomic: eyes close up involuntarily, skin flinches. I lower myself gingerly on to the blazing ground and watch the kids approach the pool. The Roaster slips over the side and wades inexorably deeper; Gracie waves to me and squints, wraps her wiry arms around her belly, and sinks like a rich American lady beneath the chemicals.

'No-one will ever understand,' I say to Clive, 'but this is paradise.'

'Paradise enow,' he answers, neatly laying out a towel and applying his skin to its knobbly surface. No further need to speak. The sun batters us into a coma. I pull my hat over my eyes and settle down on my elbows to the day's vigilance.

More Politely than Shaking Hands

It took me months to see the junk patterns. I wished to trust, and so I trusted. When events did not please me, my dreams reworked them.

On the night of the first party, I went alone. Javo was there, but he did not greet me, and sat like some sulky adolescent with his back to the room, hunched over the record player. The room was full of people I liked: I lounged about and wisecracked pleasantly with them until midnight, when I wheeled my bike outside and coasted home downhill under the big trees in those wide empty streets, sailing through tides of warm night air. I fell asleep beside my open window, and my unconscious obligingly furnished me with a more agreeable version of the evening's happenings.

I dreamed: Javo and I left the party together. As we opened the door, we found ourselves in the country, stepping off the threshold on to blond grass, a hill sloping down in front of us with a double wheeltrack half overgrown; faint evening sunlight. We ran down the hill together, laughing and exuberant, leaping over tussocks, having to dodge small clusters of brown ducks which were waddling flatbacked through the grass.

'Don't tread on my ducks!' shouted the farmer, appearing somewhere near. 'I have to sell them.'

It was easy to avoid them, though we were running so fast that it was almost like flying. At the bottom of the hill we came to a wooden fence with a stile, and stopped.

At that moment Javo walked into my bedroom, and I woke up.

He sat on the bed. We hugged each other. I sat against the bedroom wall with my knees up and my head between them.

'Oh, hey,' he said, taking hold of me by the shoulders. 'I am a self-engrossed slob. I don't want to make you sad.'

I did not want him to see that he could. So, there I sat on my bed in the middle of a hot summer night, caught between my dream and the memory of what had really happened.

If I had enough to spare, why not share it?

He touched me tentatively, as if he wasn't quite sure where to find me.

'Is that as good as it can be?' he asked humbly. I showed him how, and we fucked, we made love; we lay side by side.

'I love,' he said in a quiet voice, 'the moistureless way in which we kiss.' Exactly like that, he said it. 'I love the relationship you have with your body. I love the way your face is showing signs of wear. I love the way you talk when you're coming – the way you become a child. Your face looks twelve years old.'

I listened in astonishment.

We slept, and Gracie woke me early, and he slept on and I got up.

I found the second party in a crowded garden, its boundaries hidden in darkness. I smoked a couple of joints and took a cup of brandy to a little pozzy I found in a dry flowerbed under some bushes. I sat in my safe place, dirty and tired and not caring what I looked like. I drank the brandy and observed the social flow. The part of this which concerned me was a peculiar triangle: Javo, Martin, and Jessie whose relationship with Javo a year before had been destroyed by his smack habit. From my position on the sidelines I could see Javo's eyes on her, how he laughed eagerly at everything she said and watched her hungrily. But Martin too kept his eyes on her face, and she remained, in her demeanour, uncommitted, floating on the force of their attention, her expression changing from laughter to a vaguely detached and discontented look, her blue eyes under her thick red fringe drifting away to some private speculation. The three of them stood in a close ring, passing joints and making a lot of theatrical noise.

It was so much like watching a movie that my tired brain simply observed, and feelings scarcely registered.

I saw them move uneasily apart, together, apart again; I sensed their preoccupation with each other as clearly as if threads had connected them across the dark, leafy garden.

Javo retired to a hammock near where I was sitting with my brandy and my half-closed eyes. I got off the twiggy ground and went over to him.

'Hullo.'

He looked up with a start. His face looked strange to me, in a way I could not determine. I supposed it was because of his churned-up feelings.

'Good day, mate,' he said.

'Is everything all right?' Surely an odd, painful look crossed my face.

'Yeah. I'm really stoned,' he said in a tone which I took for an apology for his indifference. A shiver of irritation ran over me. Don't excuse yourself, bloody teenager, bloody child. Give or don't give. I'm not going to fight you for it.

I walked off and passed a woman I vaguely knew, my age, with the Eltham gloss on her, expensively dressed, too sophisticated and throaty-voiced to go smoothly amongst this bunch of desperadoes. A young man grinned passively under her attentions. I blushed in shame for us women whose guns are too big these days, who learned ten years ago to conduct great sexual campaigns with permanency in mind, while today it is a matter of skirmishes, fast and deft.

Spare us from indignity.

I saw the three of them drive away in Martin's car. Javo was looking straight ahead, his face set like a mask.

I came home alone, and mooched ill-temperedly around my room. I found his bowie knife where I'd hidden it behind the bookcase, safe from the children. I held its solid weight for a few seconds, wildly fantasising plunging it into the famous handsome picture of him in *Cinema Papers*. Instead, I dropped the knife and wrote him a letter.

'Dear Javo, there's a few things you ought to know, mostly involving things like elementary courtesy. Eh? like saying hullo; like not making that ludicrous adolescent gap between how you behave towards me at night when we sleep together and how you act in public as if we hardly knew each other. Don't get me wrong: I can recognise a desperate man when I see one. I don't want a flood of attention. Just hullo would do, so I don't have to wonder if I've been hallucinating other times we've been together. Good luck to you, Javo, I like you, but you give me a hard time. Still like to see you, sometime.'

I took it to his house next morning, expecting not to find him there – but he was there, asleep in his tidied room. I put the letter down beside his bed. He woke up, stared at me as if I were a stranger, his eyes blank with sleep, empty of comprehension, with a pinpoint of panic far inside his skull.

'I brought you a note. I didn't think you'd be here.'

He lay there, rigid, still staring.

'. . . But now I'm here, I feel very uncomfortable, so I think I'll go.'

He nodded, clearly incapable of anything more. I stood up, and as I walked out I heard him rip open the envelope.

I went into Martin's room and woke him. We talked cheerfully. I was aware that our laughing voices were audible to Javo. We went out to the kitchen and made some coffee. Javo stumped out, hair on end, face tight. He came to the table and Martin and I chattered on, our elbows resting among the mess of newspapers and orange peels. Gradually Javo's face softened, he smiled at the talk, listened with his face, spoke.

When I went to leave, I stopped in the back yard for a last word with Martin. Javo went past us and out the gate without saying anything. I said goodbye to Martin and wheeled my bike out the gate, put my foot on the pedal – and saw him leaning against a car two doors down the lane.

Adolescent!

I rolled up beside him, balanced my bike with both feet on the ground. He gave me the rueful flash with his very bright blue eyes.

'Last night,' he said, 'I was sure I didn't want to see you again. But I don't feel like that now.'

'You are not courteous to me . . . but I understand why you do it,' I said too hastily, because it wasn't even quite true. He leaped in eagerly:

'*Do* you? Well, I wish you'd tell me, because *I* don't know why I do it.'

'You don't want me to need you, even for a second.'

'No – no! That's not it!'

And we began the battle, warmed to it, ceased to stammer, started to flow.

'I find it really hard,' he said, 'to express emotion in public.

14

And you didn't understand. When I said I was stoned, I meant *smack*.'

Heart did not sink. I thought this meant a slight lessening of my naivety. I was wrong.

I looked at his cheeks, hollow before their time, lines from nose to mouth like a forty-year-old. Once he'd said to me, 'The harder you live, the better-looking you get.' Once, he'd told me, his mother had said to him, 'Don't worry, son – looks aren't everything.' People stared at him in the street, because of the way his eyes burned blue, and the scar hacked into the bridge of his nose, and because he looked wild. He couldn't believe me when I said, 'You're beautiful.'

By this time we were laughing, and I rode slowly beside him along the footpath till we came to Paddy's house. We walked into her kitchen. Martin was already there. We smoked a joint at her kitchen table. She put on an old Dylan record. He sang,

> 'I got a friend
> he spends his life
> stabbin' my picture
> with a bowie knife . . .
> I got a mean friend'

and everyone laughed. But I laughed more, because they didn't know what I was laughing at.

He would disappear for a day or two at a time. Often I'd come home at some odd hour and find him sitting at my table toiling over an explanatory note in his painstaking printing.

'Today I gave junk a nudge,' he'd write, 'like an idiot that I am and being stoned I shouldn't be here. I just managed to look the nightmare in the face that's my face today. And I decided to stop. And I decided to stop. And I decided to stop.'

When he was stoned he would usually keep out of my way. I never talked about the dope, much, being wary of crusading. I was interested in the phenomenon of his *being stoned*, and watched him curiously. I began to understand it through my eyes: I caught his face showing strange, mad planes which were not familiar to me, ugly in their strangeness. It wasn't dope as a spectre or a rival that frightened me, but the way it turned him into a stranger.

Late one night when I was asleep in my bed, he burst in at my door, wildly stoned, raving about some shirt he'd been given, tearing his clothes off, hurling himself into bed beside me. I kept dozing, full of confusion and sleep. All night long he threw himself about the bed, scratched manically, groaned, breathed loud and shallow. At last I crept out and into Clive's empty bed and dropped off by myself until morning came.

He came loping round the corner of the house to the kitchen a few mornings later. I was washing the breakfast dishes and dreamily staring at the children who were hosing the tomatoes. He was stoned – thinner cheeks, eyes wide open, pupils whited out as if the pinpoints at their centres had sucked the blue colour back into the brain. He hugged me with his gangly arms. I stood there holding the dish-mop and leaning against him. He gave me a much-folded note:

'Just writing you cause I'm going away to Hobart for the night tonite – to let you know I've been thinking of you today mate. I might stay there for a few more days seeing I've got a week of heavy thinking and working things out to myself. I might go and have a bet tonight and get a bit drunk and have a loud *externalised* time for a while. So I'll see you when I see you. Just to tell you I love your body cause it's really you there (no give) when I touch you and you bounce back which is the most important thing of all – and when we kiss I can feel the shape of your lips. Love you. Javo.'

Away he rushed to Tasmania, and my tension was reduced by half, and my nights were undisturbed. But I missed him, and missed his thin warm body in my bed; and thought about his dreadful cramps from the sweating, and his life with nothing much in it.

He came back in the middle of a night, woke me by striking a match at the door of my room, sat on my bed quiet and not stoned, told me how he'd hated Hobart except for seeing his

16

mother and winning forty dollars at the casino.

Oh Javo, your frantic life. I looked at him with no emotion except weariness and a small tinge of fear, or distaste – not for *him*, but for the eddying pointlessness of his battle with each day.

'You could get in here with me, if you liked,' I said, wanting him to. He got in beside me, and hugged me, and I felt that slow rush of pleasure, or love, at the touch of his dry, hot skin. I laid my face against his bony one and clumsily dared to love him.

'What about this junk all around me?' I asked the I Ching.

'Darkening of the Light,' it replied. 'In such times one ought not to fall in with the practices of others, neither should one drag them censoriously into the light. In social intercourse one should not try to be all-knowing. One should let many things pass, without being duped.'

Next morning we went by tram to St Kilda for the ritual turkish bath and massage, which he paid for with his winnings. We parted at the door. I took off my dress and pants and sank into the hot sea bath. I lay back and began to think about the nature of corruption, and the drift I was in, and the problem of whether there is a bottom to these things. I decided not, and immediately felt an urge to kick upwards, back towards light and order.

When we emerged from our segregated luxuries, hours later, he took me to lunch at Tolarno's, which must have cost thirty dollars. My protests he brushed magnanimously aside.

'No, no – you are always paying for me – go on, let me!'

I let him. But halfway through the meal I felt his mind disengage from mine; it veered off and wandered. I said nothing. We took a cab home. He sat comfortably beside me with his hand on my leg. At my house he said,

'I'll go on home – be back in half an hour.'

Time for a hit.

17

He didn't come back, that day or that night either.

So I began to root out of myself two tendencies: to romanticise dope, and to treat junkies with an exaggerated respect.

One sunny evening I called at Javo's house on my way to eat with Paddy. I called out: no answer, no-one home. The house was open, evening sun coming in the back door. It seemed still and hastily deserted. I walked down the passage to Javo's room. I wrote a note to say hullo. I was looking at myself in his mirror, studying my haircut, when the fatal urge to snoop over-came me.

I picked up an envelope that was leaning against the mirror. I turned it over. On the back of it was scrawled, in a travesty of Javo's handwriting,

'Sorry, Martin, my hands are shaking, I'm going crazy with this coke, yours is in the spoon, I nearly shot it all up but stopped myself just in time.'

There was a moment when my heart slithered about in my chest. I put the note back where it had been, and opened the top drawer. Right on top of his clothes was a fit, casually dropped, no attempt made to conceal it. Even a kitchen spoon, its handle bent. A small nest of evil treasure.

I closed the drawer and tried to breathe.

Terminal naivety was my disease.

I went out the back door into the six o'clock sun, past the disused car up on blocks. I got on my bike and rode away. The part of my brain which constantly and forever observes myself was reduced by shock to a very tiny pinpoint in the back of my head, as it had been when I was in labour. I heard myself gasp, and sob, and groan. The thought flicked across the black screen: one day I will find that treasure in Gracie's drawer.

At such moments, all the love in your body and mind and

18

heart and blood and cells ceases to be enough. Evil manifests itself.

I lay awake beside him through nights full of groaning and half-sleep. Once he saved me some coke, and brought it round. I snorted it and it got me through his worst night: I lay there serenely, observing dispassionately his contortions as he came down. I would have done anything I could to help him, but nothing could be done, so I lay next to him while he sweated and heaved, and the night passed.

He was off it again, but weak and fighting against depression. When I came home, days later, I found another of his letters on my table. When he wrote, he pressed so hard that the table itself bore the imprint of what he said to me:

'Came to gather some of that calming potion you manage to carry round – I had a rotten day, travelling around and fighting –

> so I thought I was never quite sure
> or never quite sure
> not really ever quite sure
> straining, but then again gently
> trying,
> never or maybe not quite bleeding,
> but then again not talking
> to anyone,
> saying what I mean
> is always a mean way of saying
> that I like a lot of you
> or I like you a lot / more than
> ever what I'm saying
> or maybe your body meets mine
> a lot more politely than shaking hands.'

I Didn't Know Where I Was

Our house was full again, people home from holidays, but the summer still standing over us. We climbed the apricot tree in the back yard and handed down great baskets full of the small, imperfectly shaped fruits. Georgie made jam. Javo and I sat in the sun on the concrete outside the back door, cracking the apricot stones with half bricks to get the kernels out. I was learning how to reach him without talking, though sometimes I was afraid he hadn't understood. We talked about this, lying on my bed with our bare legs under and over.

'Don't worry,' he said. 'I like the way you love me. I feel comfortable in it.'

But I needed bursts of other people, steady ones who didn't use junk. Georgie and I drove down through Geelong to Ocean Grove where I had lived as a child. On the road between Barwon Heads and Thirteenth Beach, as the sun disappeared completely into the ocean and the evening air turned grey and cold on our sunburnt skins, I was flooded through with an indescribable desolation, travelling across that low, scrubby coastline. I stared out the truck window, holding my arms against my chest. Georgie, out of his element, shuddered and said,

'Human beings shouldn't live this far south.'

I got work on a movie about junkies. The little speed I got hold of sent me flying recklessly through the days and nights. I flung myself right into it. When I smoked a joint during the day, I could quite clearly sense the speed and the hash slugging it out in my blood: sometimes one got the upper hand, sometimes the other, and me only a battleground.

At the script meeting for my night's shooting, I was so stoned that, when I tilted my head back to drink a glass of water, my neck muscles seemed to be in spasm. I was berserk with it, jangling with paranoia, watching people on the nod in the middle of the meeting, feeling how junk in a house oozes into

20

the very air.

In my disorientation I seized upon a small smile flashed to me across the room by a bloke with a clipboard on his knee: childishly thin, a gentle face with a big hippy beard, fine dusty freckles across his nose, skin so pale as to let the light through, and down his back a skimpy little tail of hair pulled back in a rubber band. I had lost my ability to pick a straight among the junkies.

'Who's that?' I whispered to Jessie, my only other counterpart, who was crouching beside my chair.

'That's Francis.'

'Is he a junkie?'

'No. At least, I don't think so.' She looked up sideways and winked at me.

'He looks nice.'

'He is. He's lovely.'

When I left the meeting to get a bus home, I stepped out of the house and for a few seconds *I didn't know where I was.*

'Where am I?' I asked helplessly.

'Punt Road is just at the end of this street,' said Francis who was leaning against the fence. 'The bus goes straight up to Clifton Hill.'

I walked to the end of the street, saw Punt Road, and felt the world swing and drop back into place around me.

I was sitting at the kitchen table after tea when Javo came around the corner to the back door. He couldn't, didn't try to hide it: stoned again, eyes staring, mouth dry and brown-scummed and cracked.

'Oh, but!' cried that silent, slow-thinking, straight person inside my head, 'yesterday you said, "Tomorrow I'll be better from junk." Why have you done it again?'

I said nothing. He'll always do it again.

But he came in and walked up behind me and put his hands on my shoulders, kindly, and glad to see me. I smiled at him. When I stood up, he clumsily took hold of me and bent his mad face down sideways and kissed me on the mouth.

I remembered him when he lay next to me in my bed, with-

21

drawing while I looked calmly on, full of coke, my head singing sweetly with it: our heads were side by side on the pillows, and every now and then out of his discomfort and pain he would turn his eyes to try and smile at me. Round rolled his eye nearest to me, white and frantic like the maddened eye of a steer caught in a bog.

This time I needed comfort from him. He gave it willingly, held and cuddled me, listened to my waning speedraves. I told him about the junk movie. Looking at his stoned, pale eyes, all their blue sucked out of them by chemicals, I started to want to get out of the movie, realising how little I knew about what it was trying to say.

'I'm thinking of going down to Tasmania,' he said, 'and I was going to ask you if you wanted to come.'

I thought of him in clean air, brown and hot. A week earlier I might have imagined that dope would cease to matter to him, away from Melbourne, but already I knew that was a fantasy. The day he'd said, 'Tomorrow I'll be better from junk,' I'd almost asked him, out of sheer curiosity, 'And what will you do then?'

'Yes, I'll come with you,' I said.

Oh, you steer in a bog, there's not a thing I can do to help you. Love is not enough, and you are often unwilling to take it.

Our preparations were erratic. I had to learn to manipulate him, or get round him.

'Oh shit,' he'd croak, 'we don't need mosquito coils, all that shit. I'd rather let the mozzies bite me than take all that stuff. We'll have to carry it, too, and it costs money.'

I had to go out of the room when he started to talk like that. I thought I must have been crazy to think of going to some distant place with him. But I plugged on with it, and somehow we got together what we needed.

In the night plane between Melbourne and Hobart, speed, grass and brandy alexanders combined to produce a thick layer of paranoia through which all impressions of the world outside myself had to force their way. I stared at my reflection in the dark window: bumpy head, wide forehead, small mouth held tightly with fear, skin spotty from speed and coffee, eyes drooping downwards at the outer corners. I felt small, tight and ugly. I looked as desperate as I felt. I felt that he didn't like me, that he was wishing we hadn't come. Did *I* wish that? I watched him reading his newspaper. I had seen how pale his face was at the airport. I was frightened.

I was afraid of his moods.
I was afraid of my own.
I was afraid of being afraid.

And yet on a bus in Hobart I sat opposite him and idly let my mind roll on a fantasy so idiotic and insane that it scared me out of my wits. I thought: what I will do is, when we get home I will go to the gynaecologist and have my loop taken out; and I won't say anything to Javo, and we'll go on fucking and I'll get pregnant and I will have a child, and it will have blue eyes like his but he won't be interested in living with me and it, and I won't care, so I will just go away happily to some other town, a sunny one, with Gracie and this little piece of Javo which I can love *right from scratch*, the way it's too late for me to love *him*, because of some irreparable damage that's been done to him long ago.

The fact that I was unable to speak to him even in jest about this fantasy made it double in strength. I absolutely wallowed in it for the whole of that bus ride. I had to think very hard about things I knew to be true before I could get myself back into line.

Night. Waiting for the ferry on the wharf at Bellerive. I was freezing and I crouched on the edge above the dark water slapping, trying to keep warm by making myself smaller; and he paced up and down, his boots clomping on the boards. Could this be summer? He came and sat down beside me and put his arm round me. A short-lived pleasure: away he clomped again in his inadequate jacket, and separately we froze and cursed.

23

In the casino Javo turned pale and trembled. He wrestled with the fates at the tables, and I drank by myself at the bar. Drunk by midnight, we stumbled out twelve dollars up and took a cab to his mother's studio where we slept on two hard couches and breathed air scented pleasantly with oil paints and turpentine.

Next day we took the road to Freycinet Peninsula. I had imagined that Javo would leave me behind in the walking, but I had forgotten the strength of my bike-riding muscles, and the debilitated condition he was in. He made me laugh helplessly.

''E needs a fuckin' good kickin',' he would remark viciously when a car passed us on the road without stopping. The top of his body bent over horizontal from the weight of his pack, he yelled to me at a crossroads in the coast town of Swansea,

'We could stop here tonight! Last night of civilisation.'

He dumped his pack on the motel doorstep and went in to the reception desk to negotiate. He stuck his head and hand out the door and croaked,

'Gimme seventeen dollars.'

What a whacker. I kept laughing insanely at the very thought of him. He was such a *pig*: he strewed lolly papers around him on the ground without a qualm, and raised pained eyebrows when I clicked my tongue and picked up after him.

In the motel room we collapsed on the beds. He flung back the bedspread and got under it fully dressed with his immense boots on.

'Why don't you take your boots off?' I suggested politely.

'Can't be fucked,' he grunted. 'I'm rooted.'

I started that helpless private giggling. 'Goodnight, then,' I said.

A pause.

'It's still early,' he mumbled, heaving himself off the bed. 'I'm going for a stroll around.'

I went on reading. He lurched out the door, leaving it wide open.

'Shut the bloody door, will you?'

He was halfway to the stairs, but came back and banged it shut. When he'd gone I looked up from my book. The *Herald* was all over the floor, the packs had been desecrated and their

24

contents scattered higgledy piggledy. A packet of cashew nuts, burst open, was strewn across the table, and the camera stood dangerously on its telephoto lens, from being pointed erratically at some horizon or other.

I started grinning again. My mouth got out of control. I picked up the newspaper, tidied the flat surfaces, laid the camera down on its side. Why didn't his thoughtlessness enrage me as it would have done in any other man? Must be love. Better get rid of that one. Meanwhile, I was a sucker for some kind of awkward charm he had. I liked the way he cheerfully exchanged cliches with the drivers who picked us up. I liked the way he leaned on me from his gangly height when boredom and impatience made us clown by the roadside. I couldn't resist his nonsensical claim to have the essential and definitive piece of information on every subject that came up. I liked the way he took being teased. I liked the way he used the word 'tragic'. I liked to watch for the flash from his blue eyes.

While he was out, I got up too and wandered round. In the driveway of the motel I saw a tiny baby mouse. It crouched trembling among the yellow lumps of gravel. Its coat shone in the evening sun. I could see its heart beat. I stopped to look and without warning it darted away on to the dirt and grass beside the drive.

I went back inside and lay on my bed. Two seagulls flew past the window, lit from beneath by the remains of the day's sunshine. The air was perfectly clear, the sky behind the mountains was flushed pink. Whenever a gust of wind struck the window, it made a very faint sprinkling, as if loaded with drops of sea. The timber building heaved a little and whistled in the wind.

He came back later on, after dark, when I was almost asleep. We lay in the clean sheets. The moon came through the window and the small waves hissed. We began to kiss. I took his cock in my mouth and saw the moon darken and lighten his skin, and he said my name and I felt him start to come in my mouth; I heard him groan and my heart moved for joy.

But he left me stranded, somehow – not that I expected to fuck, but he fell asleep and left my heart stranded. I needed something I didn't understand – words, perhaps. I was crying

25

out to him silently, and he didn't answer, didn't even hear me. I got up, full of loneliness and panic, and threw myself on the other bed. The radio was going quietly, jazz on the ABC and the reasonable voice of the announcer. I shoved my head under the pillow, sick with fright; got up again and squatted next to the open window and stared at the wide moonpath on the water and told myself I ought to know how to make myself calm.

I flung myself down next to him.

'Help me, will you?'

He woke up and rolled over and put me under the bedclothes and took my arm and made it go round his chest.

'Sorry mate,' he mumbled. 'I'm fucked.'

'It's not that I'm *angry*.'

'If you start feeling really terrible, you can wake me up.'

He fell back to sleep straight away, and finally so did I, but in the other bed and not till well after midnight.

Somehow we made it through that hot country. The worst part was a curved beach, two miles of soft sand into which our feet sank at every step. Cranky and black-faced, he plunged along in front of me in his stolen Paddy Pallins. What'm I doing here? Nuts. I must be nuts. I squinted out to sea and tried to dissociate myself from the toil of my legs. At the other end was Cook's Beach and a stone hut with a water tank. We dumped our packs and guzzled till we were nearly sick. Other hikers had left a logbook full of jolly comments about marauding possums and rats:

'Don't worry if the possum eats your food. He is quite clean, he has just eaten my toothpaste.'

It was all so hearty that I started to laugh. Javo did not feel like joking. He tore up great armfuls of bracken and made a big bed, upon which he flung himself, his face resolutely turned away from me. I shrugged to myself. Too tired to care.

But it got to me. By nightfall he was sitting, elbows on knees, staring into the fire. Unnerved by his silence, I wandered off along the dim track towards the beach. Someone called,

'Hey! Want a drink?'

Three kids were sitting on the ground round a fire. They handed me a bottle of Stone's Green Ginger. I took a big, withering suck of it: sickly warmth. Nobody asked any questions. The bottle passed from hand to hand until it was empty. When I got back to the hut, candlelight shone out the empty window frames and Javo was bent over in the same posture; but when he heard my step in the doorway he looked up with a start. I stopped a yard short of him, wary of asking even for courtesy, but he put out his arms to me in a child-like gesture.

'Nor – help me. I'm freaking out.'

Surprised, I stood still, then stepped forward. He hugged me round my waist, pushed his face against my stomach. I sat down next to him on the bench, but he withdrew again: his face closed like a fist, jaws clenched, eyes swung back to the flames. I knew better than to interfere between him and his sickness. I rested my arms along my bare brown thighs, imitating his posture, and stared at my thick socks and runners. He sprang up, blundered around the candlelit hut in some half-crazy distraction, moving jerkily like a puppet. I sat impassive.

On the bracken bed he turned his back to me and groaned in his sleep all night.

Next day we came from Cook's Beach over the mountain and down the other side to Wineglass Bay. It was hard walking but, because I'd learnt not to try and keep up with the manic long legs of Javo, I made my own pace and was alone almost all day, in a trance of hard work and pleasure. I raved to myself, singing and laughing and telling stories. There were times when, Javo being literally miles ahead of me, I sat down on the track to rest and fell into a waking dream, forgetting his existence and the existence of time, gazing at the water miles below and feeling the wind. I was a bit crazy. I lay on huge rocks dreaming of ancient Greece: I thought berserkly of Perseus, the wine-dark sea, the shield of Pallas Athene, the winged shoes of Hermes, the rocky coast of Thessaly – a leap in the blue.

That night we camped again, between a stagnant creek and the sea.

The only time I stopped thinking about him was early in the

morning, just after dawn, when I crawled out of the tent and left him there in his sleeping bag, and walked along the beach on my own. Two sailing boats were riding at anchor. I spiked me feet on the rocks, I waded calf-deep in the incoming tide, I glimpsed a fish a foot long lurking in the still water under the rocks. I lost the time and the situation. I was singing wildly and sweetly in my head.

By ten o'clock I was standing miserably on the sandhill. No sooner had I decided that I'd had enough, that I'd bear it as cheerfully as I could till I could get away from him, than he came up behind me to where I was looking at the sea. I turned round and he smiled, a hard-worked smile, only barely a smile, but I gave him one back and he put his arm round my shoulders and in spite of myself I was with him again.

Back in Hobart I was ironing my overalls in his mother's kitchen. Hazel and Javo were in the living room watching the cricket on television. They began to argue about politics. Instantly their voices rose to full volume and intensity. Javo's voice was almost breaking with the vehemence of his case: it was like being battered about the ears with clubs. When Hazel tried to speak, he raised his voice to an insane bellow:

'Let me finish, *listen* to me, fuck ya!'

Obviously they were used to this mode, for she didn't take the slightest offence. She shared Javo's liking for rhetorical language. When she lapsed into generalisations, I saw on her face that a cog had slipped: her eyes, like his, took on a certain opaqueness, the mouth turned up a little, the head cocked slightly, and the words flowed out too easily to be the product of real, gritty thought. It was the repetition of a catechism.

I put the iron away and went out into the garden. I sat looking over the estuary for half an hour, then ventured back into the house, thinking they would have quietened down and gone back to the cricket. But no. Worse was to come. As I opened the kitchen door I heard Javo roar,

'You just *contradicted* yourself! You're intellectually *neurotic*! You contradict yourself! Be *rational*! How can I talk to you, if you're not *rational*!'

To her eternal credit, Hazel simply let out a cackle of laughter. I glanced round the door to see how Javo was taking it. He was sprawled in an armchair, looking at his knees, elbow on the arm of the chair, one hand over his face.

I went outside again.

One day Gracie may scream at me like that.

I Heard the Curtain Going Up

I got home a few days before my scene in the junk movie was to be shot. There was one night's work in the strange house in Prahran. I had enough speed left to rev me through the night, and it let me down easy because by morning I had extended myself way beyond my limits. We finished work just before dawn, when the fingernail moon was fading in a hot, dry sky. I came out of the house and lay on the small front lawn, staring at the sky as it lightened. Jessie wandered out and lay down beside me. Attenuated, dried out, made gentle, we lay together in the companionship of fatigue.

Francis drove me back to Fitzroy and dropped me at the corner of the Edinburgh Gardens. As I scrambled down from the high seat of the VW van, I looked back at him to say goodbye: our eyes fixed together, in our fatigue and the serenity and fearlessness of that state, and I stopped in my tracks. We smiled, and smiled. I broke it, and walked to the kerb, and turned back, to see him still sitting there, one hand on the steering wheel, the other on the gearstick, looking at me. Easy contact: hearts perhaps. I hardly even knew his name. He had the gloss on him of clever parents, enough money, calm enough to smile like that at a stranger.

I walked home very, very slowly across the drying park. The whiteness of my clothes burned in the dry sun, my runners padded silently. I sang to myself, loud and unabashed,

'And the song that he sang her
to soothe her to sleep
runs all through her circuits
like a heartbeat . . .'

In the back door, across the worn matting, three steps on the lino of the hall, turn to my bedroom door – and Javo was in my bed with a thick white mask of calamine lotion on his torn skin.

'It's all right, Nor!' he burst out eagerly at the sight of my shocked face. 'It's only some pimples.'

I stood staring at him. I saw that he had been in my bed all night. I felt panicky, and tired of it, wanting to escape now, quick, before the water got any deeper.

I turned back to the kitchen, and found Clive and Georgie sitting at the table drinking coffee. I slid wearily on to a chair. They pushed a cup towards me and looked at me in silence, half-grinning about the white-masked apparition in my room. I grinned too, and shrugged, and felt again the moving of that reluctant love for him, in spite of all reason.

'Imagine,' said Clive, catching his breath and leaning forward to me, 'imagine how it must feel to be someone like Javo, thinking, "Is there anything about me that prevents her from trusting her life to me?" And knowing that YES, there's *this* – ' pumping into the crook of his arm – '*imagine the anguish of knowing that!*'

He became my sick child. Helplessly he slid further into dope. His skin was covered in infected pimples which he doctored savagely with a razor blade in front of the kitchen mirror. His face was hollow and alarmingly white. His fingertips were infected from his ceaseless gnawing at himself. We never went out together; I saw him only at night when he would creep into my bed for comfort, but his restlessness and horrifying dreams would drive me, night after night, out of my own bed into other parts of the house. Often I slept with Clive, for comfort of my own. He would move over without a word, and sometimes stroke me till I fell asleep again.

People I met in the street would take on a certain look, when they asked 'How's Javo?' as if they were speaking of a dying person.

By mid-February it was autumn already, before we had had a summer. Leaves rattled drily outside my window on the pavement. The air had a waning feeling, and moved with a touch of melancholy.

Gracie, having hung longingly over the state school fence for three days, at last became a schoolgirl. She carried a small cardboard case down the street every morning, and returned dragging her steps every afternoon. She was not interested in answering questions about school. In the second week she ran away three times, strolled into the house at lunchtime with a plausible lie to explain her early arrival:

'It was hot and we got out straight after lunch. All the grade bubs kids came home early today.'

She'd drop her case and lie on the bed with me to read or draw; then there would be a thunderous knock at the front door and a frowning man teacher in walk shorts and long white socks would be standing there, hands on hips.

'Mrs Lewis? Where is Grace?'

She squeezed out a few tears each time, but consented to return. I walked her back to her prison, feeling my treacherous heart sinking with every step. Then her teacher discovered Gracie's problem: boredom, caused by the fact that she was the only child in her grade who could read. I spent hours with her after school, drawing endless faces in profile, cartoons about the people in our household, rising suns, earthquakes, cyclones. If I had to deliver her up to her jailers every day, I would make up for it somehow. She survived. But one day when I rode past her school at playtime I saw her, very small in her brown gingham schooldress, lingering alone against a wall, watching the children moving about purposefully. I saw her heave herself away from her leaning place, and without a smile start to run with the mob.

I went to a party full of communists. I looked over my shoulder from a conversation and saw Javo come in: stoned, all right, I saw his wild eye and something in the turn of his head.

31

This time, even after five days of watching him withdraw, I didn't even involuntarily think,

'But you said!'

I just saw that it had happened. He came over to me and hugged me with his gangly arms, bending down to me. To placate? No. Because he was glad to see me. It was noisy. We walked back to my house. He talked and I listened, padding along beside him with my bare feet.

'I worked like a dog today,' he said. 'I dug up our whole back yard. And I planted a syringe tree.'

'A *what*?'

'I broke my fit and threw it in a hole and buried it.' We both burst out laughing. A plant with evil fruit.

Back in my room I lay on my bed and listened more. He sat at my table, mending the sleeve of his Lee jacket and sewing a strip of Nepalese braid on to the cuff.

I said, in a tone of curiosity, 'Did you and Martin get stoned today?'

'Nn . . . yes.'

'Did you nearly say "no"?'

'Yes, I did.'

A small flowering of confidence and trust.

I was sweeping the matting after breakfast, digging in with the corner of the straw broom, when the back gate scraped against the concrete and round the corner of the house came the hasty, fluttering figure of my friend Rita: always in a hurry, on the verge of laughter or tears, hung about with a great leather bag containing her camera, a crushed packet of cigarettes, screwed-up tissues, a blunt pencil, an apple, a bicycle pump – a bag in which she rummaged helplessly while she talked to you, shaking back bangles and cursing absent-mindedly.

'Oo hoo!' I called as she came flying up the path on her high heels. She was smiling, of course, but by the time she reached the door I could see she was only just holding on. I stood the broom against the wall, to have my hands free, but she darted past me and sat down on the red chair.

'What's up, Rita?'

'I can't – I can't –' and she dropped her shining face on to her hands and began to sob.

Her daughter Juliet, carried along invisible on the tide of Rita's entrance, appeared at the door and insinuated herself into the room: she looked at Rita, rolled her eyes round to my dismayed face, giggled nervously, and ran between the chair and the table to Gracie who was standing at the other door, round-eyed, thumb in mouth.

'Come on, Grace!' piped Juliet. 'Let's go in your room.'

Grace tore herself away from the interesting tableau; we heard them murmuring and rustling over the dress-up box in the next room.

I sat on the arm of Rita's chair and stroked her thick hair. 'So. What's been happening?'

'I'm going nuts at home,' she said, fishing a dirty kleenex out of her bag and wiping her cheeks. 'I don't know what's the matter with me. And this morning I thought, if I don't get away from Juliet today I'll fuckin' kill her. I came straight round here. Can I leave her with you today? I've just got to get some work done.'

'She can stay the night if she likes,' I said. 'You know, you really ought to live with more people, Rita.'

'I know. But it's not that easy to arrange. People who haven't got kids are so hard to get on with. I know Juliet drives them nuts, but I keep thinking that's *their* problem. What am I going to do?' The question was already rhetorical: she was on her feet, gathering up her bag, pulling herself together.

'I dunno. Battle on, I guess. It's like what Eve says: "Life's a struggle".' We both began to giggle at the mental picture of Eve the trooper, head forward in work-horse position, ready for the harness.

Rita struck a heroic pose, one hand flung out. ' "Dare to struggle, dare to win",' she intoned.

'Or – "Dare to giggle, dare to grin", as the anarchists used to say.'

'When will I come back for Juliet?'

'Tomorrow – whenever you like.'

'I'll just nick in and say goodbye.' She emerged again so quickly that I raised my eyebrows. 'At home she wouldn't leave me alone – now she's too busy to even give me a kiss. Oh, well. Thanks, Nora.' She put her hot cheek, still damp, against mine, and went off out the back door, crepe jacket flapping. I picked up the broom, but before I could start sweeping I over- heard the girls in the bedroom:

'Pretend you are a bad witch and you're going away.'

'And pretend you're dead.'

'And when you come home you find me dead on the bedroom floor.'

'And only a kiss from my mother can make me alive again.'

'Help!' I thought vaguely. 'I'm too young to be a mother. I don't know enough. I can't bring up a kid. I'm not a real grown-up. One day the real mother will come back, and I'll only have been babysitting, and then I can go home.'

I spun the broom and pointed its good side down and began to beat at the matting with sharp rhythmical strokes.

At six in the morning, as the early autumn progressed, the sky was scarcely lighter than its night-time colour. I could hear the city start to shift, and roar deeper, and the surface sounds of its life begin: doors banged, a radio gabbled, cars started up, a rooster somewhere crowed. I could tell the season was changing, because in daylight the air moved, moved cease- lessly, not what you would call a wind, but restlessness and unease which were delicious to the bones and skin.

I dreamed of a bust in a house full of people: a political bust, where nasty clever police efficiently checked and filed, and escape from their knowledge was impossible.

I went to the film co-op to see the rushes of the junk movie. The lights went out and the rushes began and the door opened and in the light from the screen I saw Francis come in. He was wearing small hippy spectacles. I took my courage and crept over to him in the dark, against the wall where the latecomers were crouching. He touched my arm, looked me full in the face, without fear.

He drove me home on his way to the night's shooting. There was something very sweet and whimsical in his thin face.

'If I get any thinner than this,' he said, 'I'll just disappear. It is this bloody movie. It is driving me insane. But it will be over by the end of this week, and then I'll be able to relate to you properly.' He was talking out of a tired face, almost waxen, the fine veins showing under his eyes. He had a way of trapping my eyes, holding my gaze for longer than my speedy head was used to, or could bear.

'I'm not complaining,' I replied, sitting placidly at the kitchen table. 'I think there's enough happening now to make it worthwhile, don't you?'

'Yes,' he said, with a smile in his eyes that narrowed them kindly. 'But – I don't know what happens in your life.'

I began to talk about Gracie and Javo, and the night in the Swansea hotel, not knowing why I chose that as the first story about myself.

He suddenly laughed and said,

'You've got amazing eyebrows!'

I laughed too. My hand went involuntarily to my face.

'Don't cover them up!' he cried.

I had lost the thread of thought.

'I'm sorry!' he said. 'Go on.'

When he went off to the shooting, I walked out with him to the VW van full of equipment.

'I'm going to give you a hug,' he said, and we were standing in the road holding each other, faces in necks and shoulders, breathing each other in. He *was* thin. Like Javo, he was twentythree.

That night I slept alone, and badly, dreaming bad dreams and feeling the night to be endless.

When I got home the next afternoon, Francis was in our kitchen. He was *so tired*. He sat on my bed and I mended my jeans and he talked, as twentythree-year-olds will, about what love means and where sex fits in and so on. It was years since I'd heard someone going through the basics so painstakingly and seriously.

'Why did you ask me my age, the other day?' he wanted to know.

'I was just interested.'

'But – this is something *I've* learnt so I don't know if I ought to try and force it on some-one else – I don't think people can

35

get to know each other by *asking* things. I think they should do it through – holding each other, and being together.'

Oh, you little hippy! I caught the feeling on my face of a mocking look – heaven forbid.

'Yes, I'm sure that's true,' I said. 'But a bit of factual information never went astray.'

He looked at me. There was a pause.

'It's rather relaxing, being with you,' he remarked, as I stitched away, cross-legged on my bed.

'Funny you should say that. Usually people find me too speedy. I seem to spend half my time trying to slow myself down.'

'So do I! Maybe we could slow ourselves down together.'

Outside at the van, he sat in the driver's seat and I stood between him and the door, holding it open with my bum. He was wearing faded old Yakka overalls; through the side slit I could see his thin, thin flank naked under the worn cotton. We talked comfortably.

'I'm sorry you have to go,' I said, 'but come round and see me again soon, will you? Because I can't really come to you, can I?'

'No, not really. Anne just couldn't . . . *understand* it.'

He took me by the shoulders, and we hugged, and kissed.

'Oh, it's strange!' he exclaimed, with his hands on my upper arms. 'I haven't *really* kissed or hugged anyone but one person for four years!'

'Have you been married?' I asked, half joking.

'No! Well, sort of.' He grinned. 'But she is going to India in a week.'

I shut the door and he drove off. Waved.

He must think I'm sharp, or hard, I thought. I might be. When I talked, sometimes he let a silence fall after I'd spoken, and looked at me quizzically for a long time, his face smiling kindly with crinkled eyes and a speculative expression.

On the last day of the junk movie shooting, I rode down to the location at the National Gallery, with Georgie. There I ran into Francis, agitated beyond endurance, stammering. He looked like an angry mouse: a frown seemed out of place on his gentle, pale face. Sweat was shining across the bridge of his nose. He smiled at me distractedly and hurried past along the empty passageway.

There was plenty of good dope around. Gracie was at school. The sun shone every day. I rode my bike everywhere. I went to the library. I was reading two novels a day. When Gracie came home from school we would doze off on my bed in the hot afternoon. For days at a time there was no sign of Javo. One night Georgie and Gracie and I went to the Pram Factory to see a play, and didn't come home till two in the morning. We rode home, speeding along, Gracie on the back of my bike like a quiet monkey. The moon hung in the deep, deep blue sky; the air was dotty with stars. We sailed serenely through floods of warm autumn air. Gracie sang a song:

> 'I useda be a parrot
> but then I met a bad witch, a bad witch,
> and she turned me into
> a dang'rous frog . . .'

Oh, that Gracie, who feigned deafness, and stole dressups from school, and smeared her face with makeup stolen by some junkie in a chemist bust, and wore a gold lame cape with a glittering G on the back, and who said to me when we met unexpectedly in the street,

'Oh, you look *beautiful*! I wish I wuz as beautiful as you.'

Whenever I worried about her irregular life, I remembered Noel Coward's poem about his childhood:

> 'I never learned to bat or bowl,
> but I heard the curtain going up.'

37

Only His Next of Kin

Javo had not been near me for a week, when Martin ran in my back gate one afternoon, with news.

'Nora,' he said, 'I've driven Javo down to St Vincent's. He was screaming with pain, he thought he was dying. I think it's septicaemia, from a dirty hit.'

Martin and I went down to casualty. We found Javo asleep in a cubicle, dressed in hospital whites with blue stitching. One arm dangled out from under the stiff sheets. He woke: those blue eyes in his battered face. His skin was still erupting in huge pus-y sores.

Martin stood at the end of the bed and I crammed myself between the bed and the metal chest of drawers.

'I want you to bring me another set of clothes, in case they hide these,' said Javo, pointing at a supermarket bag beside the chair.

'Why would they do that?'

'They might want to keep me here longer than I want to stay.'

He was raving, slightly.

Martin sulked, pursing his small lips, arms folded, looking at the floor. I felt like the mother of two headstrong, opinionated boys. My bones flooded with weakness. I stared at the metal bed. No-one spoke. I stopped caring about seeming straight, or motherly.

'I think you ought to stay here as long as they make you. They won't keep you any longer than necessary – people are out there clamouring for beds.'

'But I'm better already. They didn't give me nothin'. My body's beaten it.'

His skin was burning and dry, his eyes were pale with fever.

'Anyway,' he continued recklessly, 'I know people who've had it, and who only needed to stay in for a day.'

'Who?'

'Schultzy. A guy called Schultz.'

I couldn't even laugh.

'I'll come in tomorrow and bring you some fruit, and something to read.'

Martin and I got up to leave.

'Yeah – go,' urged Javo, meaning *Don't think I need you, I'm all right here, I don't need you.*

Martin went out first. I paused, turned back, put my hand on Javo's arm, kissed his hot forehead. Out of Martin's sight, his face changed. He rolled on to his side, looked up at me, tried to smile, cast his anxious eyes up to me sideways.

'Sorry, mate,' he whispered.

'You don't have to say that!' I cried in confusion, pushing my way between the foot of the bed and the curtain.

Next day I rang the hospital. They told me he was 'satisfactory' but that only his next of kin might visit him. Forced to be his mother, sister, wife. But of course when I got there in the evening no-one questioned me and I walked straight into the ward. I gave him a joint and he smoked it behind the *Herald.* He had a drip in his arm, sticky-taped on to his punctured inner elbow. His fever had gone down. He was restless, complained of the people in nearby beds – a hopelessly spastic boy beside him, who groaned without respite, and an old man dying in the bed opposite. Martin came in and they conducted a staccato conversation about a house they were going to rent when Javo came out. I stood leaning against the cream-painted metal bed and stared at the clean, clean lino tiles. My impatience rose up in my throat to choke me. When I kissed him goodbye, Martin was waiting for me, and it was a cold farewell.

I went home in despair, unable to wish him well.

The next evening I was riding home for tea before going to see him at the hospital. At the bottom of our street I met Eve going in the other direction.

'Hey, Nora!' she shouted as she passed. 'Javo's there, in your room.'

'*What?*'

'He just got there. He's waiting for you.' She sailed past, raising her eyebrows and turning down the corners of her mouth.

My heart beat so hard it blinded me with rage. I dropped my

bike outside the back door and went into the bathroom to hide from him. I was eating my anger. But he came in there after me. I was sitting on the edge of the bath. I looked up at him. I would have opened my mouth to berate him, but I saw the great scabs healing on his face, and I saw the way he looked at me, dumbly; looking into his eyes was like looking down some hollow, echoing passageway straight into his brain. He said nothing. He stood there in front of me with his hands dangling down. My anger evaporated.

I put him into my bed.

'What happened, Javo?' I took his hand.

'When you came to see me last night, I didn't know how to start telling you how good it was that you were there. I'd been waiting all day for you to come. And when you left, I started feeling really shithouse. It got to be nine o'clock, and all that night ahead of me, and that fuckin' kid moaning. So I got up and got dressed and nicked off.'

I started to shake, imagining him pulling the drip out of his arm in the dark ward. My stomach clenched up hard.

'And I came straight round here,' he went on, his skinny arms lying out upon my purple sheets, 'but there was no-one home. I went to Nicholson Street, and Queensberry Street, but no-one was around anywhere. And at the tower there was only Jessie home, and she didn't want to know about me.'

'Well? What did you do then?'

'I went back.'

'To the *hospital*?'

'They didn't even notice I'd gone. I just got back into bed.'

'But how'd you get out this time?'

'I told them I had people to look after me. They said OK, if I could get a doctor to say he'd take responsibility, so I rang Mac, and he said he'd do it. They gave me a script for some penicillin. Mac will come round later and teach you how to give me a shot.'

O will he indeed. Must I be your mother? This house was the only place he could go for proper looking after; and yet, I couldn't resist:

'I thought you said you didn't like it here. You told me it was "too homely".'

40

He said nothing. His eyes were dark. He looked desperate in his soul. I was sorry I'd spoken, because I did . . . love him, was that it?

I went out and cleaned the fridge to keep calm. I finished the job, scrubbing the old yellow enamel with Ajax and polishing it with the warm dishcloth. Then I smoked a joint in the kitchen with Georgie, who was carefully not making any comment, and crept back into the bedroom to look at Javo. He was almost asleep. I lay on the bed beside him, flat on my face with my arms at my sides. The hash had done the trick: I found I could direct my imagination with my will. I saw a painted blue sky with scallopy clouds, and I soared up into it, borne up effortlessly and not too high by tides of warm air. Slow, easy flight. I fell asleep on the wing. Javo too slept still and deep, with no thrashing or groaning. Whenever I woke, I put my arm around his skinny body.

He stayed home, in my bed, all next day. Impatient at my tentative fiddlings with the syringe, he hit himself up with the penicillin: tossed the fit into his own bum like a dart into a dartboard. He barely flinched. The rest of us stood round him in a ring, reluctantly respectful of his nonchalance, except for Gracie, who sang out in warning,

'*Don't do it, Javo!* You'll want more and more!'

It was the first time any of us had laughed in two days.

When I came home I found he had written me a poem and fallen asleep:

> 'Let me be just that other wall
> cause there's no need to try breathing gentle
> near me
> just to look at your respect
> contains me – happy –
> not my mother – your body warmth
> is there – can feel it with just looking
> it's just a matter of looking . . .
> from anything other than blowfly
> with a pin between his wings –
> can try being anywhere right now –
> except back in that specimen jar –

you just keep teaching
without telling
keep loving
without expectation
maybe that thing you call clinging at your dress
mother –
is just me staring
almost blinding gaze
at "STRONG"
I'm learning something new
all the time
all the time getting better at liking this flesh of mine.'

Respectful of His Fragility

Francis sent me a note, to say he was living alone. I went to visit him. We talked as people do who know nothing about each other from other sources. He asked me to stay and I did. Hot, thin body, thin hard arms.

'I used to be an athlete,' he said. 'I used to run a hundred miles a week. I was sort of crazy.'

We were in the bed he had shared with Anne for four years. He was very stoned, and I was afraid for him.

I was bleeding. I bled and bled, dark red flowers on his coarse sheets. I wondered if he minded. I was used to people who didn't mind, who hardly even noticed. I couldn't find his mind. I searched for his eyes but they were closed. His body was thin, thin, thin. I think he was frightened. Once, I thought he spoke. I took his face in my hands.

'What did you say?'

'Nothing. I was only breathing.'

And again, later, he said the same to me:

'What did you say?'

42

'I didn't speak.'

The blood. It ran everywhere. And for her memory's sake I was afraid of not being beautiful – or, of being more weather-beaten, marked and scarred, looser than the young girl. No, not *afraid* of it, but regretting it, wishing something perfect or new; respectful of his fragility.

We slept too lightly for rest. Early in the morning I climbed over him from the wall side of the bed, pulled my clothes on over my bloody legs, and wheeled my bike out his front door. A wild yellow sky, dry grey air full of turbulence. The street surfaces were burnished, blown clean as a bone. My bike tyres, pumped up hard, whirred on the glossy bitumen. Autumn, air, air, moving in dry warm blusters.

I got home and walked into the still house and found Javo asleep in my bed. He turned over and opened his eyes. His intelligence swam up behind the daze of sleep. He said nothing, but looked.

'I didn't know you were coming, Javo.'

He tried to smile: unhappiness blurred his face like a veil. He didn't ask me where I had been.

'I stayed over at Francis' place.'

'I thought you might've.'

'What made you think that?'

'Oh, somebody told me you'd been fucking with him lately.'

'But I haven't! Last night was the first time. Who told you that?'

'Oh, I dunno. Someone.' He took my hand. I sat down on the edge of the bed.

'But I would always tell you if I fucked with anyone else! How could you think I wouldn't?'

'I suppose ... maybe you thought I already knew about it anyway.'

'Oh *shit*. People's lives are just gossip fodder.'

I got into bed with him and we lay close together, not talking, held there by sadness as the day began.

It was raining, pouring warm rain. Francis and I left his house at two o'clock one afternoon and walked up to Lygon Street.

We were passing the Commercial Bank when the door of the University cafe flew open and Javo and Martin stepped out. All four of us stood still. I took five steps towards Javo and without a word we turned and walked off down the street towards the city. His arm went across my shoulders. I glanced back and saw Francis grin and shrug at Martin. Together they went back into the cafe.

We walked in the Exhibition Gardens, along the dripping avenues.

'I can't live with it. I'm too jealous,' said Javo. My left shoulder fitted exactly in the hollow of his under-arm. 'I am going away with Martin for a couple of weeks.'

'Where to?'

'We are telling everyone else it is to Perth. But it is really to Asia. We want to get into Cambodia.'

Nothing surprised me any more. I knew it would be wiser not to ask how he proposed to pay for his ticket.

We sat on a wet bench in our sopping clothes, close together.

'Let's go to my place,' he said.

We walked dully past the kids' adventure playground, across the carpark, and up the broken stairs to the series of empty rooms over the Italian grocery, where he had a mattress in a corner and a heap of things he called his. On the wall he had pinned some photos of Freycinet, where we had struggled over the mountain. We stripped off our wet clothes and lay on the bed. We held each other for comfort, and made love as we always did, in spite of trouble: falling into each other's eyes.

'I think I'll have a sleep,' I said.

He got up. 'I'm going downstairs to clean up the kitchen.'

I dozed off, but couldn't quite fall asleep. I went downstairs in bare feet to the dunny, through the chain of rooms. I came round the corner into the kitchen and he looked up, shocked, and backed against the bench to hide what he was doing. I said nothing, and went past him out the back door. When I came back he had the belt on his arm and the fit ready. I stood watching him curiously. He was clumsy; could not get a vein in his left arm; seemed oblivious of my presence once the ritual had begun. I saw how his face turned pale, his hands trembled most dreadfully so that all he could do was butcher his flesh, for all he wished merely to make love to himself. Blood trickled in the crook of his arm. He cursed under his breath, and took off the belt and put it on his other arm, awkwardly manoeuvring the fit with his left hand.

I didn't wait. I went back upstairs to his room and lay on the mattress under a blanket, looking at the mountain I had climbed, and the sea at its feet, and the moonpath on the water outside the motel room at Swansea. I was careful not to think. And I fell asleep.

No Fade from Distance

I was sitting at the kitchen table while the rest of our house slept. Gracie stirred in her bunk in the next room. The clock ticked on the window sill. The matting was crammed with tiny scraps of food and other matter which I could feel with my bare feet. The pigeons flapped and . . . out came Javo, tousled and foul-tempered, heading for the dunny in his levis. Today he and Martin were going away, thank Christ.

My head was fat with the secret of their destination. They had a pack each. The rumour had run round that they had ordered white tropical suits to be made for the journey, which were not ready by the day of their departure. I was hard put to deny the implications of this gossip when people brought it to me.

Martin arrived. His small curly head moved impatiently as a bird's while Javo chaotically forced clean clothes into his pack. Martin was wearing a brand new pair of blue and white brogues: spiv shoes. He did not take the teasing well, being too agitated. At last Javo pulled tight the last buckle on his pack and heaved it by one strap on to his back. He accepted the farewells of our household with a nod, never having learned to be gracious.

I took that well-worn route to Tullamarine: turn right on to the thunderous freeway and slide easily into the shining flood. We were all in the front seat, Martin in the middle, Javo disdaining to fasten his seat-belt. We didn't speak, but simply barrelled out along the freeway, full of our own troublesome thoughts. My elbow was out the window into the dull warm air. Javo was biting his nails, or what was left of them. He had washed his hair, and freed from its customary mattedness, it flopped and shone. He was wearing painfully clean jeans and a denim shirt. He glanced at me across Martin, ventured a tight smile.

I brought us all to rest in the carpark. Martin was at once the organiser. His head was thrown back and behind his rectangular spectacles his green eyes darted eagerly. His voice took on a sharp, peremptory note which Javo responded to, unconsciously perhaps, by doing everything a shade more languidly than he would have otherwise. I didn't open my mouth. I felt like a mother, as if my face wore that expression of tight-lipped but amused tolerance to be seen on the faces of parents who, being tired of interfering, are letting their children slug it out between themselves.

Out there at Tullamarine the air was almost country, between the blasts of aviation fuel; and the sky was immense, with empires of blue- and pink-tinged clouds. I dawdled behind the busy heels of Martin's blue shoes, dreaming about the country. Javo waited for me, turned and put his arm around my shoulders. I got a whiff of his sweat, the sharp smell that made my heart shift.

Martin got the baggage out of the way and we were standing, suddenly forlorn, in the great shining echoing terminal, with half an hour to kill before it was time.

'What about a brandy alexander?' I suggested.

'They are sixty-five cents a hit now,' said Martin, dropping his schoolmasterish demeanour at the prospect of a small pleasure.

'What the hell,' croaked Javo. 'I'll pay. Come on.'

In a rush of belated generosity he ordered up two each, and we drank them in silence, planting our feet on the ugly carpet and avoiding each other's eyes, for fear of a compromising emotion. I looked out through the wall of windows at the great jets blundering about on the ground.

And of course I bungled the farewell, as one always does. At the 'first and final call' we hastened to join the mob banking up at the departure lounge behind the metal detector. For a second I quailed at the thought that Javo might be carrying some absurd macho weapon as part of the fantasy: the bowie knife? Something worse? But he waited in line unperturbed. Their turn came and all in a rush I threw my arms round Javo, wanting to tell him *take care you big idiot, I love you* but instead I instruct, 'Write to me, eh?' and sound dry in spite of myself. He bends down to hug me but there's no time to get the fronts of our bodies together and he turns away to the colder embrace of the security guard who runs a metal bleeper up and down his lanky body and presses him forward to the little archway. I kiss Martin: it always was easier, he is my height; and he too turns and offers himself to the metal detector. I am leaning over a wooden railing, I see them being sucked away from me towards the doorway and I'm seizing them with my eyes, *oh, you are incapable!* and just before he disappears, Javo gives a glance back over his shoulder and flashes me a rueful smile. Gone! that's all. And just as well, says the little head-prefect on my shoulder, you don't need 'em, you can get back to the proper business of your life. OK, OK.

I walked back along the bright passageway and slowly through the carpark, and got into Martin's car which was to be mine for longer than any of us had thought: and I drove home thinking about Javo's long legs driving him crazy in an economy seat all the way to Singapore.

I took to my bed for a couple of days. It was like a holiday. At night I slept clear and still, waking in the morning with the impression that I'd only just closed my eyes.

A letter came, written on the plane. 'A love with no fade from distance in it,' he sent me.

I went to the Kingston to hear Willy's band. I drove there on my own in Martin's car and sat at a table with Paddy and Angela and Nick.

Paddy nudged me. 'Look at Willy!'

His blue shirt was open to the waist, his eyes were closed, his blond head rolled back: the public ecstasy of musicians. I laughed, admiring and envious.

'Isn't he beautiful!'

'I always want to fuck him when I watch him play,' sighed Paddy, who until recently had lived with him for years. She rolled her eyes comically.

'Wouldn't mind, myself.'

Angela, always attuned to the sound of Willy's name on other women's lips, heard this. Her face seemed to contract a fraction. She tossed back the rest of her glass of Southern Comfort and turned to me where I was sitting beside her on Nick's knee.

'I've been wanting to say, Nora,' she began, having to lower her voice suddenly as the music stopped, 'that I don't hate you any more, like I have been for the last six weeks.'

'Hate me?' Nick, probably scenting trouble, gently pushed me off his lap and followed Paddy to the bar. 'I didn't notice. I must be a bit insensitive.'

'Yes. Well, that's part of the trouble, actually.'

I noticed she was rather drunk. I was in for something I wasn't going to like.

'I'd been thinking,' she said, 'that you were . . . you know . . . a kind of predator; that you assumed a certain sexual privilege when you wanted to fuck with someone, and didn't care much about the effect this would have on whoever else might be involved.'

'Like when?'

'Oh . . . with Martin, I guess . . . and putting it on Willy last year . . . I was thinking you had this habit of using people up and throwing them away.'

I stared at her in dismay.

'But it's all right,' she added, 'because I don't think that *now*.'

There was nothing to be said. The music started again. I put my head down on the laminex table and the music burst around my ears and I began to cry. Angela was alarmed, and hovered at the table, not daring to make gestures of comfort. I got up and stumbled out to the car. I cried as I drove along, and I cried when I got home to my room, and I cried till my eyes were bunged up and my chest ached. Georgie came in, and I kept on crying and trying to talk. Francis arrived and I felt ashamed of the state I was in, and foolish, and began to make jokes.

'It is all so monumentally *boring*!' I shrieked, lying back on the pillows and blowing my nose. I almost laughed to see their two horrified faces bobbing in front of me in the flood of tears.

Francis stayed with me and was patiently kind to me; but when we were fucking I began to cry again out of weakness and fear that he was *fucking me*, as a man *does it* to a woman; or out of fear that I liked it. I couldn't find his mind, or his heart; he was away in his own travelling.

Dark rain flooded the house. Eve was out and Grace and the Roaster were asleep in her bed. Waking to the battering of the rain, I ran out to her room and found the kids doggedly huddling, still asleep, in a growing pool of water which the leaking roof poured on to the bed. I picked them up, one by one, and carried them to their room. Grace went into her bed without waking.

'Francis,' I said, 'can I put the Roaster in here with you while I make his bed for him?'

Before I'd finished speaking he had thrown back the blankets and his arms were out ready for the blinking bundle.

'How is it you're so good with children?'

'B-because I used to be one,' he said.

Francis and I drove the VW van to Peterborough for the weekend. We parked it at the very edge of the cliff beside the Bay of Islands. I lay about, in the van and outside it on the thick turfy grass, dozing and reading and thinking and keeping my mouth shut. I woke at six in the morning and saw a red sky. The wind was mild and blustery and I walked on the clifftops with Francis' dog. The wind flattened yesterday's waves, deep green combers, into smooth bumps which worked hard to heave themselves to breaking point.

For hours neither of us might speak. I watched Francis, who

sat cross-legged on the floor of the van, his eyes blank with thought, staring out the open door at the silk-coloured sea. Rain splattered lightly on the van, and the wind buffed and rocked it.

I fantasised in full detail about living in the country. I thought about how daily life might be different: the air would be cleaner, the days emptier of people, the evenings more silent and perhaps lonelier, the house uglier. But in the yard I would have a dog, and some chooks, and we would ride bikes, and the children would wander more slowly home from school.

At home again, alone in my bed and my neat room, I fell asleep at eight in the evening and woke at dawn, still in the rhythm of the weekend just past. I dreamed I was in bed with Angela: I pushed my face between her big, soft breasts. At six in the morning I heard Gracie moan in her sleep; she stumbled into my room, all broad forehead and gold earrings, and crept in beside me, to suck her thumb till breakfast time.

So, when the news came, I was not prepared.

I got a telegram from Julian, one of Martin's brothers, asking me to meet him at Tullamarine: he was passing through from Asia where he lived and where the smack was cheap. I stood at the barrier and saw him come through.

'Hey, Jules!'

He turned his head. Even his Harris tweed jacket couldn't disguise his irrevocably bent nature, the translucent, fined-out pallor of the ex-junkie. His cheekbones protruded in his worn face, his hair was dry and bleached with sun, pulled back in a rubber band in an attempt to look straight for the customs, but escaping round his face in wisps. The coming and going of the blood in his face showed through a screen of suntan. His eyes sat deep in their rounded sockets, green as bird's eyes, very clear and steady, fringed with pale brown lashes. He put his cheek against mine.

'Hullo Nora.'

I didn't know he had news for me. He hissed it to me as we bumped clumsily through the heavy doors into the bar.

'They're in the pen.'

'*What?*'

He took hold of my elbow and pushed me gently into a chair. He fixed me with the unmistakable eyes of his family: Martin's eyes.

'They got busted in Bangkok.'

'*What for?*'

'Stealing a pair of sunglasses.'

My stomach started to roll.

'Oh, come on. *Sunglasses*. It was dope, wasn't it. Come on, Jules – you can tell *me*, for Christ's sake.'

'I *know* I can. No. I actually believe it *was* the sunglasses.'

'What's the bail?' Incredulously I heard myself asking all the correct questions, in my sensible voice; but somewhere in the back of the world I could hear Javo's voice, or something that sounded like it, calling me: '*Nora!*'

'A thousand American. Each.'

'*Each?* You're not bullshitting me, are you?'

'Would I? Look, Nora – anyone in jeans in South East Asia these days would cop that much bail.'

I kept grinning, with shock, and the irony.

'What are we going to do?'

'Is there any way you can get the money together for Javo?'

The backs of my hands started to prickle. I was laughing on the other side of my face.

'A thousand *bucks*? Are you kidding?' Stupid tears came into my eyes.

'OK – OK.' He held out his hand to calm me. 'I'll ask father.'

'Does he know?'

'Yeah.'

'How did he take it?'

'Pretty cool, really. He's used to Martin.' He gave a shrug and a crooked smile.

'But what about the junk? He can't avoid finding out about that, can he?'

'I guess not. He got used to it, all right, when I was down there coming off, myself, a while ago. It's amazing what they can handle, if you tell them the truth.' He turned the glass of scotch in his thin, brown hands. 'You probably won't like this

51

much, but it's karma, ou know. What you give out, you get back. It manifests itsel clearer in Asia than anywhere else.'

We said goodbye at the foot of the escalators. He changed hands with his bag and I hugged him and he held me tightly with one arm. I could feel his thin body inside his too-big, respectable clothes.

From outside our back gate I could hear the music. I walked into the kitchen with the car keys in my hand, and found Georgie bopping to himself in front of the mirror. Clive was hanging over a frying pan on the stove. Eve came in and saw my face. Her gat-toothed smile of greeting faded.

'What's happened?'

'Javo and Martin've been busted.'

Everyone stood still. The music clamoured in the room.

'Turn that fuckin' record down, Georgie,' said Eve. Georgie's mouth was open. Clive ran into the next room and the house was suddenly full of silence.

'Here, Nor, sit down.' Eve put on the kettle and reached for the packet of Drum. I told them what I knew. Clive stood behind me with his hands on my shoulders. I must have looked green.

'They've done it this time,' I kept repeating idiotically. 'They've blown it.'

In the middle of a night Martin's phone call came. When I recognised his voice, unreachable and yet close enough to touch, I broke out in sweat all over my body.

'Nora? How you doin'?'

'I'm all right, mate. What the fuck have *you* been up to?'

'Got sprung, I guess.'

I couldn't believe how casual he sounded. His laugh came crackling down the wire. But I knew that fleeting manner of Martin's, how his eyes would slide sideways to dodge the direct question. I could have screamed with the tension.

'How's Gracie? Tell her I've got her a present.' He was maddeningly casual, almost debonair.

'*Listen*, Martin, will you? How'd you get out? Where's Javo?'

'Julian bailed me out. But Javo's still in.'

Bad connection: the air between us roared and hummed. His voice swam meltingly, drifting as if under water.

'What? What? I can't hear you.'

'I said, *Javo's still in.*'

'Why?' I could hardly hold the receiver, for the sweat; my heart was thundering.

'They doubled the bail. So I got out and we are still hustling the money for Javo. Also . . .'

'*What?*'

'. . . They've moved him to another prison.'

'Have you seen him?'

'Yeah. I saw him today . . .'

'– Is he all right? Did you talk to him?'

'Through the bars. We could just touch palms. He looked OK – they've cut his hair, though.'

Javo shorn, Javo on his knees. I couldn't open my mouth.

'Nora?'

'Yes. I'm still here.'

'He gave me a note for you, Nor. I'll post it. Listen, Nor – for Christ's sake *don't worry*. Julian knows what to do. He'll be out in two days at the most. I have to go, mate – this is costing me a fortune. I'll write. OK?'

'OK.' Hardly heard myself speak. 'OK, Martin. Take care will you? And send him my love?'

And I hung up in a turbulence of emotions: panic, impotence, rage, fear. *I was unable.*

I waited. Javo's letter came: 'I need strong love,' he wrote from prison, so I started to give it, writing to him every day. He didn't write back.

At last Julian wrote to me from Bangkok:

'I have bailed them both out. I threw Martin's fit out the window of the hotel a couple of times, but I don't suppose that did much good.'

Martin wrote to me:

'Javo was pretty stoned before we got picked up. But that time has passed for both of us now.'

Liar.

53

I ought to weed out the whole fantasy from my mind. But I couldn't help remembering Javo, his thin limbs and wild face and blue eyes. He had been out of jail for ten days, and I had not heard a word from him. Junkies like other junkies. But I went on writing anyway.

I went to Anglesea with Paddy. On the Point Roadknight beach the tide was in and the air was full of salt and sharpness. I was eating dried figs.

'Do you want a dried fig, Paddy?'

'Look,' she said, 'I've got such a mad eating binge on that I'd eat a turd if you sprinkled it with sugar.'

We lounged on the beds, talking about junk and our households, speculating and exchanging anecdotes about broken resolutions and night-time freakouts and lies told and tears shed and love refused.

In Melbourne, every morning I went running with Rita in the Edinburgh Gardens. The yellow leaves were coming down, lying in drifts along the gutters. Javo waited in some hotel room in Bangkok for his trial; I wrote him dozens of letters. Scared to write; lonely not to.

I remarked to Georgie,

'I miss Javo, you know.'

He laughed incredulously. 'You miss him like you miss a piece of glass in your foot!'

I wished for him as he had been, occasionally, in the past. I wished there were no such thing as junk. I didn't wish I'd never known him. I wished there were some way for us to love each other. And I wished he were out of trouble so my mind could rest.

There was a life to be made.

At last he wrote to me. The letter came on one of an endless succession of empty mornings.

'I am thinking of your room, Nora. It was the hole in the arm that brought me undone – I am in this trouble just because I wanted something to hide being stoned behind. I wish you were here then we could go down to the sea and walk and talk. I just wish I was standing beside you sharing some sights of

54

things peculiar and things funny – smiling and talking and laughing and getting sunburnt – then having a shower, getting cleaned up and eating and fucking resting together like those two spoons in a drawer.'

I went to salvage his possessions from his house over the grocery store, which other junkies and cops had plundered and wrecked. In Javo's room I found: his photos of Freycinet, still pinned to the wall; a bottle of eucalyptus oil; his greasywool socks from Hobart; the mattress where we had fucked together, in hopeless sadness, the day it rained and rained and I surprised him in the kitchen with the belt on his arm.

In another room I found an exercise book of Gracie's, in which Martin had written at her dictation:

> NO THINK IS TRUE EXCEPT THE
> WORLD.
> DO YOU KNOW ANYTHING THAT'S
> TRUE?
> NO.

I walked round his house, tired and dull. Tears kept filling my eyes; my stomach was weak with sadness.

It was still all an absurd fantasy. I remembered only the good and lovable things about him, and not the wretchedness he caused me, and the dope and the resentments and silences and the half-crazy outbursts. I remembered his smell and the colour of his eyes and his head thrown back to laugh; these things were a second away, in time, but the others I dredged up dutifully, knowing I must, for the sake of truth and sanity, try to keep the balance.

I dreamed: Javo was back in town and the word was out, but for some reason it was appropriate to stay cool. I came out the front door of a small house with Paddy, going somewhere in a business-like manner. I saw Javo lying back with his feet up on some kind of chaise longue in the front yard, which was concrete with nothing growing. We passed him and under the influence of this social cool I didn't speak to him but gave him a salute as I passed his chair. He raised his arm to say goodbye, just as cool. Paddy and I were halfway down the street before I realised that what had happened was not enough for either of us.

'Wait for me; I want to say something to Javo,' I said, and ran back to the yard. He was still there in his long chair. I ran up to him and flung my arms round him, got my face in his neck and smelled his skin, and we held each other tightly, and *were both very happy*.

When I woke up I stumbled out to the kitchen, found it was the middle of the afternoon and that I had been dozing with the book still in my hand. On the table was another letter from him, ten pages toilsomely printed. I read it greedily.

Willy's Trick Parcel

By May Day they were still in Bangkok. The sun shone that afternoon in Melbourne, and I made an insignia in red letters for the back of my shirt, saying HO CITY for the Vietnamese and the liberation of Saigon. It was like being stoned all afternoon, marching to the river and singing. Somebody quoted Ho Chi Minh:

'What could be more natural? After sorrow comes joy.'

But in my own life it was the other way around. Our house was sold and we had to go. Some wept, some raged, some shrugged and went off searching. Like a fool I did some acid in the last week. I lay on my bed for a long time, listening peacefully to the strange orchestration of conversation in other rooms. I gazed at the yellow curtains which were rippling in the breeze from the open window, and they became the yellow wall, and I became part of the room and the curtains were my fine yellow skin rippling smoothly like ribs of sand on the Sahara. When I left that house, ragged ends of myself would be left hanging. I was the last one of the household left to sleep

56

there, in the empty shell. I wished I had someone to love.

Gracie and I went with Rita and Juliet to an old house near the Victoria market, small and square as a sailor's cottage, bare of furniture. Rita had two weeks of her old lease to fulfil; Gracie and I camped in the cottage in the beginnings of winter. Used to a big clashing household, we stared round us in the night silence, huddled in my bed with our clipboards and the big tin of textacolours.

'Draw wit' me, Nora – draw wit' me,' she'd say, every morning before it got light. When we woke, those mornings, I'd gallop up the wooden stairs to the second storey attic room and hang out the window, hands on the crumbling sandstone of the sill, and peer eastwards to the yellow face of the brewery clock. Quarter to seven on the knocker every time. I'd turn to the south, lean out a foot further, and right at my elbow would loom the dark towers of the inner city, towers of Mammon, picked out against the infinitesimally lightening sky by hundreds of tiny squares of light: windows behind which cleaners were already at work.

Every day Rita came and we bandaged our heads with scarves and painted and chipped at the old walls, and ate absent-mindedly, standing in the bare kitchen with handfuls of bread and sausage.

I was starting to notice that I hadn't fucked for a long time. It wasn't the fucking I missed: I wanted *love*. I felt sad and hungry, or greedy rather, wishing to comfort myself. I ate small snacks all morning, felt disgusted with myself, and returned to my room upstairs to pick away at the walls hour after hour. Lou came to visit me. He worked with me all one afternoon. He kept dropping his scraper and dashing over to me and hugging me ferociously, kissing me and hugging me and making much of me, saying,

'Ooh, isn't this sexy work!'

He stopped me from feeling sad in the flesh.

'I haven't fucked for weeks,' I remarked. 'I dream all the time about fucking with guys I know.'

'What'll you do?' asked Lou, interested, pausing in his scraping and shuffling his Adidas runners in the mess of crumbling plaster we were standing in.

'Oh,' I said with a laugh, 'something will fall in my path sooner or later.'

The only thing that fell in my path was a trick parcel: but I was too lonely to tell it from the real thing. One night I was watching television at the tower with Willy. Everyone else had gone out. And something odd happened. Willy had a way of talking largely in political generalisations, then of suddenly saying something intensely personal in the same tone of voice, which always had a rather shocking effect. This night he delivered himself of some opinions on the nature of romantic love and its damaging effects. I listened placidly, silently agreeing, staring at the screen: then he dropped his head over the back of his armchair and said, looking at the ceiling,

'What I feel for *you* isn't romantic love. But it isn't just sex, either. I'm finding it really exciting being in this room with you, and I'm going to be ex-treme-ly pissed off when the others start coming back in.'

Immediately he sat up again and looked at the television, without a direct glance at me. I stared at the side of his head, too surprised to speak.

People did start coming back in, but when it got late and they had all gone and I stood up to go home, he said,

'Why don't you stay here?'

He was half-laughing, the caricature of the European student, all silvery and golden in gleaming spectacles, his short blond hair precisely cut, one wrist still bandaged from his eternal karate injury.

'I can't,' I said. 'I'd bleed all over you. And anyway, if Angela came in in the morning it'd freak me right out.'

He laughed. 'She won't.'

'Of course, you could come to *my* place – but you wouldn't be able to stand the early rising.' We kept looking at each other, laughing. 'I bet we'd really have to slug it out,' I said. 'For example, you wouldn't come to my place tonight because if you did you'd be admitting I'd won the first round.'

He said nothing, laughing so his regular teeth showed, looking me right in the eyes. I got up and stood between his knees. We smiled at each other because it simply didn't matter if we stayed together then, or later, or never. I leaned over and kissed him goodbye: slight prickle of his short blond beard, his mouth surprisingly soft. I put my hand under his jacket, under his arm, accidentally on the curve of a muscle.

One evening, a week later, I was driving up Elgin Street in Martin's car and caught sight of Willy in the laundromat. I stopped the car, parked it, and walked into the humming fluorescent brightness. He looked up from his newspaper and nodded.

'Want a lift home?'

'Yeah. My stuff's in the dryer. Can you wait five minutes?'

I waited while he sorted his clothes; he concentrated completely on the task, working quickly and neatly, folding his lips together in a line.

In the car I remarked, 'I have so many dreams and fantasies about you, I can hardly tell which is which any more.'

He glanced at me with a half-smile. 'Easy. Dreams are when you're asleep, fantasies when you're awake.'

'Yeah – well, I don't quite know what to do about 'em.'

'Nothing – if you want them realised. Because then they wouldn't be fantasies any more.'

I felt as if I'd been given a push in the face. The car was full of the smell of his clean washing, warm and homely. I drove on in silence. Aware of overkill, he said, probably thinking he was changing the subject,

'I'm really digging getting good at karate. Now, whenever anyone starts anything, I just adopt a half-fighting stance, and they drop back.'

I dropped back.

I dreamed: Javo and I were walking along a beach. There was no-one else in sight. We walked side by side for miles. I was talking to him. I was saying very fulsome emotional things. I said,

'I love you so much that if I thought you didn't love me, I'd want to die.'

We trod and trod together through the sand, heavy going. I stopped talking. He said nothing. I looked sideways at him, waiting for him to speak, but he remained silent and did not look at me. I realised that he didn't love me like that, that he was confused and embarrassed and didn't know what to say.

I lent Willy my car and he drove me home to Peel Street. We talked awkwardly for half an hour beside my cold fire. He was sick, I was tired. I kept thinking of my bed and getting into it to go to sleep. At last I said,

'I'm going to bed, Willy. You could come with me if you liked.'

A pause.

'No . . . I think I'll go home.'

'OK.'

A pause. He was standing next to my chair. We both stared at the fire.

'I hope you get well,' I said.

'Yeah. I'll take lots of that white stuff tomorrow, and try to get better.'

'You ought to fast.'

'Yeah, I know, but it's so hard. Hunger's like a disease: it has to be tended.'

So is loneliness.

He bent over, both hands in the pockets of his thick blue coat, and – I would say kissed – put his mouth against mine. His lips felt cold.

'You're not pissed off with me, are you?' he said.

'No. Of course I'm not.'

'I'll see you tomorrow. Probably.'

'OK.'

He went out my broken front door, having to slam it hard to make the lock catch. I went straight away into my room. I turned on the lamp and knelt on the bed to move the cushions aside. Tears came almost to my eyes.

'I'm lonely. I'm lonely.'

I thought perhaps he would get as far as the car, and come back.

Men never come back.

He didn't.

I lay in my bed in the empty house. I thought, when Javo

comes back, his presence in my house might be just as difficult, painful and *wrong* as Willy's. Oh no! I imagined him behind me in the room, like Willy, pretending to read *Rolling Stone* while I stared at the fire and fiddled with briquettes, wondering how to ask him to stay, and whether I really wanted him to, and whether he would refuse with grace or hurtfully. But I wished for him. Maybe he had gone over the river into Laos, maybe he would end up in jail in Bangkok for six months, or longer. I wished for him, with his great lanky limbs and thin face and bright, bright blue eyes.

Was That Somebody Knocking?

Where are you, Javo?

I kept feeling he would walk in any day. Sometimes I swore I could feel it in my bones.

I was tired out. I worked like a dog on my room. As I scrubbed vigorously at the skirting boards I thought, I've never cared this much before about doing the job properly: why do I care so much now? Javo's face flashed in the corner of my eye every now and then as I worked. I would like to bring him into my room, make him lie down, listen to him talk, look at his bony face.

'Let's go to the tower,' said Gracie.

'OK. What for?'

'To see Jack. And because round there they always buy the Sunday papers, and they have in them carturns, and horse racing, and stories about girls who fuck with men to get money.'

'You mean car*toons*, dingbat.'

At the tower Gracie went into her father's room, and in the hallway I met Jessie, just back from Europe. Her face was pale and thin, under her straight fringe of red, red hair. She put her hand gently on my arm and smiled right into my eyes. No wonder people love her forever. Jessie and Javo together: a bed full of blue eyes.

I dreamed: Javo was back. Everywhere I went people were telling me,

'Hey, Javo is back, Nora, and he's looking for you!'

I didn't know whether to stay where I was (on a farm, up a sandy road) and wait for him to come to me, or to set out myself and start searching for him round the households. I was full of joy and anticipation. As the dream progressed, this joy drained away and I realised that it *was* a dream. I woke up desolate.

Martin and Javo were in Kuala Lumpur. Julian had got them out. I knew my feeling was right. I kept dreaming drunkenly about seeing them come back through that airport door I'd watched them disappear into two months before. The day I met Martin's father there, and we kissed cheeks, I bumped his spectacles; when I met Julian he trod on my toes; when I see Javo we will wrap ourselves around each other effortlessly.

This was a fantasy.

I had to be ready for anything: he would be traumatised, and so would I.

Come home, Javo, and let me work it out from there.

Days passed, days passed.

It rained, and the long autumn was over. Rita and Juliet came to the house. I dreamed that Rita had the power of altering, by sheer willpower, the cellular structure of my moral fabric.

Javo and Martin had been granted travel papers and could leave Kuala Lumpur. Martin, his father told me, was going to Europe; *and so was Javo.* My heart turned over. But how, I said, can he afford to travel in Europe? I lent him the money, said Martin's father. The old familiar rage crept out of its lair.

O, o, you bastard, if you can afford to go to Europe you can afford to send me a cable. Death, death in the crook of his arm – what's a cable here or there?

'Javo, I could say you owed me a letter. I wish I could stop the flow. I have leaked myself away towards you for nearly two months now. I ought to put the plug back in, fill up the tub again for myself and other people; and I try, but all the time there's this stubborn little trickle running away, running away towards some unknown place where you are killing yourself. Where are you? What'll I do with this letter?'

In the evening I was washing the dishes and talking with Rita who was sitting by the fire.

'Was that somebody knocking?' she said.

She got up and went to the door. My heart leaped up into my mouth. It's Javo, would he knock so quietly? At the old house he always walked straight in. She was opening the door.

'Oh – hullo!' she said.

My memory brought his scraping voice so vividly to mind that it grated in my ears. My heart was not beating. I leaned back from the sink to see and it wasn't Javo. It was somebody else.

I must be going crazy.

No word from him. We live and don't learn. Maybe he'll shoot himself to death in K.L. Maybe he's gone to Europe. What a nasty flight, coming down off a habit that big. If he'd walked in at that moment, I'd have moved over and made room for him. What's love? Being a sucker, I suppose.

I dreamed: I moved with Gracie into a new house in a swanky part of town. I was walking along the street. I saw an expensively dressed couple, glossy like Bunuel's bourgeois, playing with their two groomed children on their front lawn. I introduced myself as a new neighbour. They appeared to be Belgian diplomats. We were chatting politely when a telephone rang beside the woman in the grass. She answered it, listened, registered surprise and pleasure. She took notes on a piece of paper, spoke briefly, hung up.

'Who was that?' I asked.

'It was Javo!'

What! and she hadn't told him I was there, and he hadn't

asked! I was dumbfounded. She showed me her notes.

'He's started school in America,' she said. I looked at her scrawly writing and couldn't decide if it said *Michigan* or *Canada*.

Clive came rushing into our house and thrust a postcard into my hand.

'From the old house,' he panted, just off his bike.

I turned it over and saw an English postmark. 'Darling Nora . . .' – what! Javo would never write such a thing. I looked at it properly and saw that it was from his *mother*. What a trick of fate. I hid my disappointment. I fell back into my state of aimless waiting. I couldn't get free of it. Every morning I woke up empty.

Life was getting thin and sick. I lay on the floor in front of the fire and listened to the litany of gossip sung by my friends. The loneliness was drying me out. I reached the bottom one Friday night. I lit a fire in my room, for animal comfort, got into my bed, turned off the lamp, looked at the fire. Dry, dry and aching.

In the morning I got up and went about my business. I got home from the market at half past eleven. There was a pack and a red and yellow string bag on the doorstep. I stared at the bag, my arms full of shopping, Gracie and Juliet jostling at my legs. Through the weave of the bag I saw packets of Lucky Strike, and a big book bulging with paper and covered with Asian stamps. There could be no doubt. The children peered curiously at me.

'Your face has gone all red!' squeaked Juliet.

'If it's Javo, I know!' said Gracie. 'You're going to cry of happiness!'

He was nowhere in the house.

I faked calm and climbed the stairs to my room, but my dry heart was swelling up fat. I was standing in my room doing nothing when I heard the knock at the door, and I was halfway down the stairs when the kids opened it, and I was so close to him in the small white hallway that I'd hardly had a chance to

64

see him before we had our arms round each other without missing a beat.

It Makes You Forget Your Friends

That night when our skins touched, for the first time in months I felt perfectly sure that I wanted to be with the person I was with. We kissed, I remembered him, he looked straight into my face, and my heart and body were in tune with each other. What *is* it about him? I want to align myself with him, be his ally.

He was weak, half ill, terribly thin, only five or six days off a big habit. He came just from touching and kissing. My heart, hollow and dry for months, slowly filled up.

'My heart's full for you,' I whispered, ashamed of the words but having to say them.

He smiled at me out of his lantern head, his eyes shone way back in their caverns:

'I don't ever want to stop loving you.'

He fell asleep, but started twitching and groaning and crying out, and thrashing hard in the bed. I didn't know how to comfort him and take away his fear.

Five days, he lasted.

When he came back, all the splinters of my life started to make sense again. But straight away we misunderstood each other. Driving in the afternoon, we saw a man and a woman in the street stop and kiss. We all smiled and I said,

'Oh, ooh! They must be in love!'

Gracie writhed with laughter. 'I hate love! I'm never going to be in love!'

'Good on you, Grace,' said Javo, grinning. 'Love's shithouse.

It makes you forget your friends.'

'Oh, go on, you old grouch,' I protested, to hide that idiotic flinching of the heart. 'Do you think that's what's happened to you? You're on your way to see your friends right now!'

'No! What I meant was – it makes you forget you *are* friends!'

I drove him to Easey Street, his old junkie haunt, and Gracie and I came in with him for a moment. The ring of white faces looked up from the fire at Javo who stood grinning in the doorway with Grace and me hovering behind him.

'Javo! Where did *you* spring from?'

'Bangkok, mate.' He gave out a gust of nervous laughter, tossing back his shorn head. Mark shifted to make room for him at the fire.

'Plenty of cheap dope over there, eh?' They all laughed the conspirators' knowing laugh.

'Yeah. But I'm off it.'

'You got off?' Mark's face sobered in surprise. '*Well done!*' There was genuine respect in his voice. I couldn't help grinning at his tone. He saw this and turned away with a smile. 'G'day, Nora.'

'Hullo Mark. Well – I'm going, Javo.' I took Gracie's hand. 'See you later on.'

'OK. See you, mate.' He touched my shoulder. 'Thanks for the lift.'

In my room I made a fire of wood. The window was open only a crack but a thin wind was edging through. Gone again, already.

He came back with a Stevie Wonder record, and played the same song over and over: 'They Won't Go When I Go,' crouching desperately over the fire trying to warm the frozen marrow of his bones. No matter where I went in the house, I couldn't escape that voice, its attenuated weeping, the shameless moan of its straining after holiness.

I didn't want to hold him, or stop him from hitting up, or be with him twentyfour hours a day. There were times in those five days when I was ready to beat my head with the rage of not being able to make myself clear to him: stupid, bloody tears kept rolling out of my eyes, it was *so hard*. But when we looked at each other sometimes, or he put his hand on my back in the street, or his arms round me in the night, everything fell simply and momentarily into place.

On the fifth day, (days thick with difficulty and his sickness and his cold bones), he came out with it:

'Every time I go to Easey Street,' he said, 'I suppose I'm hoping there'll be a hit waiting for me on the table. If there'd been dope, these last few days, I'd have been into it . . . so how can I have an honest relationship with you, when that desire's still there? You said you wanted *me*, not me and a bunch of fuckin' chemicals.'

I was paralysed: what he was saying filled me with uncertainty, I could barely make sense of it. He was in a chair facing away from me, and I was sitting on the floor in front of the fire looking at his back and side.

'I have to go and pick up Gracie from school.'

He was still sitting in the chair, with an empty plate on his lap. I pushed my head into his neck, I said,

'I love you, Javo.'

Tears ran off my face on to his blue jumper. He put his arms round my shoulders and started to cry too.

'I love you too,' he said. I was bent over him, the plate was resting on his thin thighs; I had to stand up and leave.

When I got back he had fallen asleep on my bed. He woke up bad-tempered, sick in the bowels; he asked me to drive him to Easey Street. I did it, I drove him there, no social visit this time but the purpose in it; I drove off feeling as if I'd delivered him to the lion's den.

Alone in my house. Javo did not come back. I might have gone looking for him the night after, but I had the children to look after, and I read them a story and put them to bed with a plate of cut-up apple, and no-one else came home, so I went to bed myself. I comforted myself with the thought that his things were still in the house – oh, but what if he comes for them while I'm out and I come home and they're gone, no word?

I shall see what I shall see.

In the morning I ran into him accidentally in the tower,

where he had just woken up. I could see the dope still in him, but we'd been together in the car for twenty minutes before he said,

'I got stoned last night.'

We both laughed.

He was being scrupulously courteous and pleasant to me; but gradually he became offhand, in a way he had, until I ceased to exist. He picked up his camera from my house so he could walk down to Russell Street and hock it.

'I might see you later on tonight,' he said, kissing me goodbye. I was sitting at the living room table. He went to the front door without looking back. I said,

'Do you mean you'll come back here?'

'If I can get a lift. It's such a fuckin' long way!' he said, invisible behind the front door. 'Jack's invited me to the tower for lunch – isn't that nice of him!' His laugh was almost a sneer.

I heard him but I sat there and said nothing.

'See you,' he sang out, and banged the door behind him.

Oh well, oh well.

No more tears in me for him, not yet a while.

The fire was drying the towels. I ironed my shirt and tidied my room. I was happy in the quiet house. I felt as strong as a horse. A person would need to, to try and go on loving a junkie. Javo: the rolling eye, the head rearing back, the smile which is a ritual gesture tinged with fright. Rubbing the crook of his arm.

I saw him at the tower – or rather, he heard my voice in the middle of the morning and called to me from the little room at the top of the stairs, where he had slept. Lifts his pale, dry head from the pillow. Croaks to me,

'Nor!' Puts up his arms to me like sticks of kindling. He is not stoned.

I go out on an errand, and when I come back fifteen minutes later he's had the first hit of the day and is cooking something in the kitchen. I hear Willy shout, and Javo answer, also shouting.

'You're doing it to *yourself*, mate!'

'What? What?'

'You're *stoned!*'

'Yeah – well, so what?'

The rest I can't hear from Jack's room where I am playing with Gracie. I go out again to the shop and come back up the stairs. He hears my voice.

'If you're lookin' for me, Nor, I'm up here.'

I climb the creaking stairs to the bedroom where he is lying in his crumpled clothes, boots on, eyes rolling up under half-closed lids. I sit in the curve of his body. His arms are like the forelegs of a praying mantis, seeming oddly jointed and moving at random. He takes my hand, I take his between both of mine and feel the weight of his thin arm. His sleeves are rolled down past his elbows.

He nods off, wakes again, launches himself on a perfectly coherent explanation of his feelings towards me. Whenever he pauses, his eyes roll up and close and his breathing becomes noisy for one in-out; then he opens his eyes, focuses on me, and continues to talk, slowly and deliberately, as if the pause had not happened.

'I can't promise to give up junk . . .'

'I never asked you to.'

'I know you didn't. But . . . I've been using shit for two years now, and I can't cut off the past . . . because there are good things connected with it too, you know. It keeps me warm on cold nights, and it makes me feel young again . . . you know, physically.'

I listen. How did I teach myself to listen to this kind of thing without those small spasms of death in the heart?

Our faces are very close together. The pupils of his eyes, tiny from the dope, have receded like tides from their immediate surrounds, leaving a ring of almost white between the black centre and the blue, blue iris.

'That's why my eyes look mad,' he says.

This close, we smile at each other with the flesh of our faces.

'You *are* beautiful, Nor. What a good face you've got.'

He kisses me, we start to kiss.

I can, I can taste the dope on his mouth. It is like medicine,

69

faint and poisonous, but not unpleasant.

'I can taste it on you.'

'*Can* you?'

I lie next to him, we kiss, I stroke his belly on which the skin is smooth and winter-white. His nipple stands up hard.

'Unfortunately,' I say, 'you are the only person I want to fuck with at the moment.'

He laughs. ' "Unfortunately" is right!'

'It makes my sex life pretty spartan.'

'It'd be spartan whether I came over or not.' ('Too wasted to fuck,' he'd told me in my bed.)

We are laughing, right up close to each other. Now we kiss again, it is easy for him now because he is stoned and loose in the body, not afraid. I can feel him go loose, he lets his breathing change and his voice travels gently on his breath.

Jessie calls out to me from the hallway and I have to go. I sit up and feel my cheeks warm from his unusual tenderness. He holds me in his curve. His face is soft too, even his white eyes.

'I feel better now,' he says. 'I feel good about our touching. I didn't, before. When I first came back, I didn't feel right.'

Because you weren't stoned, Javo; and the rest is not enough.

Outside the tower I buttoned my jacket and strode down Elgin Street with Jessie.

'How's it going with Javes, Nora?' she asked, grinning at me under her woollen cap with its earflaps.

'Ah shit, I don't know, Jess,' I said with a twist of the shoulder. 'Bloody dope. You know what it's like.'

'You're not kidding.' She laughed.

'How did *you* manage it?'

'I didn't! I was so sick, trying to keep up with him – he was way ahead of me. Even snorting it used to make me spew, afterwards.'

'I wish there was no such thing as smack,' I grunted into my collar.

She laughed. 'But the reasons for it would still be there.'

'Yeah. I s'pose you're right. Well, fuck it.'

We paced along, hands in pockets.

He won't come tonight, because he is too far away and he wants the dope, and he won't come near me when he's stoned. Not yet, anyway. And he says he won't come over while he's coming down. If he sticks to these resolutions, I'll never see him. He talks about 'keeping it under control', which means using it when it's around and talking bravely about his freedom from it when it's not.

And when he did come round, he was stoned, but still in the honeymoon phase: it hadn't got him by the throat. He got into my bed in the middle of the night and wrapped his thin limbs around me, and we fucked with a joy so intense and peaceful that our hearts were in our faces and we gave them to each other without a word. I came three, four times; once we rolled apart and I lay with my back to him in the curve of his body, but before I could doze away, he turned me back to him with a hand on my shoulder, brought me round to face him, insisted gently against my sleepiness until I came up out of it to join him, and thought,

'Oh, I will fuck you till I die.'

That was the terrible trick of the dope: one more step into its kingdom and Javo would be lost to me. But now we swayed dizzily on its borders, each in our own ecstasy.

Next day I spent an hour with Javo in a restaurant at lunchtime. He said he hadn't had a hit since the afternoon before; but he was cheerful and goodhumoured, and we laughed and chattered like real people, not like a junkie and a woman with a puzzled attitude towards his obsession.

I said to him as we walked along Lygon Street to the car,

'Some days I love you, some days I hate you, but today I *like* you.'

He laughed. 'That's best!'

'Oh, no – they're all good. But I like you; I think you're terrific.'

I drove him to Easey Street and he kissed me goodbye,

affectionate and half-laughing.

What'll happen next?

I found his fit in his shirt pocket: in fact, going through his pockets before throwing his shirt in with my washing, I withdrew my hand with the fit hanging painlessly from one fingertip, where it had imbedded itself.

He got up in the middle of the night for a hit. I was afraid (next morning, when I found the fit and pieced the time-fragments together to account for my bone-knowledge, in sleep, of his condition) that Rita or one of the girls might have gone downstairs in the night and found him hitting up in the kitchen. I was guarding them all from each other.

White eyes.

But we loved each other. In the night we touched, or held each other warm. I wanted to make him cry out, for love or pleasure. I heard his voice through his breathing.

At the film festival I met Francis again. I sat beside him on the carpeted stairs of the Palais, and while we were talking he suddenly kissed me. He drove me back across the river and I might, had circumstances allowed, have stayed with him; but the jaw-faced sailor in *Sweet Movie* had made me think of Javo and his hot, bony face, and all evening I was moving back towards him, thinking of him as my man.

He told me about a woman he was working with, in a play he had begun to rehearse.

'I would like to fuck with her,' he remarked.

She was a junkie too: I saw her once: thin, white, with red plaits on top of her fine head.

'I would be jealous, I suppose,' I said unwillingly.

'I know. But that wouldn't stop me,' he said, without the harshness the words might have carried. 'Though I would *think* of that; I would *think* of it.'

The fact that *he* might be jealous wouldn't stop *me*, either.

I wish . . .

I wish it would, but only if it would stop him, too. As it is, I must learn not to need him, because when I need him he will have nothing to give.

I ask the Ching: 'What about him and junk and me?'

It replies: 'Only through having the courage to marshal one's armies against oneself will something forceful really be achieved. One should submit to the bad time and remain quiet. It is impossible to counteract these conditions of the time. Hence it is not cowardice but wisdom to submit and avoid action.'

'What is it that each of us desires? This morning I got up filled with happiness and confidence . . . but I walked round the city on my own and stared at the strange faces and received my own fair share of mocking or puzzled looks . . . splinters stuck in the memory: how you glanced up at me as your fingers threaded the beads, and you gave me a crooked smile which made me suddenly afraid that you were at that moment leaving my house for HER, the OTHER who exists (faceless yet more beautiful, ghostly yet more fleshed out, outside time and yet more temporally real than ME) in the cobwebby corners of my mind and imagination which are not illuminated by my confidence in you. This is not your fault! Or rather – the lit areas are confined, or limited, by my fear, and my need (born of old scepticism and pain) to protect my flank from your thoughtless kick or the rot of neglect and forgetfulness.

'Javo I will live for now and not read between the lines.'

Night again, cold again. We saw *Lenny*. I kept remembering what his wife said about him, with tears in her eyes:

'He was just so goddamn *funny*!'

He OD'd in a bathroom. Oh Javo! One day I'll find you on the bathroom floor. I don't know how to talk about that unless I make a joke of it.

But we fucked, we held each other in the night, we made love. In the night whenever we half-woke we turned to each other and felt that old electric charge. If we acted on each one, we would never rest. That night, he said to me when we were all but dissolved into one another,

'Where do we go from here?'

Further, deeper. Somehow.

'I love you *very much*!' I said to him.

'But what happens when that stops?'

I drove the kids to Anglesea, sang to them, told them endless stories, my invention never flagging as I drove and they hung, open-mouthed, over the back of my seat. When I left Melbourne, Javo was still asleep. When I came back that night, the bed was cold and messy, and I found a big splattering of blood on the concrete floor of the dunny.

'*Red water in the bathroom sink*,' I sang absent-mindedly. I sponged up the blood. I got a fire burning in my room and roasted my back; I was going to mend my shirt, but I was too tired to think of using a needle and thread. I ought to sleep, ought to. The children are already silent in their bunks. I think about him, as we dozed off in my bed, turning me towards him and mumbling,

'Kiss. Kiss before sleep.'

Will he come back? Not worrying me, but I think of him and wonder 'where in the city can that boy be?'

He came back days later; I was asleep. He was coming down pretty hard, but waiting on two sleeping pills he'd taken before he left Carlton. He lay next to me, stiff and straight.

'You don't seem very happy,' he said. I turned away from him, sick in the heart. I was afraid to talk about loving him when he was in that cold, rational frame of mind, because I didn't want to be ... left behind, or something.

There was no bodily warmth between us. The withdrawing

seemed to take everything away.

But he actually rang me up and said,

'Nor, my rehearsal doesn't start till eight – do you want to do something between now and then?'

I said yes, by all means. Good grief! An invitation, an acceptance, courtesy, like ordinary people! I went to Easey Street and stood by the fire with him. He had had a shower, washed his hair, put on clean clothes. Prison haircut growing out elegantly in two points at his cheekbones. His face was open, cheerful, his eyes sparkling. He was always pleasant on methadone, the worst poison of them all.

I said, 'You freaked me out the other night, talking about how unhappy you think I am.'

We laughed.

'Well,' he said, 'you sometimes seem pretty ... gloomy, when I come in late at night.'

'Gloomy, do I! But what about when we're fucking? Do I seem gloomy then?'

'No!'

'Well – it's only one, two ... *three* nights we haven't been fucking.'

'Is it? It seems like weeks.'

I wondered how he meant that. *I* missed the fucking: it had stopped when he started to withdraw.

I went to visit Francis, and talked merrily with him in his cramped, woody house. His two big dogs clamoured round our legs. Dogs at his place, children at mine. I wished I could see clearly into his in-turned, mysterious, determined mind.

Javo, eating a slice of orange in bed, wedges the peel between his teeth and lips and mumbles,

'Do you love me? Just like *Planet of the Apes*!'

In the night we laugh so much that I am always saying,

'Shhoosh! You'll wake up the whole house!'

'Keep talking!' he says. 'I love gossip!'

Javo's play was ready and I arrived at the back theatre for the supper show at eleven o'clock. I paid my two dollars and went in. I heard straight away from behind the set Javo's voice raving his lines in the loud hysterical tone I'd heard him use only once before: the day I did the acid and he hit up more and more until by nightfall he was blackened round the mouth, blazing-eyed, manic in his speech – *that voice*! with a note of maniac laughter in it, his face grinning madly. I dared not go near him, for fear of a swipe from his swung arm, an accident but proceeding out of his absolutely *not caring*. Once at the old house he pushed me aside in the hallway, staring past me with pale eyes; he went two steps further and remembered who I was and that there were social forms which people expect to be observed. He came back and hugged me perfunctorily, his limbs trembling and stiff, eyes still going past me.

So it was in the theatre. He either didn't see me, or wasn't going to meet my eyes. Turned from my eyes. You bastard, Javo.

I didn't wait for the show. I got in a cab and came home. Not unhappy, but tired in the heart. When I got home, it was like having escaped from a stricken city. I sat by the fire and talked with Clive who had been with the children, and as we talked, the thought formed itself in my head,

'Time coming in which I must survive without a lover.'

If I can do it.

But he actually came back in the middle of the night. What'm I going to do? He is out of the human phase, is like a black-lipped spectre which eats, sleeps and groans.

What a Wonderful Guy

My own modest crumbs of coke I hoarded for solitary moments. I crept upstairs with the mirror and the razor and the rolled-up banknote and snorted it secretly in the stuffy little attic room where the children kept their toys. Up I flew. Wasn't it already the shortest day of the year? Winter solstice. The coldest days and nights were still ahead of us. My brown gloves smelled leathery and perfumy, like the inside of my nanna's handbag. In my pockets I found scraps of paper with lines of songs scribbled on them: 'everybody's cryin' mercy', my head raced ahead of itself and my mucous membrane became fat, but it was worth it! Fickle stuff, though, specially when mixed with fatigue. I sailed off to the film festival, chilled in the hands but full of warmth for the human race and all material things . . . I was early and called in to visit Paddy, who was crouched on the floor over a poster she was designing. She turned her thin face up to me, smiled her dry, absent smile, her eyes behind the spectacles still preoccupied.

'Nora. What are you up to?'

'I've just had a huge snort of coke,' I cheerfully announced.

'Ooh, you lucky thing! Haven't got any more, have you?'

'No,' I lied, sitting there in her room with an envelope of it in my back pocket.

What's *happening* to me?

But, as if in revenge for my greed, as I left her house the coke turned around, gave a twist and a wriggle, and fled away, dumping me unceremoniously in a limbo, skew-whiff and desolate. I drifted through the rest of the afternoon in a puzzled dream.

And when I came home I decided not to waste another snort, but to wait till my body was clear. I sat down at the table to transfer the coke to an uncrushed wrapper, and idly sniffed up the residue as I worked. How thoughtlessly you can persuade yourself that what you're doing at any particular moment is not *actually* getting into dope, or eating, or smoking, or whatever it is you've rationally decided not to do; that it's just a small aberration, or to make sure something is not wasted – or it's not anything at all because your mind has slipped its moorings, disconnected itself for that moment from your body. The left hand doesn't know what the right hand is doing.

So! I shortly found myself feeling *fantastic*, and went on feeling that way till ten o'clock, when I got into bed and fell asleep. I dreamed that I opened up a cut I had in waking life in the biggest finger of my right hand, and took out a shining white fish-bone, three quarters of an inch long.

Trouble.

Javo the monster. I don't know him when he's like this. I wish he would go away. He barely gives me the time of day. He blunders into my room at night, drops his great boots from waist height and crawls into bed beside me. This is *not Javo*. I know he doesn't care, and somehow neither do I. But I want him back, the way we used to be, when we loved each other with open hearts.

'Have you noticed,' I said, 'that we never see each other in daylight any more?'

'Yeah – it used to be like that with me and Jessie, when she was working on a show and I wasn't,' he said. 'It'll be different when the season's over.'

My mind ceased momentarily to compute, out of sheer amazement. I realised that I *never looked ahead*, with Javo, more than half a day.

He kissed me goodbye in the street outside the tower.

Rita told me she had seen him with a 'red-headed girl'. In my imagination I erected instantaneously a great castle of paranoia with glittering towers and battlements. I examined it. I dismantled it brick by brick, and left it in a corner of the yard.

We slept together every night.

In the street, on a sunny, windy day, I ran into Javo on his

78

knees outside the film co-op chalking up a footpath sign for that night's supper show. He was stoned but sparkly-eyed; incredibly dirty, grey-skinned, black-lipped.

I said, 'Wanna come for a cup of coffee in Tamani's when you've finished that?'

'OK,' he replied. 'See you over there in a few minutes.'

He came in, sat down at the table, and somehow he was with me but not with me. He kept looking over my shoulder, and I hesitated to start talking because I got the impression, halfway through a sentence, that I was talking into the phone long after the other person had hung up.

He asked me what gnocchi was, and if I'd buy him some. I said yes, and he went to get a cigarette off Lillian at the other end of the restaurant, and sat down with her for ten minutes; and I sat on my own at my table feeling my heart go heavy and sink, feeling used again, paying for a meal I'd invited him to and ending up sitting with my chin in my hand staring out at the street while he talked with someone else – and to make it worse, with Lillian, long-legged goodlooking Lillian in her ragged fur coat, who shared with me a past of such bitterness that it was all we could do to greet each other without a grimace, the rigours and theories of feminism notwithstanding. I was about to leave the price of the as yet unserved gnocchi in his box of chalk and go off quietly when he came back to the table and sat down opposite me, smiling with his bright eyes in his filthy face.

'I had to tell the Bangkok story yet again,' he said. 'You know Lillian, don't you? She's too much!'

But when we crossed the road together, he took my arm.

I had a second try at seeing his show. Every fifth person in the audience was either nodding off or just about to: junk oozing in the atmosphere. I had learnt my lesson and did not trouble myself with Javo. When the play ended and the rock and roll began, I kept a safe distance and lounged with Paddy in the high bank of seats. But Javo seemed a bit concerned. He kept glancing over at me from the other side of the theatre, and when our eyes met he would give me one of his rueful smiles;

once, when I grinned at him, he nodded vigorously at me, a sign of allegiance. I went over, in the end, and sat down beside him. He put his arm round my shoulder in an affectionate and unconsciously proprietary manner. We sat there happily for an hour or so. When the music finished I said,

'I think I'll go home now. Are you . . .?'

He looked worried and said, 'No . . . I'm going round to Easey Street to have a shower, first.'

A hit, you mean, I idly thought.

Chris said politely to me, 'Want to come round for a cup of coffee, Nora?' She smiled at me with a tinge of the same anxiety I saw on Javo's face. It was a pleasant charade we all played out, me and the junkies, either to spare what they saw as my delicate sensibilities, or to be genuinely courteous: a social code with a sub-text that they meant me to grasp intuitively.

'No thanks, Chris,' I said, fulfilling my part. 'I think I'll just go home and crash.'

Throwing cool to the winds, Javo took hold of my arm, kissed me on the mouth, and said, looking me right in the eyes, 'See you, mate!'

I got a cab home, smashed out of my brain, and staggered into the kitchen. I made myself a bowl of cold curry covered in yogurt, guzzled it standing at the open fridge door, fell into bed and into sleep, and woke up again at four in the morning when Javo pushed open my door and burst in with his wet hair flopping and his dotty, pale eyes burning.

'Are you mad at me? Did I behave all right this time?' he mumbled as he tore off his clothes and crawled into bed next to me. I started to laugh. He had brought me an orange and a cup of blackcurrant cordial. He kept nodding off at first, but then we fucked, first time for a week, and talked a bit, and laughed, and fell asleep.

In the morning when we were getting dressed I said,

'Hey Javes. Do up my press-studs for me, will you?' I stood still, head hanging.

'Sure!' he said, always eager to perform a small service. Breathing heavily, he wrenched and forced the defenceless studs on my jumper neck.

'What a wonderful guy!' he croaked, laughing at himself.

All day I kept thinking of his clumsy ministrations, and a great plug of insane laughter would rise in my throat.

'How do you feel about knowing you'll be sleeping with the same person every night?' asked Rita.

'I love it.'

'But you *don't* sleep with him!' she said, laughing at me. 'You nearly always go upstairs to the spare bed!'

I did, too: Javo crashed into my room at 2.30 or 3 or 4; he nodded off into a noisy sleep and I crept out of my bed and up the creaky stairs to the bed I called the cloud because it had three mattresses into which I would gratefully sink. I slept so utterly deeply there that the night seemed no longer than the blinking of my eyes.

One night I went to bed at about seven o'clock. My room was warm, a fire was burning in the narrow grate, my bed was clean and comfortable with plenty of blankets. I read for a while and fell asleep at my ease. I was dreaming that I was in Bangkok with Martin's father, when Javo came in and I woke up. He got undressed and came into bed, asking,

'What did you do today?'

I told him a blurry account, being mostly still asleep. But he began to give his ill-considered opinions, and I argued with him, and woke up completely. I became discouraged and fell into silence. There was a long pause, both of us wide awake.

I became aware of some very peculiar bodily sensations coming to me from outside my own skin. My stomach seemed to contain a big, aching hollow with a small point of discomfort, approaching pain, in the centre, and a frill of nausea at its edges; and my limbs, especially my legs, were bitterly, deeply cold.

I said, 'Are you awake?'

'Yes.'

'Geez I feel shithouse.'

'How do you mean?'

I described these sensations. He laughed, and said,

'You've got my withdrawal pains.'

'Have you had a hit today?'

'No. I haven't had one since yesterday.'

This is ridiculous, I told myself. I lay there on my side, aching on his behalf, staring wide awake into the darkness and waiting for ordinary reality to reassert itself.

'*You* must be feeling pretty bad,' I remarked.

'Yeah. But it's in the head, too.'

'You mean psychological pain?'

'Yes.'

I breathed as calmly as I could, and after quite a long time I fell asleep. He slept very quietly behind me.

Maybe one day I will feel his flash.

I went out all day and didn't see him till six-thirty in the evening, when I found him in the theatre. His pupils were large. He did not seem pleased to see me, and was offhand and cold. I went home and did four loads of washing at the laundromat. I washed his shirts and jeans and socks. Why do I do it? I do it for love, or kindness. Women are nicer than men. Kinder, more open, less suspicious, more eager to love.

Blind White Eyes

Javo blundered into our house at teatime, Hank and Chris behind him.

'Listen, Nor – I reckon you ought to hand Martin's car over to Hank.' His eyes remained fixed on the floor. 'He can fix it when it breaks down. And he needs it.'

'I've given it to Willy,' I said. The kids clamoured behind me in the small room. 'Shutup, Grace – Juliet – let me think. Why should I change that now?'

'Because Hank *needs* it,' raved Javo, eyes still averted. Hank

82

was smiling uncertainly at me, hands in pockets, shifting from foot to foot: the dirty angel. 'And you *said* you couldn't keep it over here because of the parking tickets. You *oughta* give it to Hank – he's got a job, after all; and Willy hasn't.'

'So fucking *what*?' I felt that run of rage up my windpipe, as I stood there holding a teatowel, face flushed from the stove. Juliet's piercing voice went straight through my head:

'*Don't*, Gracie – DON'T!'

I slapped behind me without looking. One of them set up a wail.

'It's not fair, Nora, it's *not fair*!'

'Will you kids bloody SHUTUP?' I was nearly crying. Javo stared doggedly at my feet. Hank saw I was about to go off the edge. He plucked at Javo's sleeve.

'Come on, mate. We'll talk about it later. See you, Nor.' He pulled Javo out the front door, and Chris followed, having observed the altercation with an impassive face. I was choking with anger.

I was asleep at four in the morning when he knocked at the front door. I let him in, and stumbled back to bed while he made himself a cup of Ovaltine in the kitchen. He came in, got into bed. Very, very stoned. I had already half fallen asleep again. He put his arm round me: that moment at which total capitulation was always a possibility. I held back.

'What's wrong, Nor?'

'I'm really pissed off with you. I don't like the way you burst in here tonight, telling me what I ought to do with Martin's car.'

'But Hank needs it. He can fix it.'

'It's too late. It's Willy's now, you knew I was passing it on to Willy. How come you didn't say anything before?'

'Because Hank didn't even *drive* it till last night.'

'Anyway, the car's not the main reason why I'm so mad at you. When you came in here tonight I was right off my brick with the kids, and you didn't even notice. You just don't give a shit about what I have to do in my life.'

'Well . . .' His voice took on the blurry, uncertain tone of the dope. 'What do you want me to do?'

I began to talk at length, angry and despairing; but I could never say more than two sentences before his breathing became louder and slower and he nodded off. I was nearly crying with unhappiness and frustration. Again and again, at my impatient movements, he would drag himself back to consciousness, mumble a few slurred words, and drift off again.

At last I gave up. I got out from under the blankets, meaning to climb quietly up to the cloud and sleep the rest of the night there on my own; but by the time I was sitting on the edge of the bed, I was overcome by a fit of discouragement. I sat there in the half-dark and stared unhappily at my yellow feet on the blue floorboards.

He woke up.

'Wha – wha – where are you going?'

'Upstairs to sleep.'

'*I'll* go there. At least you should have your bed for one night.'

I stood up between the bed and the door, edging my way out. He was struggling with his mind up towards me, trying to speak or persuade, but lying flat among the blankets while I moved away from him.

'It's all right – I'd *rather*,' I said; I wanted to contain his wretched and disorderly presence within the part of the house which was specifically mine. As I turned the corner of the stairs I heard him mumble and fade,

'I hope you're not upset, mate . . .' and the old wood creaked under my feet, oh, what's the use of trying with him? He says it himself:

'You have to be a rat to be a junkie – a junkie'd kill his best mate for dope,' that posturing to make the petty sordidness dramatic.

I fell asleep huddling myself in the cold bed, up in the roof of the house.

In the morning he woke up when I came back into the room after the children had gone to school. He got up and began to pack his clothes. While I was in my room he went down to the bathroom and had a shower and came back white-eyed, with a spoon handle sticking out of his jeans pocket. After Rita had gone out to her studio, I found him rummaging through her drawers.

'What are you *doing*?'

'Looking for a jumper.'

'I think you'd better leave her things alone,' I said dangerously, my stomach turning over with anger and disbelief.

'But I'm *cold*! I've got no warm clothes!'

He reared up from the drawers, turned as if to make for her other chest of drawers. I saw his blotched, peeling face and blind white eyes. I kept on standing there, stubbornly forcing him with my presence to drop his search and come out of her room. You dare, Javo, how do you dare.

We walked over to Carlton. In the cold sunlight I looked at his face again.

'I don't know what this smack's been cut with,' he said. 'Must be bicarb soda or something.'

His skin was coming off in patches of dark pink and scaly white, and his glands and sinuses were swollen. He looked filthy and neglected. I felt like crying. I wanted him to go away (he was carrying his belongings on his back: 'I'll stay away for a couple of days,' he said, 'and *you* can come and visit *me*.') because he was driving me crazy; but I wanted him to stay because when he was himself I loved him.

We said goodbye at the counter of the University cafe. He kissed me openly, as he always did now, and I walked away full of agitation.

That night I went to bed with a wood fire burning low in my room. And he *came back*. I half-woke when someone knocked at the front door in the middle of the night. I stayed in my bed and Rita went down.

'Who is it?' I heard her whisper through the closed front door.

'Javo.' She opened it.

I lay quite still. He pushed open my door and came in. I was breathing. I wanted him to disappear, and I also wanted to say 'Hullo' as I always did; but he stood there in the middle of my room, and I lay there in my bed with my eyes closed, and after a minute he turned round and crept loudly up the stairs to the cloud bed overhead. I heard him drop his clothes and shake my room with his attempts at quiet: he got into the cloud bed and everything settled again.

Agitation! The house filled up with his anxiety.

> 'True joy ... rests on firmness and strength within, manifesting itself outwardly as yielding and gentle.'
>
> *I Ching: The Joyous*

Five days later I came home at lunchtime and found on my table a note:

'Dear Nora, I have been here looking for my pawn ticket for my camera – and to say hullo – but I feel strangely uncomfortable, like as if my presence isn't any longer allowed. I have been staying at Grattan Street for the last few nights where there is a room in which I may prop: but I think I should say that I miss you a lot.'

At my table sat the author of this note, pen poised to sign his name. I sat on his knee and we hugged each other. We went to the city and ate a meal. He borrowed ten dollars from me and bought himself a blue cardigan. We walked back to the tower with our arms round each other, companionable and cheerful.

In Willy's room he struggled into the new cardigan.

'Nor, do you want me to come home – I mean, back to your place – tonight?' he said, looking not at me but at his cuffs as he wrestled.

'Yes.'

'OK, mate. I've got to rehearse, though. So if I don't come, don't worry. I mean – don't sleep light waiting for me, because if we work till two o'clock I'll be fucked, I won't feel like walking all that . . .' Realising he was bungling it, he pulled fitfully at his cuff and tried again. 'I *want* to come, but it'll be so *late*.'

I sat in Willy's armchair nodding accommodatingly. Maybe I looked sad, though I didn't feel it, for he came over and sat awkwardly on the arm of the chair, and kissed me with his crazy, bent face.

I went to the bank. He went to score.

I found his fit on the dining room table at seven o'clock in the morning. I picked it up hastily: Rita was still under the impression that he was not hitting up in the house. I held the fit in my hand. I remembered hearing how Eve got Lou off dope: she smashed his fits, jumped on them, tipped his dope down the drain. Not my job. I dismantled it and took it upstairs to the cloud room. He was lying on his back, his face contorted even in sleep with some nameless dread. His arms were half across his face, as if he had fallen asleep in the moment of raising them to ward off an attacker. His head was turned stiffly to one side. I stood watching him, sick with pity and anger. He opened his eyes with a start, threw up his arms, groaned, saw me, froze still, and relaxed.

'Oh – g'day, Nor,' he croaked, his voice thick with sleep.

'Javo. You left your fit on the dining room *table*.'

He jerked his head from side to side.

'I left it *here*,' he cried, pointing wildly at the chair beside the bed.

'Don't be stupid, mate! Do you think I fuckin' hallucinated it? Here it is!' I stuck out my hand like a doctor's tray. 'Rita doesn't know you bring dope here. Why do you make it so hard for me?'

'I *told* you, Nor. I left it right *here*!'

I looked at him silently. War with the eyes. He capitulated. He looked down.

'It's getting too much for me, Javo. I can't handle the dope,' I said gently. He nodded, listening as I spoke. 'I want you to understand – I love you a real lot, but I can't live with you when you're like this. So, maybe it would be better if you found somewhere else to sleep, at least till you've got it under control a bit.'

He looked at me quietly.

'Nor, I *want* to get off dope. But I can't, now.'

'When *will* you be able to?'

'I can't stop while the play's on. I couldn't perform

coming down.'

'I know.'

'Nor, when the show's finished, I'll get off it, we'll go away, we'll go up north.'

'*How* will you get off it?'

'I'll take a cure. I'll go cold turkey. I can get off it.'

I looked at his wrecked face, skin in great lumps and boils, eyes whited right back to pale. Where's your bright blue, Javo? I want your blue eyes back again. I wanted to have faith in his promises, but only a fool would. I suppose.

He got up, kissed me goodbye, and left the house.

I heard of him wherever I went.

'Javo looks terrible.'

'Isn't Javo living with you any more?'

'How can you handle the dope?'

'Javo was out of it when I saw him today.'

Angela said to me, 'Javo is quite convinced of his immediate future. He says that as soon as the Brecht show finishes, you and he are going to Queensland together and he's going to get off dope.'

I can't 'go to Queensland'. I have to look after Gracie, and I've got no money.

Gracie slept with me, and in the middle of the night I woke up and put my arm round her small body. It was the first time I'd missed Javo's body. And only a twinge.

I came in from the laundromat with a basket of clean clothes in my arms, and met Javo on the stairs.

'What are *you* doing here?' I asked, in a not particularly unfriendly tone.

'Just leaving you a note.'

The window of my room was open and a steady stream of dark air made the palm leaves rattle against the wall. He sat at my table and buried his dirty face in a newspaper. He was stoned, but not very. I read the note.

'Dear Nora, I nearly banged the door down trying to get in just now. I am scared of what happens to me outside tonight in

88

the night – I don't know what to say. I have got to that terrify-
ing point of looking around and seeing no-one there, just ugly
reflections of my own image. I think maybe I have left it too
late to come in your direction – seems like I've worn out abuse
at your house – so here I am as usual caring for no-one but
myself – using a peculiar medicine with its handsome
accessories like a fat contradiction with your choice of knobs,
buttons or dials. Anyway I'll probably wait and talk. Javo.'

I made him wash his face and hands.

We held each other, touched and stroked, looked at each
other's faces for long, long moments. Nobody knows what I get
out of Javo, or out of knowing him. I don't know how to
explain. It's that when we fuck, or can be together quietly
sometimes, *we touch each other*. No-one else gets that close to
me. He behaves towards me, then, with tenderness, holds me
when I'm half asleep, he says my name and looks into my face.

But up, and down again.

At Grattan Street I yelled to wake him for a message from
his lawyer. I thundered on the door in the morning. He
shouted back in rage, opened the front door, his face creased
with sleep. He stared at me as I delivered the message in a
level tone. I felt a strange smile on my face. I stopped talking.
We stood looking at each other. He was sorry for yelling at me.
He'd had a shave, and was holding his unbuttoned jeans up
with one hand. He reached out his thin, ungainly arm, took
hold of my shoulder and kissed me. I ran off.

That night I finished reading, closed the book and fell
asleep. Some time after midnight I was woken by somebody
knocking at the front door and softly calling my name. Stunned
with sleep, I reeled down to the door and it was Javo. I had my
hands caught in the sleeves of my nightdress: I blundered into
his chest and he hugged me, jerky with dope, and thrust at me
some photos of Cambodia that he had printed. I was too sleepy
to see. I went back to bed and he followed me there. He put his
arms around me. I drifted off again just as he said,

'I'm sorry about this morning, Nor.'

When I left in the morning I said,

'How about you pick me up at one o'clock and we go and have lunch?'

'Great!' he said, seeming enthusiastic.

I worked till one, and of course he didn't show up. I waited till one-twenty and went home. I wasn't surprised, and for that reason I didn't care. I found he'd thrown back the blankets, taken my clean greasywool socks, left his dirty ones on the floor, and gone.

Well, fuck him.

> 'Misfortune to him who does not know when to call a halt, and who restlessly seeks to press on and on.'
>
> *I Ching: Preponderance of the Small*

I met Javo at the University cafe. He said he was into the second day of withdrawals. 'I feel shithouse,' he said. However, he appeared softer, pleasanter, more gently smiling.

'Let's go up north as soon as you can, Nor,' he said, taking my arm as we stood side by side at the high bar. 'I need to get healthy. I'm sick of the junk scene.'

I said nothing. I looked up into his face. His eyes were normal, almost blue again. He kept smiling at me, waiting patiently for my answer.

'I'll be able to come as soon as we've pasted up the next issue of the paper,' I said. 'But I can't go any further than Sydney – I can't take that much time, and Gracie's at school. Is it worth going only that far?'

'I reckon.'

I put my hand on his shoulder. I saw us on the road with Gracie, looking like a ragged family. He took hold of my hand and we stood together comfortably, liking each other and feeling hopeful. Up north the sun will shine on us and turn us brown. I wanted to go.

But I would have to be a mediator: between him and Gracie, between him and the rest of the world.

It can't be spring so soon, at the end of July, but the senses say otherwise: sunstreams through open windows, daffodils in yellow masses at the market; clear, deep blue skies at night, and blue moonlight; air shifting ceaselessly as at the change of season; day after day of sun, of benevolent wind, of yellow patches on the bedroom wall when I wake up in the morning.

In this mysterious mid-winter spring I got stoned at the supper show in the back theatre and danced till two o'clock in the morning, by myself, with a head full of strange fantasies. I saw: my striped sleeves, Mark's thin hands on his saxophone, Rita dancing with her eyes shut, Chris singing the words to herself as she danced, Javo on the other side of the theatre catching my eye to smile. We came home together. In the night he said to me, his face right up close to mine,

'My love for you never seems to get any less. There is something new there, all the time.'

And as the day began we lay together in my bed in the empty house and made love: we went into each other. I looked at his face and it opened and blossomed under my eyes.

Do You Wanna Dance?

One afternoon, when I got home from working on the paper, I found Javo asleep in my bed, fully dressed except for his boots. He woke up and I asked him how he was.

'Shithouse,' he croaked. 'Nauseous.'

'Is it the withdrawing?'

'Yeah.'

'Do you want some orange juice?'

'Yes.'

I made him a drink, and a boiled egg each and some toast. He sat up in bed to eat, propped his tall back against the wall, smiled sheepishly.

'The women down at the paper know about you,' I remarked as we ate. 'You're a bit of a standing joke down there, actually.'

'Yeah?' He laughed. 'What do they know?'

'They know I have a date with you every Wednesday at one o'clock, and that you never turn up.'

We finished eating and I lay on the bed, full of speed and chatter.

'Lillian's been coming to the play a few times,' said Javo. 'She came on to me . . . you know, she gave me the looks, it was coming off her real strong.'

'What was?' I asked, sick, knowing it already before he told.

'She wanted to take me home with her.'

'Oh.'

'But I don't like that, I can't do it that way. I have to have a friendship with someone before I can do that.' He laughed. 'So I kept it all on a friendly level – you know – let's go and have a cup of coffee, give us a lift home, that sort of thing.'

Lillian, blight on my life. She broke into it, once, years ago, before any of us had heard of sisterhood; she looked round to see what she could take, sampled Lou and quickly put him back on the shelf, saw the weightiness of Jack and decided to take him with her. And did. And that was the end of everything, between him and me. She had it, the knack of engulfing, of making sharing impossible.

'How come you two don't get on, when you've known each other so many years?' asked Javo.

I began to tell the old, bitter story, and as I talked I felt the old, bitter turning of my stomach and heart, envy of her beauty, fear of her mockery, uncertainty at her changefulness.

Javo was half-laughing at the way I looked when he talked about her: it made me feel *upset*, thinking about her. I lay curled up on the bed, miserable and afraid. He flicked the blankets back off his legs and started talking about Jessie.

'Everything between us is only OK as long as I'm up,' I said, watching the stripes of my jumper reflecting in the tiny round mirrors sewn into the cushion cover.

'Yeah? What do you mean?'

'Well . . . if I feel miserable, I don't *get* anything from you. You seem to think, "That's *your* problem, you work it out for yourself".'

'It *is*! When you're talking about past stuff, anyway.'

He's right. I suppose.

I asked him to pick up the kids from school. He wouldn't. I didn't expect him to. Why don't I? I expect nothing, on that level, and I get nothing.

Next day he slept all day. In the early afternoon I sat at my table patching a sheet. The wind came in at my window and I sewed neatly, green cotton on white. I heard him stir and looked over at him. He saw me look, and smiled at me like a child, from under the bend of his arm.

'I've just had a terrible dream – a nightmare,' he said, stretching his long limbs. 'You had fallen in love with Mark, and you were having a scene with him.'

'Yeah? Were you jealous?'

'Of course. But what freaked me out was that I *hit* you.'

'What!'

'We were in a very tiny room, about as big as a phone box. And I hit you, slapped you very hard. You looked at me, with an expression of absolute amazement on your face. It was *awful*.'

That night it rained. But I didn't know till I woke up in the morning and the wooden wind chimes had stopped clacking outside my window. Still, wet morning, like England in summer. I dreamed I brazenly stole three pairs of expensive wool socks from Georges in Collins Street.

Work, work, work.

All alone at a rickety table on the first floor of the women's centre, I typed long strips for the newspaper. No-one came near me. Sometimes, when I started hallucinating or getting too far into the whirring of the IBM, I stumbled downstairs for a reality check, for a bit of human contact. One of those soft, warm nights, I was up there typing in the ugly bare room, copying an article about government attitudes towards the Halfway House, when music started in the dancing studio across the lane. It was Bette Midler singing 'Do You Wanna Dance?' They played it over and over, a dozen times or more, and as my fingers obediently typed, my imagination went soaring off into those fantasies of violins and dim lights and perfume and dresses and arms holding me, oh *yes!* I wanna dance! and the music came in through the dirty windows, along with the sweet night air.

I finished work and took a bus to Carlton. On the bus stop I had to fight the housewifely urge to make things simple, to stay in the groove, to go straight home. I had an hour before the time I'd promised to be home for the kids, and I needed to be sociable.

I turned the corner of Faraday Street and saw the big, wide-shouldered, smooth-headed figure of my friend Bill step out the front door of the tower. I whistled and caught up with him.

'Wanna come and eat with me?' I said. 'Just the two of us?'

'Ooh, yes, that would be lovely.'

Between the tower and the restaurant I nicked round the corner to post a letter. I vaguely heard someone shouting. I took no notice, dropped the letter into the box, and turned back to join Bill. We'd taken two steps towards Lygon Street when Javo burst round the corner, running.

'Oh,' I thought, 'he's stoned.' But he stopped a yard short of me, his hair flopped back on his forehead, and I saw that his eyes were dark, not white.

'Hullo!' I said. 'Was that you shouting?'

He nodded, out of breath; smiled.

'We're just going to the Shakahari for tea.'

'Oh. Yeah – OK.' And he backed away up Elgin Street, right of his beat, smiling at me sideways over his shoulder as he turned and we parted. I'd expected him to say he'd come with us. Bill and I had crammed ourselves into a corner table at the Shaka and commenced a spirited discussion of the latest collective upheavals, before the penny dropped. Javo was being *tactful*. I remembered what he'd said to me, days earlier, after his dream about me falling in love with Mark and our conversation about Lillian:

'I do sometimes think about fucking with other people, Nor. I'd like to fuck with Lillian, for example, and with Jessie again only she won't have a bar of me these days. Don't blame her. Who do *you* want to fuck with?'

'Oh ... Bill, I guess,' I said unwillingly. 'And Mark, of

94

course, but that's everybody's fantasy – he's such a golden boy.'

He laughed. 'That gives me a bit of a twinge.'

'Don't be dumb! What *is* this – some kind of game, or something?'

'Course not. But for you to go off with Bill would be sort of – it would be about as heavy as if it was Mark.'

'You reckon? Listen, mate – if you want to know – I've known Bill for years now, and it's been on the cards for ages that we might get round to fucking.'

'Don't worry, Nor.' He gave me a push, grinning at my discomfiture. 'Don't get hot under the collar. I could handle it.'

I could let my heart sink, sometimes, in spite of the way work buoys it up. It wasn't being in love, or loving, that made the difficulty: but the awful silent fear of not being loved in return.

So, an hour later I was home in my clean bed, looking after the kids while Rita went to the art school ball. And I kept wondering, what did Javo think in the street tonight? Which of us tries harder to be cool? or in control? Will he come back to sleep with me tonight? Will I care if he doesn't? Should I scramble back out to the solitary life I led when he was away in Asia? Can I live without being loved? Is it true what Lillian said once, years ago, that I've always been too good at *giving it all away*? And on a practical level, is there a supper show tomorrow night? And if there is, can Rita and I find someone to stay home with the kids so we can dance the night away?

I wanted to get stoned and forget what I looked like and dance till I was loose all over.

'Dear Javo, you said you wondered if the trip we're supposed to be going on is worth it for such a short time. Well, I'm definitely going on Monday, and if you feel doubtful about going, please say so *now*. Know what I think? I think you see me as not much more than a lump on the other side of the bed. I think maybe you want to fall in love.

I think you've got the look of someone who's on the make.
I think that, if I'm right about this, it's high time for us to call it a day, throw in the sponge and so on.
I am afraid of painful, long-drawn-out endings to things. I got a fright, the other day, at the gloom I experienced when we talked about Lillian; and you talked once again about Jessie in that way that makes me feel you are saying, "My relationship with Jessie was the high point, the great love of my life", and that's OK, it really is, only I get to feel a bit like some kind of charlady keeping the home fires burning after the princess has passed by.
I want to be with you, laugh and mooch round, travel if we can. But I'm not getting anything back, I'm running out, I need love. And if you don't want to give it any more, will you please say so? I'm telling you, Javo! I'm lonely! Are you reading me? . . . over . . . Nora.'

I asked the I Ching, 'What about my feeling that it is all hopeless with Javo?'

It replied, 'Times change, and with them their demands. Changes ought to be undertaken only when there is nothing else to be done. A premature offensive will bring evil results.'

I left the letter for him, just the same.

He came in the middle of the night and read it downstairs while I dozed. He came up to my room again and sat on the end of my bed, pulling off his boots.

'Did you read it?'

'Yeah. We'll talk about it tomorrow.'

'No, that won't do – because when I have to leave, you'll be asleep.'

He got into bed. Before he had come in, I had been fast asleep, and comfortably warm; but when he was coming down, his awful coldness drew the warmth out of my body and left me lying in a chilly envelope of discomfort. He did talk, for an hour or so. Every few minutes he'd groan and roll over, complaining of restlessness and pain. He said,

'One trouble is, that you like me best when I'm off dope, but *I'm* always happier when I'm into it.'

'No, no, you're quite wrong,' I said, throwing caution to the winds. 'The times I'm most comfortable with you – and it's because of your own attitude to yourself – are when you've just started back into dope, before it gets you by the throat.'

'Maybe I never really liked myself much,' he said, with a faint bitterness, 'before I found dope.'

I tried to talk about needing love.

He said, 'Sometimes, when you're giving out affection and love towards me, it's . . . missing. I don't mean *absent*, I mean . . .'

'You mean not hitting the mark?'

'Something like that.'

I didn't understand what he meant, and, discouraged, thought better of asking. There was a long silence. He heaved a great sigh.

'Well . . .' I said, 'what about going to Sydney, Javes? Will we still go?'

'Yeah. I reckon. We both need to get out of here for a while.'

We both needed something, that was certain, but neither of us knew what it was. I wished stupidly for something steady and complete. For someone steady and complete. What's *that*? No such thing, no such person.

By nine o'clock on the morning of the big departure for Sydney, Javo was still asleep. Gracie and I fidgeted, our enthusiasm waning by the minute.

'Are we gonna be late for Sydney?' she asked, looking up from her drawing.

'Too right we are,' I snarled.

I stumped furiously up the stairs, and yelled at him from the doorway of my room.

'Come on, Javo! It'll be fuckin' midnight before we get to the border!'

By eleven we were out on the highway. Not a smile out of him, scarcely a word. I was kicking myself for having forgotten the lesson of Freycinet the summer before. It rained. We ate chocolate by the packet, in a vain attempt to make the situation look less pathetic. Javo dropped the papers where he stood.

'You bludger, Javo,' dared Gracie, smiling her evil smile. To my astonishment he burst out laughing, against his will.

A huge wheat transport picked us up as dark and cold fell just outside Holbrook. It bore down on us in the remaining light, brakes shrieking. Grace clung to my leg and screamed with fear; I stepped back in panic on to the grass verge. But Javo turned to me with a laugh of triumph.

'Come on, Nor! It's our ride to Sydney!'

I slept a little on the hugely vibrating sleeping-shelf, which shook my bladder and gave me indigestion by disturbing a hamburger I had eaten at Gundagai.

'I'm going to stay awake *all night*, till the morning comes!' announced Grace, sitting up like Lady Muck behind the great gear stick. Three minutes later I glanced over and saw her head droop and her eyes close.

At three o'clock in the morning the truckie dropped us at a blighted all-night cafe thirty miles out of Sydney. The girl serving us was bare-armed in a cotton dress. Two coppers stood drinking coffee in the kitchen. The fluorescent light turned us into corpses.

Gracie added up brightly at the laminex table and ate a fruito; Javo wolfed down a plate of baked beans on toast. We were not looking at each other. Outside the cafe we started walking towards Sydney. It was a bitterly cold, icily clear night, with a sky miles high and light coming from somewhere far away, the stars perhaps for there was no moon. A dog barked from a driveway. The cops stopped in a black maria and brought us to Liverpool station: in the back of the van Javo grinned at Gracie's round eyes but pretended I wasn't there. I was too cold to care. At the station he clowned with Gracie on the turnstiles while I crammed myself with my book into the ticket-puncher's booth. The first train came through at 4.20. It was full of shiftworkers huddling themselves inside what was left of their body warmth from bed. We were the most wide-awake people on board.

Outside Central Station at six o'clock. Javo foul-tempered again, Gracie tired and frightened. I have to keep us together somehow. Frozen and miserable, we trudge along the colonnades looking for a taxi. Grace whinges and at last I pick her up and lug her on my hip. Javo is always twenty steps ahead of me. I can't keep up. At 6.20 the cab drops us outside

Peggy's place in Annandale. Cold sky, dark before dawn. I tap nervously on the front window. Peggy opens up, brings us in quietly, insists that we take her big bed, and moves into the spare room. In the bed still warm from her body our limbs thaw and we fall asleep, not touching.

By the next night I was homesick. I was still tired, though I had slept all afternoon while Peggy played with Gracie. Javo was behaving as if we hardly knew each other: everything was in ruins. I began to hate him.

He came and got into bed hours after I'd gone to sleep, tired and sick in the heart. He put his arms round me. I couldn't even swim up far enough from sleep to acknowledge, to turn over to him. We tried to talk to each other. He said it had hurt him that I seemed so little interested in his work on the play. I said I had never guessed that he cared one way or the other about my attitude towards his work: that if I'd known, I'd have been eager. I said it hurt me that he didn't make friends with Gracie, who called him 'Javaroo' in her foreign accent and was just waiting for the moment, for him to open the gate and let her in. We spoke sharply, out of weary sadness.

He lifted his skinny arm and put it round me, but somehow kept his shoulder turned to me.

'When you are cold to me,' I said, 'it makes me feel you think I am ugly, and stupid, and boring; and I give up, and wonder why we go on bothering.'

He said something I didn't hear.

'What? What did you say?'

'It's all right – nothing.'

'Please tell me what you said.'

'I said, "Maybe you're right".'

He went out late in the morning, to 'visit people'. He barely said goodbye to me, didn't kiss me as he once would have done as a pleasant matter of course. A few minutes after he had left, Gracie and I set out walking to the shops. We turned the corner of the street and I saw him a hundred yards ahead of us, the red shirt collar showing between his leather jacket and his rough head. I fell in love with his long legs, saw him getting smaller in the distance, felt him pulling one of those long strings out of my heart. Nothing to be done. I held Gracie's hand tightly, for comfort.

It doesn't matter, it doesn't matter.

But in the night he began to kiss me ('I've got a tooth-ache,' he warned) and I got my hands on his round belly, we fucked in the dark, I could just make out his lantern head under my eyes. When I came I was almost laughing with the ease of it.

Every day he would disappear and come back hours later, stoned, white-eyed, obsessive about washing his clothes and cleaning up after himself. Maybe, I thought, torturing myself, he is in love with somebody, with Ruth perhaps who was here with her two children and Micky while I half-slept. I heard Javo say,

'Want to go to the zoo tomorrow, kids?'

You bastard, you holiday uncle. You never give Gracie the time of day, at home. Must be trying to impress someone.

Too much loneliness. I got so sad.

In the night we talked about splitting up.

'But *I* can't do it,' he said.

'Why not?'

'Because I'm the one that's in the wrong.'

How was I going to think about *that*?

What's *love*?

I mean, what *is* it?

Grace and I talked in the bathroom in the morning.

'How did you get on at the zoo with Javo?'

'Well . . . good . . .' she hesitated. 'But he was a bit nervous.'

'Nervous? What do you mean?'

100

'Whenever I spoked, he'd go, "Oh, *no*, Gracie, you're *not* going to . . ." ' (turning her head in mimicry of his disgust) . . . '*you* know, freaking like that.'

We slept together every night. No fucking, no loving.

'I'm confused in my head, I'm anxious,' he said. 'I'm freaking out.'

I dared not try to comfort, scarcely dared to touch his back which was turned to me.

In the morning before it was light Gracie woke up in her floorbed and asked me for something to eat.

'I'll get you a piece of bread and butter,' I said, dropping my feet out of the double bed.

'Hey, Nor – get me one too, will you?' called Javo.

I got them, in the dark kitchen in the sleeping house; and when I came back to the bedroom they'd both gone to sleep again. So I ate one of the slices of bread and thought a bit, and climbed back into bed and lay on my side and read *Flying*. And the day began.

I Just Can't Keep from Crying

Grace and I went over to Balmain with Peggy. We bought flowers for Micky's birthday and she dropped us off at his house in Darling Street. We knocked. Javo opened.

'I woke up,' he said, 'and the house was empty. I thought you'd end up over here, so I came over.'

No touching, he won't touch me, he won't allow me his body. But, as usual when I was being of service, he cheerfully accepted an omelette and a cup of coffee when I made lunch for everyone. Mistakenly interpreting his smile, I finished cooking and threw myself on the big bed beside him. No

101

response. I started to feel really bad, not daring to have anything to do with his body even for friendship's sake, watching his face become animated only when he spoke to Ruth or Micky, or when he paid attention to their conversation with each other. I got off the bed, humiliated. He fell asleep. I talked with Micky in the kitchen. I heard myself yelling.

'*I'm so unhappy, it's just ridiculous!*'

I would have liked to shake the teeth out of that Javo, lying there under the rug, boots hanging off the end of the bed. There was a sickness in the air of that house: it was the awful pointless temporariness of waiting to score. Micky chirped and chattered, like old times, but his face was white with it; Ruth's gaze was abstracted. And we infected each other: they with their loneliness in a strange town, we with our blank wall between us and our fear of speaking the truth.

Fear of being loved; fear of not being loved.

I decided to leave. Gracie came with me. We walked sadly down the hill.

'What do *you* feel about Javo?' I asked, in a kind of dull curiosity. To my surprise she had plenty to say, several theories to put forward, and some advice to give.

'I think it's because he's a drunkie,' she opined, trotting along beside me holding my hand.

'Junkie.'

'Yes, junkie. Well, I think you should leave him alone. Because if you talk to him nervously, he will get nervous, and won't talk back. And if he was *alone*, after he'd taken a pill – '

' – Stuck a needle in his arm, you mean.'

'Yeah, a needle – well, after he'd stuck a needle in his arm, he might *think*, if he was *alone*, well, I'll *try* to stop, and not be a junkie any more.'

'Do you think I talk nervously to him?'

'No, not much. But you should talk to him nice, like he talked to me once when I was with him and Willy in the car going to the tower. And you should leave him alone.'

I thought about that.

It was a dull, grey afternoon. A grubby wind blew, and the houses in the street looked depressingly delapidated. We walked along, keeping each other company. I thought about the patterns I make in my life: loving, loving the wrong person, loving not enough and too much and too long. What'll I do? How much of myself will be left hanging in tatters when (*if: I don't want to end it*) I wrench myself away this time? I have this crazy habit, a habit as damaging as his, of *giving it all away*. I remember a line of Villon, which Bette Davis quoted in *The Petrified Forest*:

> '. . . nor cease to serve
> but serve more constantly . . '

Serve what, serve whom?

Go on taking it, it means. No more of this ancient, courtly masochism.

I have to get free. But there is this incomprehensible bond that keeps us together. The night we talked in bed, he put his arm over his face and said,

'Why do you put up with me?'

Giving it all away.

I talked about Javo to Peggy, and felt better. And while I was washing the dinner dishes, in walked Tom, the perfect person to save me, all light and speed, his brain sparkling with bombs and crackers. I thought I was too tired to talk, but we sat down and began, at quarter to nine, and gradually the old magic made itself felt, talking about ideas and words; our minds raced each other joyfully until one o'clock in the morning.

And yet, as my fatigue took over after midnight, I began in spite of myself to listen for footsteps at the front door, a knock, a sign that Javo had come back.

He didn't.

He did. I heard his voice, and a woman say his name, in a laughing conversation outside the room in which I was falling asleep. I didn't get up, but let my mind slide away. Hours later (it must have been nearly dawn) I got up to go to the dunny and found him sitting alone in the living room, writing in a small notebook. He looked up at me dully.

'Hullo,' I said, passing his long legs. 'Are you coming in to sleep? Because I'll need to move Gracie out into her bed.'

'Yeah. I'll be in soon.'

He came in, thumped into bed beside me, folded himself along my curled-up shape, put one arm round me, for all the world as if nothing had happened. So I talked, he talked, both of us sighing, stammering and starting again in a dogged need to *say it*.

'I'm neurotic,' he said. 'I do this over and over. Whenever I get something good, I destroy it.'

'But everyone has these patterns which they can't break. I've got one – it's just different from yours.'

'Yeah?' he said, interested.

'I go on giving it all away.'

So sad. I get so sad.

'I'll go back to Melbourne in the morning,' I said at last.

'No. *I'll* go. It's me *doing* this to you. *I'll* go. You stay. It's your holiday.'

We fell away into silence, lying side by side in despair, bound to each other yet pulling away, him pulling away from me, but for a few moments in a truce . . . he took hold of my head gently, made me kiss him, brought my face close to his and looked at me for a long time. His gaze out of that bony lantern head. The light was coming faintly, dawn already, and I got his cock in my mouth and my cheek against his familiar belly, made him groan a little; he lifted me back up to his equal level and we fucked, he came and the delight of watching his face dissolve brought me to join him with no effort. Light on his skin, bones and skin under my eyes.

We fell asleep.

During the day, once the end of it all was in sight, he was as pleasant to me as he usually was at home. We spent hours lying on the bed, his head on my hip, with a book in French about Luis Bunuel, which he toiled through, asking me to teach him.

'Aren't you bored with this?' I asked, laughing at my rusty attempts to translate.

'No – I'm learning!'

He wanted us to communicate on some intellectual level where we didn't usually function together.

The house was full of people, and while dinner was being prepared Javo and I lay on the bed, talking and waiting for his taxi to arrive. I kept looking at those blue eyes he had, still bright blue in spite of the dope. In these last few minutes it was possible to say things crudely, in haste not to leave them unsaid.

I said, 'I love you.'

He said, 'I can see myself in three or four weeks, coming back to you and begging you for forgiveness . . .'

I said, 'I don't know how to break off sharp like this. I keep remembering things which give me hope.'

'Like what?'

'Like – there's no-one I ever touch, the way we touch when we fuck.'

He said, 'I'll go back to Melbourne and put myself on the rack.'

The cab came. Javo thrust his mouth-harp into my hand.

'Here. Give this to Gracie.'

He hugged me clumsily, heaving his suitcase towards the front door, but it wasn't enough, and I went out to the car with him and we kissed properly, face to face, and held each other.

' 'Bye, Javo,' said Gracie, who was standing quietly watching with her thumb in her mouth.

'See you, Grace,' he mumbled, getting into the front seat. The taxi drove away. He didn't look back.

It was already dark outside, and cold. We went back into the house. I went into the kitchen and stood at the sink with my back to the light, ashamed to show the rush of grief I was feeling. I put my hand into the bowl where the fruit salad had been, picked at one or two passionfruit pips that stuck to the enamel sides. Peggy, working beside me at the table, said in her brisk voice,

'Does this outcome satisfy you?'

I shrugged, not daring to speak until I could fight down the weeping. I wanted to turn to her and throw myself on her thin shoulder and her surprised kindness – help me! I'm so sad – -

but I was afraid of crying out of control.

I whispered, 'I can't talk right now.'

'Oh! ... yes – all right,' she said, perhaps not daring to follow an urge to comfort.

Somehow, with that kind of grief, the moment for weeping passes, and after it, to weep would require a small forcing. The meal was served, and in the clatter and conviviality I perceived an oblique kindness, for which I was grateful. I went to bed with Gracie, who slept, and outside the closed door of the bedroom people were laughing and clashing plates.

In the morning it didn't seem so bad. When I woke up, beside Gracie, in the sunny room, it occurred to me that this was the first morning in three months, give or take the odd dope binge, I hadn't woken up next to Javo. I felt a bit empty, staring out the window and wondering where he was and what was going to happen when we got home. Then I remembered what I had dreamed:

Javo and I were in a very expensive women's clothing store on the upper floor of a building. I was flicking through the dresses on a rack, while Javo, good-humoured and courteous, wandered over to the window and waited for me. While he stoood at the window, *somebody shot him*, out of one of the slit-like upper windows of the building opposite. The bullet entered his neck. He was not killed.

Respect

Peg took Gracie out for the day and I went off by myself. The sun was shining and I travelled on the top deck of the bus and I was afraid of the openness of myself – as if, one lover gone, I was opening up in the search for an immediate replacement. Smack habit, love habit – what's the difference? They can both kill you. For the bus journey I fell in love with a woman who smiled at me. The motion of the bus made her thick mop of fair curls tremble. We talked about desperadoes.

'I am fatally attracted to them,' I said. 'In fact, I probably *am* one.' The idea had never occurred to me before.

I thought I was going to veer in and out of tearfulness all day. I got myself out to Bondi, where Tom lived, but when I reached his door and knocked and no-one answered, I sat down defeated on the concrete and would have liked to throw back my head like a dog and howl with unhappiness.

The door opened. There stood Tom, naked except for a towel.

'Oh, it's *you*!' he cried. 'I was asleep. Come in.'

We sat at his kitchen table. He went about the room awkwardly making coffee. I looked round the small white room lined with weatherboard. He had pinned a Matisse print on the wall. My trembling insides began to settle; I sat there accepting his shy hostliness.

'If you look out that window,' he said, 'there is the sea. I am going to have a shower. Will you mind waiting?'

'No.'

I stepped over to the window and, indeed, the sea was there: the bungalow was only yards from the cliff edge. It was the ocean. I stood weakly at the sink and pressed my face against the small sealed window with its four panes. I stared. I felt my breath go in and out.

He led me down to the cliff path. We lay on our fronts on the bare rocks, staring dizzily down at the water smashing itself underneath us. We must have lain there for hours, talking drunkenly about what we knew of the world. When we stood up, the sun had moved across behind us and we were chilled right through.

'We must be the last of the big-time ravers,' said Tom. 'Let's go to the movies.'

We saw Leni Riefenstahl's *Olympiad*. Tom sat beside me hissing irreverent remarks. I pointed out that the German runner had not made a showing in the marathon.

'He's probably picked up the vibe of the whole event and headed for the border,' said Tom. We snorted and giggled behind our hands in the front row.

The sun was shining after a night of rain. I sat on the back doorstep of Peggy's house, the sun warming my right side; I squinted my wrinkly eyes in the light and tried to read a magazine.

'What are you thinking of, up there?' inquired Peg affectionately from the yard where she was hanging out wet clothes.

'I was thinking,' I replied, 'that I have got right over Javo leaving.'

'That's good.'

'And I was also thinking about something Tom quoted once, from Reich – "love and work", he said, that's what it's all about.'

'Do you want to work?'

'I'll go back to Melbourne and work on the women's paper.'

With Javo gone, I had had sweet sleeping at night, slow thinking as the light came in in the morning, and the company of people who liked me. It was time to go south, home again. I booked a sleeper for me and Gracie, and I kept thinking about: her asleep, me looking out that cold glass at the moon passing, the ground rushing, remembering for the thousandth time that poem of Judith Wright's, *Train Journey* – 'glassed with cold sleep and dazzled by the moon'.

On the phone I said to the railways booking clerk,

'Can we get anything to eat on this train?'

A shocked pause.

'This is the Southern Aurora – it's one of the best trains in the country, woman!'

'Us poor people don't get around much, you know,' I retorted. We laughed.

I fantasised again and again our street with its centre parking metres, the green carpet in the hall, the flattened square of sunlight that hit the wall of the first landing of the stairs, and my room with its blue floor and thin red curtain, oh the joy of going home, it choked me in the throat.

Not a person.

A place.

But alas! I was too poor to afford the Southern Aurora. I spread the contents of my purse on the booking office counter. A hard-faced clerk inspected the ceiling. I stood helplessly, my eyes filled with foolish tears. I should have known that the 'best train in the country' was not for the likes of us. Condemned by poverty to sit bolt upright for fourteen hours on the Spirit of Progress. Gracie took my hand.

'Come on, Nora,' she said. 'Let's go. *That's the way life is.*'

And indeed, she charmed me with conversation and drawings, while she was awake, and slept peacefully across my knees as we rattled southwards all night long. While she slept I stared at myself in the dark window. I thought, when I get home I will have all my hair cut off. All, all.

The sun rose up in the morning and shot its beams horizontally through the dining car where we sat eating greasy bacon and eggs at $2.25 a hit. The gum trees turned pink in the new light: mist rose off the tree-filled water. We slid past farms and towns. In Melbourne it was raining. We came home in a taxi and crawled into my bed at ten o'clock in the morning. I backed up to the small burr of warmth coming off Gracie's foot, and for a second I longed for it to be Javo behind me, big, so I could back into his curve and be warmed. But it passed. I slept.

I went to an expensive hairdresser in Little Collins Street. I sat in the chair, pointed to my hair, and said,

'I want it all off. Short all over. Understand?'

'OK,' replied the imperturbable technician. And he took it all off, and left me with a crewcut and a pointed tail at the back of my neck. I looked like a pre-war German scientist. It was not a matter of liking or disliking it: I saw the bumpy shape of my skull, I saw myself shorn and revealed. I wandered in a dream around the city, glimpsing in shop windows a strange creature with my face. I was alarmed. My neck was bare. My ear-rings gleamed publicly. I crossed a road. An oaf in a big transport yelled at me,

'Hey, *spunky*! Do you fuck?'

'Not with the likes of you, shithead,' I snarled under my breath, maintaining an outward composure.

In Flinders Street I met Paddy. She laughed and made me turn round and said,

'Oh, it makes you look delicious!'

We went to sit in the dark and watch *The Godfather Part 2*. I kept running my hand across my skull, disbelievingly. We caught a tram to my house. We charged merrily up the stairs, talking loudly about the film. Just as I was pulling my left boot off, the door of my room was shoved open, and Javo walked in.

Not stoned. Plenty of colour in the eyes.

Instantly my mind jumped out of my body into his to look at my shorn head. I started to feel awkward about his being there. Paddy went out to put the kettle on. He sat on my chair and I looked right at him. He looked dirty and was wearing a slightly hangdog grin. I fronted up, straddled his knee, hugged him. He turned his face away, didn't take his hands out of his pockets.

'Just come for the TV, have you?' I couldn't help asking, but laughing in spite of the cynicism. I stepped away from him, registering 'He thinks I'm ugly'. I wanted to ask him directly, 'What are you here for?' I tried to phrase the question a little more tactfully.

'Oh . . .' he shrugged. 'I just thought I'd come and see you.'

Small fantasies of being in bed with him popped on and off my screen. Oops! Wrong way to go. But I made a joke:

'Been getting any fucks?'

'No.'

'Neither have I.'

'But I fell in love with Jessie again for a couple of days.'

My heart began to ache.

'What does she think about that?' I asked.

'I dunno.'

'Does she know, when that happens?'

'I dunno. Anyway, it doesn't matter.'

'How's that?'

'Because it's all fantasy.'

We went downstairs and drank the tea. Paddy left. We sat in silence, me facing him, him turned in his chair to one side.

'Did you get into dope a lot when you came back?'

'Yeah.'

'What's the situation now?'

'I'm comin' down today.'

'No dope around?'

'I'm broke. Worn out all my friendships.'

We laughed.

110

I said, 'I've got to go down to Spencer Street. Want to walk down with me?'

'Jeez, mate, it's a fuckin' long way. I'd be worn out before we got that far.'

I said, 'I am going upstairs to see what I need to take with me.'

I went upstairs, feeling plain and awkward, and instead of going on with the enterprise I lay disconsolately on my unmade bed and read a dozen pages of *Murder on the Orient Express*. Half an hour later I went downstairs to have a shower. He'd gone, leaving the radiator blazing away in the empty room.

I went out by myself to the theatre to see the new show. It was two weeks since I'd been there, to the heart of this particular ghetto, and it was like a homecoming: people stroked my furry head, laughed, hugged me, made much of me.

'Oh, oh, oh!' said Bill, seizing my head in his big hands and tousling me against his chest.

Javo was there. He sat up on the mezzanine, hunched over, staring down at the floor where the play was happening. I was so engrossed by the performance that it only crossed my mind once or twice to glance round for a look at him. But when the puppet play began, he walked over and sat down beside me and we watched the show together. When it ended, I said,

'I'm just going to the dunny,' and ran off.

When I came back, he'd gone.

Well.

Lou drove me home and would have liked to stay, but I said no, too tired, and we parted friends. The truth was, I was afraid of not wanting it enough. And I slept with Gracie, my daughter, who stroked my face in the morning.

I spent a day on my own in the empty house. In the afternoon I mended a dress and listened to the ABC news and some baroque music. I was cold, and went down into the back yard to chop some wood for a fire. Tentatively I stood a great lump of wood on the chopping block and brought the axe down on it.

It flew into two perfect halves. Such was my elation that I ran inside, put on our ancient cracked record of Aretha Franklin singing *Respect* and danced all by myself for half an hour in our living room, without inhibition, almost crying with jubilation – not just about the wood, but because I could live competently some of the time, and because that day I liked myself.

I was asleep in the night. Someone knocked at the front door and woke me, just a quiet knock but my heart jumped about in my body like a cracker and I went down the stairs on trembling legs.

'Who is it?'

'Javo.'

I let him in and stumbled back towards my bed.

'I've come for a talk,' he explained. It must have been, I thought, because I had taken his belongings over to the tower that day and left them there with a note. I got into bed, wearing the big socks he had once given me and holding a hot water bottle against my stomach. He sat on the side of the bed and we talked. Everything in his life seemed dull and pointless. He was anxious about the fact that he owed fifty dollars to Chris and had no way of paying it back.

'Did you come over hoping I might lend you the money?' I asked politely, feeling polite.

'Oh, come *on*.'

'Where are you going to get it from?'

'I dunno.' He stared at the floor between his thighs. 'I might as well go out and shoot myself.'

A pause.

'Can I ask you something?' I said.

'What?'

'How come you acted so cold the other day, when I went to hug you?'

'I wasn't sure about anything,' he said, 'about who I am or why I was here – and you reacted with this incredible burst of emotion. I didn't know *what* I thought.'

'What *do* you feel towards me?' I asked, by this time wide awake. 'I want to know.'

112

'Well . . .' He hesitated for such a long time that I thought he was struck dumb, and remembered someone I'd been in love with once asking me in exasperation, 'What *do* you like about me?' If I'd been perfectly honest, I'd have said, 'At this precise moment, nothing.'

At last Javo replied, 'I like you when you teach me things.'

'Yeah? Like what?'

'I liked it in Sydney when you made me read that French book out loud; lying on the bed. That was *great*.'

'I liked that, too.'

'And I like you when we walk round the city.'

Riding drunk up Bourke Street last summer; drinking in the Southern Cross; strolling up Russell Street to Sam Bear's to buy the last pair of Lee overalls in Melbourne.

These things won't happen again.

'Do you want to sleep here?'

'I *can't*, mate! I've got to go out and hustle that money.'

But we talked on, and he decided to stay, and I made him have a shower because he hadn't washed for a week and he stank. He got into my bed, put his damp head on the pillow; and we lay sides touching, and fell asleep.

In the morning when he woke up, we had a strange conversation. I sat on the chair fully dressed, my head caked with henna under a towel; he lay in bed, his face hidden by the hump of the blankets. I said, with a sense of daring, what I thought about dope. I told him he was living a sordid life, which he tried to make dramatic by saying things like 'I might as well go out and shoot myself'; that he was cutting off his options one after another, and so on.

He thought.

He said, 'Do you know what you're doing, Nor, even if you don't realise it? You're prodding me in the chest and saying, "Say you don't love me, go on, tell me you don't love me any more".'

'You're probably right,' I admitted. 'In fact, that's probably the most perceptive remark I've ever heard you make. Well – why *don't* you tell me?'

Of course, he didn't in so many words.

'Before,' he said, 'we had something to lose. We didn't go to

113

extremes because we had something to lose.'

'You think there's nothing to lose, now?'

'Yeah, and so do you; because you never would have said all those things to me three weeks ago, before we went to Sydney. I nearly got up and left.'

'All the time I was saying them, I was thinking, "I never would've said these things three weeks ago".'

He went downstairs. I was making the bed and I heard him pick up the phone and dial a number. I eavesdropped.

'Can I speak to Jessie, please?

'Good day, mate. It's Javo. Listen, I'm ringing to ask you to do me a favour ... please. Yeah. I need to borrow some money. Yeah? Great. Thanks very much. OK. I'll see you. 'Bye.'

He came upstairs again smiling, looking a bit triumphant. 'Well, that's settled *that*!'

I felt mean. *I am not mean.*

I glanced up at him as I pulled the blankets together, and on my face I felt a wry, unpleasant smile. Our eyes met, and held. He was half-smiling. He went out of the room again, and I sat down, feeling unhappy and upset, at my table. I read on in *Murder on the Orient Express*. When I went down later, I found he had gone along the street to help Rita paint her studio.

My hair meanwhile had turned bright red. I walked to Spencer Street on my own. People stared. I cared, a bit. I was too unhappy to feel ugly as well. When I came home, Javo had gone.

I stepped out the door of Tamani's with Jessie, and saw Angela coming up Lygon Street from the newsagent, forging along in her lairy crocheted coat. She took one look at my red, short hair and let out a great shriek,

'WOO, WOO, Nora! It looks fan*tas*tic! – but I'd uncover the ears.'

She ran up and seized my head in both gloved hands and buffed it from side to side, cackling quietly to herself.

'You're blushing, you are, you're *blushing*! You look fuckin' *amazing*. Well, I'm going in here for a spaghetti. See ya, baldy!' She pinched my cheek and vanished into Tamani's in a cloud

114

of perfume and flying sleeves.

Jessie and I paced along together for a block.

'I've been wanting to say something,' I said to her. 'It's something that really shits me about Javo. He has this way of presenting you to me as a wondrous love affair, and hugely talented, so I feel hopelessly drab by comparison.'

She laughed, striding with her loose strides beside me down Faraday Street. 'He talks like that about you, too,' she said. My anxiety and envy simply disintegrated in her reasonableness.

'Juliet said something funny this morning,' I said. 'She said, "Javo is always lazy. He should busily work".'

We burst out laughing.

'You can imagine Javo *manically* working,' said Jessie, 'but *busily*! Never!'

In the evening when the children had gone to sleep and the house was quiet, I sat in my room and stared at the fire. I could hear Stevie Wonder singing somewhere outside. I opened the window. Someone in our street was playing very loudly *Fulfillingness' First Finale*. The music made me lonely. I remembered Javo when he first came back from Thailand, sick and cold and thin as sticks, fighting himself to stay off dope, and as it got closer and closer to the moment when he couldn't hold off any longer, he got more and more nervous, and we wept helplessly next to the cold fire, and I drove him round to Easey Street and left him there.

No use, no use. Gone now.

The lawyer rang with an urgent message for Javo. I hadn't seen him for days but I knew he would be at Easey Street waiting to score so I walked round there just after dark. Micky and Ruth were standing on the doorstep as I approached and we all knocked together. Chris opened the door and we went in. In the living room were Javo, Mark and the baby Nina, a large crowd of us in the small room. Mark said hullo to me in his friendly way. I squatted down next to Javo, noticing his round belly, his jeans too tight from his scrounger's diet of bread and cereal. I told him the message.

'You have to be in court tomorrow.'

'What! Dressed? Fuck, I haven't got a suit to wear. Oh, fuck it.'

'You can wear my suit,' said Mark calmly, peeling apples by the fire.

I got up to go, wondering why Javo's eyes were so blue and his pupils so big.

'Thanks for the message, mate,' said Javo hastily; he wasn't looking at me. I headed for the door. Mark glanced up.

'Is that all you came for?' he said, and grinned.

'Well, it's like this,' I said. 'Javo and I aren't on very good terms, so I don't feel comfortable, you know, hanging round.' As I spoke I backed out into the hallway: Javo's face was hidden from me behind the door. From the hall I saw Mark's face turned up towards me from his seat: he had a wry, still smile on his face. I backed away towards the front door, raising my voice as I moved: the words just rolled out, not willed by my conscious mind:

'*I'm* on good terms with *him*, but *he's* not on good terms with *me*.'

I was out the door, had closed it behind me, was out in the dark street.

'Hoo, hoo!' crowed Micky, who had followed me out. 'You really laid it on him!'

I didn't want the commentary. 'Fuck him,' I snarled, 'he gives me the shits.' But I couldn't help laughing, to think that he was almost certainly saying the same thing about me at that very moment.

Lou was going to come and stay with me, but he didn't show up, and I woke in the morning surprised and a little relieved to find myself alone. He walked in at lunchtime, when Gracie and I were sitting at the table eating an artichoke. He came straight over to me and kissed me on the mouth, and hugged me. He said nothing about not having come round the night before. I didn't care at all. There's a warning in there somewhere.

He shared our lunch, pleasant as always, but distracted. He had a rehearsal and made to leave. I darted beside him to the door. He stood on the the step outside, I stood on the carpet inside.

'Hang on, Lou!' I touched his arm. 'Is everything all right?'

He gave an odd smile and looked away over the brick wall, hands in his jacket pockets.

'Ye-e-es . . . except for one thing . . .'

'If it's not turning up last night, that's all right,' I jumped in, too thoughtless to wait for him to speak. He ignored what I'd said, and went on,

'Selena's got to go and see a doctor on Monday.'

'What's she got?'

'She's pregnant. And she can't keep it because of the hep.'

'How do you feel about it?' I said, thinking instantly that he would hate it because he was a *romantic*.

'Ohh . . .' he shrugged.

'What about her?'

'She couldn't keep it, anyway.'

'Well, then. She'll be needing . . .'

'Support. Yeah. She will.'

'OK. Well – will you give her my love?'

'I sure will. I'm going to rehearsal now. I'll call round afterwards, maybe for tea. Hey, Gracie! Learn a new vegetable by teatime. Zucchini? See you!'

And he went off over the uneven bricks.

I wished that we would have the grace to fall back without endless explanations.

Gracie and I went to the theatre and stayed there from seven in the evening until two in the morning. I danced, very stoned, by myself and with Gracie who kicked up her stringy legs in black tights and did not need me for her partner. Through the crowd I could glimpse Bill way up at the other end of the theatre, juggling three silver balls, his shorn dark head dipping and bobbing gracefully.

'Hey, Nora,' said Clive, sidling up with a grin. 'Want to sleep with me tonight?'

'Sure do.'

Early in the evening my unhappiness about Javo had got on top of me, and I'd had to drag my heart round after me like a tin tied to my ankle; but now I was flooded with the possibilities, the theatre was full of people I liked and loved and whose work was joyful to me. Child beside me, friend to sleep with, body loose from dancing and laughing. Coasting! for a while.

I came home with Clive and Gracie. She went to sleep in her bunk, and we fucked in the silent house, and fell asleep peacefully, tenacious old lovers, friends forever perhaps. In the morning we drank orange juice and talked about everything.

In Lygon Street we passed Willy: spiky silvery-yellow head, blue and white striped jumper, a hard-edge image, absolutely distinct from his environment. He looked at us with his smart-arse grin.

'Are you two in love again?'

'Never been out of it,' I lied for the sake of laughter. 'But it's funny you should say that, Willy, because when I saw you coming up the street I thought to myself, "I bet Willy will say – Are you two in love again?" And so you did.'

Two Bob Each Way on Everything

Javo came to my house a few afternoons later. He had been in court all day and was wearing Mark's brown suit. His eyes were bright blue, and his hair had grown. We talked quietly, but some terrible things were said.

He said, 'You said one thing, the other morning, which made me think, well, that's it.'

'What did I say?'

'You described my life as *sordid*.'

We looked at each other steadily and defiantly.

118

'I do think that.'

'Well – that's what I mean. It's *not* sordid.'

'Do you think I meant *morally* sordid, or sort of *materially*?'

'Just *sordid*. It's got a meaning!'

'Yes, but what do *you* think it means?'

'Just *sordid*!'

Had to drop that tack.

He said, 'When I came back from Sydney and started spending more time by myself, I also started using a lot less dope. And I realised it was because my life, away from you, was much less complicated. I reckon if I'd had a place to live over the last few months, I'd have been hitting up a lot less.'

Probably true.

'I find *my* life a lot simpler, too, when I'm on my own,' I said. 'But I want to say – I miss you, and I miss fucking with you; because even when things were really difficult, I always felt we made real emotional contact when we fucked.'

'Yeah . . . but you've got to realise that the dope had a lot to do with that.'

'I *know*! You don't understand my attitude towards dope.'

'Yes I do. It can be summed up in four words: YOU DON'T LIKE IT.'

'*It's not that simple*. How do you think we kept going so long, if I felt that simply about it?'

'Well – with the feelings you've got about dope, it's a wonder you didn't stop it a long time ago – you *should* have.'

I was struck dumb. I felt my face change as under a blow. Tears would have come to my eyes but for my dry stare. He looked defiant, pugnacious almost. I got up and walked out of the room, needing care on the stairs to preserve an equilibrium inside my head. In my room I stood and stared at nothing. I thought that if I didn't go down again he would leave without telling me, or saying goodbye.

I went down again. He was still sitting there.

'What makes me saddest,' I said, 'is the way you're physically closed to me. It's not just that I want to fuck with you. It's that in the ordinary daily run of things it's not possible for me to touch you. You do *this* to me' – shielding my face behind my arms – 'so I end up with nothing – not the passionate stuff, and not the friendly touching either, that people feel comfortable about doing ordinarily.'

He looked exasperated, and smiled.

'But, Nor – maybe that's the way it has to be, when things finish between people: that blank-out.'

'How can you say that? You believe in change, don't you?'

'Look – before you, the last person I was really involved with was Jessie. That's over a year ago. The other night after her show I went up to her and hugged her, and she flinched back – *still*, now, she wonders "What the fuck's going on?" when I touch her.'

Resign, resign myself.

'You've got all the cards.'

'I just don't think about it like that,' he said.

You mightn't, my old lover, but that's the way it is.

I went out to the kitchen and put the kettle on. When I came back, he had fallen asleep in the chair beside the fire. I set up the board and began to do the ironing, glancing back at him over my shoulder from time to time. I saw the way his head fell a little to one side, his hands stayed clasped between his thighs. In spite of myself I filled up with helpless tenderness. He half-woke and crept down on to the floor, and Rita came in and put one of the children's eiderdowns over him. He slept for several hours. We did our housework, the children came in from school, we drank our tea and clattered our plates, he didn't stir. At seven o'clock Willy came to pick us all up to go to Paddy's party. Javo woke up, struggled to his feet.

'Can you give us a lift to the tower?' he croaked to Willy.

He came that far with us, sitting silently hunched in the middle of the front seat. We stopped, he got out, glanced at me.

'See ya.'

' 'Bye.'

At the party I got stoned very methodically. Willy and Angela turned on one of their appallingly funny arguments about the state of their relationship, and I laughed till my face was stiff with it. Bill came home with me, and we sat together in the car with the sleepy children babbling on our knees. Gracie told us how to remove a tic from your skin.

'You don't do it way of clock-ticking,' she explained. 'You

do it *wrong way of clock-ticking.*'

Being ignorant of tics, and too stoned to understand, I thought she was talking about the two words *tic* and *tick*. But Bill looked at me, astonished, and translated,

'She means *anti-clockwise*.'

In my room we were so stoned we could *not* stop laughing. But at last we did stop, and gently fucked, very easy and simple, the outcome of six or seven years of friendship. He flowed along under me, beside me, a kindly lover. When he came he sighed and his voice was soft. We woke in the morning to gossip pleasantly about the world and our small, intense part of it.

'Dear Javo, by *sordid* I meant something quite particular: the way it has become necessary for you to live with an eye to the main chance, two bob each way on everything, wild swings and lurches in the twinkling of an eye, losing your centre as you do it. I think perhaps you mistake this lurching for flexibility. Things you said to me yesterday made me feel really terrible. You jerked the rug out from under me. But it's good that it was all said. I wouldn't want to go on thinking that my illusion was the reality. You've given me some frights, and at the same time I believe you have misrepresented some things which were good and true and which did happen between us. Also I don't think my attitude towards dope is as moralistic as you make out, but that's really academic, because we are forever divided on that score. I want to say, I love you, and wish you well, and like you, and firmly believe that it is ALL WORTH IT and always was. Nora.'

I really thought it was the end.

'In times of adversity it is important to be strong within and sparing of words.'

I Ching: Oppression (Exhaustion)

Paddy came to visit, and stretched out her thin legs by the fire. I told her about the awful conversation I'd had with Javo.

121

When I repeated his comment about my 'moralistic' attitude towards dope, she clicked her tongue in disgust.

'That's absurd,' she said. 'You're the only one who's stuck by him.'

I had never thought about it like that.

Last time he was in my house, he walked down the stairs in front of me; as he turned at the landing I saw the angle of his cheek, and the tousled back of his head, and a double feeling of tenderness and revulsion ran over me. There would never be an end to it, because I couldn't hate him as I had (for a while, at the end) hated other people who had hurt me. He was too helpless to be hated wholeheartedly.

And besides, I loved him.

It wasn't that I ached for a sight of him, or wished to seek him out. I'd just made a place for him in myself, and he needed it in spite of himself, and I needed someone exactly his size and shape to fill it.

Rita moved a bed into her studio along the street.

'Listen, Nora,' she said. 'What would you think if I told Javo he could crash there? He's got nowhere to live.'

'He'd come along here all the time and eat our food. You'll regret it,' I said, thinking of his long body in that bed over the cold stone floor. Warm yourself at my fire, Javo; I've got enough for both of us, if you were not too proud to share.

Teach Me How To Feel Again

I went with Bonny to a screening of the junk movie I'd worked on the summer before. We rode our bikes up Brunswick Street in a cold and gritty wind.

'Did Bill tell you he stayed with me that night after Paddy's party?' I asked, wondering why it still required a moment of force for me to be honest. 'I hope it's all right.'

'Of *course* it is. It's not a matter of jealousy – not with you, anyway, because I love you. It's just that he's given me the bum's rush. He never comes round any more. If I want the relationship to go on, I have to do all the legwork. It's all the same, to him. He reckons he's "got his own life to live".'

'Why are they *like* that?' I said, looking at her friendly, cheerful face as we struggled up the hill past the big flats: her cheeks were rosy in the wind, half sunk into the collar of her blue pea-jacket.

'It's that old thing about "having room to move",' she said. 'They're afraid of being emotionally pressured . . . you know, the old fears of manipulation, of moral pressure – because of course for centuries women have been the conscience of the world.'

She flicked her eyebrows comically. We laughed, propping on our bikes at the lights outside the Rob Roy Hotel. I remembered Javo that last afternoon by my fire, how he had lifted his chin and opened his eyes wide, and declared,

'Anyway, I'm never gonna get off dope.'

My hands fell apart in despair. 'I never – I never – I never asked you to!'

Javo was at the movie. He sent me a signal, hullo. For a second I would have liked to sit with him, but he was with the prestige junkies, Chris and Mark, and I was in the front row with the straights, Bonny and Willy and Angela and Eve and Lou. So I stayed put, keeping my side of that unspoken social pact. Watching myself on the screen, my heart dived about all over the place and I shook in my seat. But it was only five minutes, and the rest of the time was crammed with the faces and voices of people I knew, and I forgot myself, staring at the moving pictures, listening to Angela sing and Willy play, amazed at the concentration of talent in this group of people with their chopped hair, rolled up pants, sceptical expressions and idiosyncratic shorthand speech.

At the end, when we were leaving, I caught up with Javo and said,

'Hey! I've got something for you.'

I handed him a silver ear-ring which I'd found left over from a pair. He'd sold his gold one, in jail for cigarettes. 'Here you are. If you've still got a hole left.'

'Thanks, mate.' He took it, smiled at me, disappeared in the small crowd.

I answered the phone one morning. Someone dropped a coin, pressed the button.

'Is Rita there?'

'No,' I said. 'Who's that?'

'David,' said the voice, which I dimly knew. But I didn't know any *David*.

'Do you want to leave a message?'

'No,' said the voice, becoming more familiar every second. 'No . . . I'll try ringing back later.'

'OK,' I said, and before the receiver hit the stand I had recognised the voice – Nick. I finished hanging up and went back to bed, pondering on the ruses people will employ. He must have known it was me. But perhaps he didn't know how distinctive his own voice was: flat, broad accent, sharp; pauses while he thought, then the words came out in a flat, hard clatter.

I suffered a terrible compulsion to find out what Javo was thinking. Gracie and I got to the tower before ten o'clock one morning. As we clomped up the stairs, that familiar voice croaked,

'Uh – uhh! Hey – whazza time?'

'Ten o'clock,' I answered. 'Where are you?'

Not in Jack's room. I went up another flight and found him in the little bolt-hole opposite the dunny. I stuck my head round the door, and he lifted his off the pillow. He was so stoned – pin-eyed, skin breaking out again – that I involuntarily glanced at the floor for the fallen fit. None there. He grinned at me.

'It's nearly ten,' I repeated. 'See you.'

I went off down the hall. There I saw his journal sticking out of his calico bag. I whisked it out and into Jack's room and sat down to snoop: hands trembling, mouth watering. He had glued to the inside of the back cover an old photo of me, stolen from one of Jack's boxes of history.

'Nora said my life was *sordid*,' I read. 'The word is stuck like a piece of gum to the inside of my skull; in fact I'm almost getting to have a feeling for it. Rita came to see me at Easey Street, offered me a place to sleep in her studio. She's the warmest-hearted person I've met in a long time. She asked me what I thought about the fact that she had fallen in love with Nick. I felt happy about that, in a way . . . but also a bit thrown because I'd fancied the idea of some kind of scene with her myself. Well, that's that.'

I put the book back in the bag, and with one dexterous flourish I turned my jealousy against *her*: anything rather than estrange myself further from *him*. What a mechanism. With a head full of dark thoughts, I wandered miserably up again to the room where he was lying, and stood at the end of the bed.

'I've read your book.'

He smiled, I smiled.

I said, not understanding the urge to hurt myself, 'Why *don't* you have a scene with Rita?'

He looked at me, opened his mouth and said, shaking his head,

'No. I don't want to.'

I stood there silently, suffering *pain in the heart*.

'Well,' I said, ' 'bye,' and stepped down the step. I heard him speak, went back. 'What?'

'Come here a minute.'

I went over to the side of the bed. He reached up his arm, took hold of my shoulder, pulled my face down into his neck, his face half turned away.

'My face is cold from the wind,' I stammered, not used to him touching me. He turned his face to me and kissed me on the mouth. I stayed leaning over, held against him, for seconds. He let go and I straightened up and went away down the stairs.

Stoned, stoned, stoned again. Coke madness. Sitting up in my

125

well-made bed, all alone on a Saturday night, my tongue numb from licking up last night's coke crumbs off the mirror, I pondered the nature of dissipation and pleasure. My nose began to bleed weakly from the left nostril, probably something to do with the quantities of coke I had absorbed into the mucous membrane the night before, first with Jessie in the tower kitchen when I was supposed to be stirring the soup for supper, and again later with Bill, in my room after the show. We were stoned when we got home; but we snorted more and lay back, and I talked compulsively for a while and then lapsed into a silence, struck dumb by the flood of fantasies which came pouring through my head. Visions of strange countries, Arab or South American; 'urban delirium'; memories of a room where I once gave in to hepatitis in Bill's old house in Sydney. I remembered the last time I'd been so coked: the night in summer when Javo brought me some and I snorted it, and lay awake all night beside him while he came down hard after days of shooting it. His eye rolled round to me again and again, his face tried feebly to smile.

Bill and I fucked one ordinary, human fuck, and then the coke took over and we were doing something else: my head raced and plunged away into other worlds, and my body flowed on a tide of uncontrollable fantasy, singing sweet and high the while.

I slept two hours barely; and the next day I kept going only by smoking huge quantities of black hash. I went to a party at Eve's. Clive was there.

'Come and stay the night with me, Nora!' he said, taking my hand in his callused palm; but I *couldn't*, I was so exhausted.

'I've been fucking my arse off all night,' hissed Eve to me as she passed me a plate of food. Jessie and I made each other laugh till we were nearly sick.

Everybody was out of their heads.

And when I passed through the tower on my way home, I found Javo had left me a note pinned to the board at the top of the stairs.

'Dear Nora, I'm sorry for trying to make you my conscience

126

and I don't know how to go about making that any different right now – I'm just a fool with a stupid burden that I can't shake off – without lumps of it hitting other people close by. I'm a self-centred ratbag – and probably because of that ugly fact – my love for you is in short bursts with long self-engrossed advertisements in between that last so long you lose track of the story, like Hal Todd on Night Owl Theatre. And my other strong fear was for a time there losing grip on knowing emotionally I wouldn't freak out if there was no-one there beside me. It's just like reassuring yourself that you can do more than just survive, being by yourself. Things will have to change – I can't say when – but only you can say if it's too late.'

I came back from the laundry, walked in in my boots and rolled-up pants. Rita was home, standing at the stove. She turned her bright face to greet me, smiling away there with the wooden spoon in her hand.

'What have you been doing since I last saw you?' she asked.

'Oh – starving myself, and getting stoned, and fucking, and slugging it out with Javo – I'm exhausted, trying to work out how it all got blown.'

She nodded, stirring the food with one hand and ruffling up my hair with the other. I looked at her flushed cheeks, and without having to think about it, I suddenly threw my arms round her waist and said,

'Give us a hug, Rita! I've been feeling badly towards you, because I thought Javo was going to fall in love with you.'

'Oh!' she laughed, hugging me back. 'I thought – I wondered why – how can you have thought that?'

'I read his diary.' We both burst out laughing.

'Oh no!' she said. 'I went to see him because I was afraid that my attitude towards dope might have had something to do with you and him breaking up. And anyway, I saw him today in the street, and he acted as if we'd never met, he was so stoned – and I thought, poor Nora! If that's what he used to do to *her*, well! . . .'

'I guess I feel pretty good now, though,' I said. 'And tomorrow I'm going up the country to stay with my parents for a couple of days.'

'Good idea. Get out of town for a while.' She banged the spoon on the edge of the saucepan. 'Right. Food's ready. Do you want to call the kids?'

When I got up in the morning, Rita said,

'Javo came round last night.'

'What? I didn't hear him. What time?'

'About three in the morning. He wanted the key to the studio; he's asleep along there now.'

My heart turned over at the thought of him passing my door and waking Rita instead. The willing prisoner. Won't this ever end? I went down to the studio and glanced in at him, still, under the blankets, his face hidden and his hair standing on end. I didn't go nearer, *fearing to be uncool*.

What *is* this, that we all do?

I was so tired.

Up in the mountains – or rather, in the winding valley at their feet – the air was thick with pollen.

I felt a freak there: short hair, dulled and anxious look, nothing comfortable to talk about. My mother showed the dam to me, and the underground spring behind the house. She had gumboots on and leaped across channels. I puddled gingerly in my city runners. Lethargy stole over me, the way Javo described smack: warm lead poured through the veins.

Gracie and I walked a mile or so to the post office. I heard a quick rustle in the grass and remarked,

'I wonder if that was a snake.'

Gracie, city child, went completely white and clutched my hand.

I would go nuts in the country. I was already nuts in the city, but had learnt to handle it.

I was washing my hands at the basin. I imagined that the phone would ring and it would be Javo, saying in his hoarse voice,

'Come back, will you, Nor?'

Idiot. This is not going to happen.

I should have let it all pass, but I was unwilling to. The pain of it was by no means unbearable. Sometimes I could sidestep it altogether. I remembered Anna Wulf in *The Golden Notebook* saying to her psychoanalyst,

'I came to you so you could teach me how to feel again.

Maybe one day it would come to that.

Meanwhile, I breathed the polleny air and waited for dark, for another twelve hours of bottomless sleep.

I woke, and the whole sky was falling in rain. It rained steadily all night, and was still raining by morning. At three in the morning my father went outside with a torch: at first I thought it was lightning, but then I heard his step crunch on the gravel as he passed my window to find the source of a leak in the spouting. The house was tight as a drum: not a drop of water came in. I lay there, protected in my bed like a child again; and at Peel Street Javo comes in in the middle of the night, up the stairs, past my door, into Rita's room, stands beside her bed till she wakes, says,

'Let me sleep with you.'

'No,' she says, 'I won't because of Nora'; but she wants to, and his presence persuades her; he gets into the bed and they fuck, and he comes quickly with that gasp of breath he makes, and Rita thinks,

'Is that the way he and Nora used to fuck? How come she was so happy with it?'

Out rolled this fantasy, smooth as butter; and I fell asleep and dreamed about the sea: my children drowning, beyond my help, my screams unheard.

My back ached and ached.

I daydreamed of an end to this pain, and of another attempt at Sydney. I sat on the grassy hump behind my parents' house, armed with a stick against the magpies which zipped mercilessly about my ears whenever I went outside. I talked out loud to myself, half crazy. I thought about Javo and his gawky limbs.

I went up to the dam in the middle of the afternoon to pick up the yabby nets. The sun was shining out of a clear sky, a cool breeze passed over the paddock and the water before it struck my skin. I took the nets in my hand and started back towards the slope that led away from the dam. But for a few minutes I stood still on the lip of the grassy slope and held the nets and stared at the countryside: mountains a couple of miles away in front of me, the dam and a sloping paddock behind me, the house down there to one side almost out of sight. At my feet wet strips of marsh grass, and in my ears the endless rhythm of the small frogs cricketing in the dam.

Just in that moment when the senses' intake, hearing and seeing, began to melt into one impression, Gracie called me from the house and it all broke apart again into its separate categories. But for a few seconds there it was like Joni Mitchell's song:

> 'And you want to keep moving
> and you want to stay still
> but lost in the moment
> some longing gets filled . . .'

Home, home, home.

We drove forty miles down the Hume and my back stopped aching.

No-one home. I walked into my room and looked at my face in the mirror and was surprised to see that I had a slight suntan, and that my hair had grown, not just longer, but thicker.

Javo had been in my room. A lump of cigarette ash lay on my table between the opened letters: no-one else would have dared.

That night I had a terrible dream: I came into the house and found it full of the dense feeling of two people sexually involved with each other: Rita and Javo had been fucking, and I was totally excluded. I could *not* break through. I was dreadfully upset. I tried to talk to Javo, half-crying, full of grief, but he adopted an airy tone and brushed my questions aside.

'Is it that you just aren't interested any more?' I asked, almost pleading.

'Yes, that's about it,' he replied, not looking at me.

130

There was no communication between me and Rita in the dream, only my wretchedness and jealousy. The atmosphere of it was thick with misery. I woke up out of it and found it was the very early hours of the morning, and the house still, but I could not fight my way out of the thickness of that dream. I lay there wide awake, battling with it and with my feeling of shame, and very slowly it began to dissipate itself, and release me. But the room was full of his presence, and of my fears. What *was* I afraid of? Nothing much, by the time daylight came, and I began to use my brain.

Damned Hide

Lunchtime in Pulcinella: me, Rita, Bill and Willy grumbling over a mediocre pasta.

'Ah – there he goes, the star of stage and screen,' remarked Willy nastily. I looked up and saw Javo, white-faced and rough-headed, stumble past the window, heading east down Elgin Street, looking for a hit.

No pain.

At one o'clock in the morning he loomed in my doorway, hesitating till I woke up properly and said hullo. Both on our best behaviour, 'being friends', we talked awkwardly for a while. When conversation flagged, he mooched round the room and picked up his Bangkok journal off the bottom shelf. He sat on my chair and read over what he had written months ago, when he had been frightened and even more strung out than he was now.

I lay there watching him, saying nothing. He was a bit stoned, I observed. I looked at his face, which changed as he read. His hair had grown out from the prison haircut, and looked thick and dry and matted.

'I'm keeping you up,' he offered absent-mindedly as he

turned a page.

'No, it's all right,' I said politely.

At last he got up, his head nearly touching the low ceiling. 'It's getting late. I think I'll go to bed.' He turned off the light, and was hesitating between me and the door, about to start off for the studio.

'Give us a hug,' I said, because I wanted to touch him. He sat down on the edge of the bed and put one gangly arm around me. We hugged each other, and I began to stroke his face and hair, for the pleasure of feeling him again. He flopped his lantern head on to my shoulder, and let me go on stroking. I thought, no-one has touched him since he left me in Sydney. His eyes were closed in the dark, and I stroked him over and over, while my head filled with fantasies of what might happen in the morning if I asked him to stay with me.

He sat up, rested his elbows on his knees, and stared doggedly in front of him in the dark room.

'I would like to ask you to stay, but I don't want to get kicked in the teeth again in the morning.'

He sat silent.

'Do you want to stay?'

'I don't know, mate. I just don't know.'

I put my hand on his thigh and began to stroke his leg, both because I liked the feel of it and because in some perverse way I wanted to make him stay with me, to seduce him to stay, perfectly benevolently, to coax him to drop his pride, or fear, or whatever it was around his neck like an albatross.

'Get in here.'

He started to pull off his boots. He took off his clothes, awkwardly, and got in beside me. When I pulled off my shirt and we lay down together, I was glad. No anxiety.

But he was inscrutable. I heard him give a small sigh at the moment when our skins met, but after that no sign from him; and I tuned myself to his inscrutability, and myself became opaque. I did not say a word. Our wariness and politeness extended itself into the way we fucked, though our bodies remembered each other without strain.

And finally we turned aside from each other to sleep, and I folded myself round his long back for a minute, put my knees in the curve of his knees.

'Goodnight,' we said, the only word we spoke. We even kissed goodnight, as we always used to do, and it was a gesture of goodwill.

He slept till three in the afternoon. When he got up to leave, well into the sick part of his day, he came across to my chair and hugged my face clumsily against his hip, meaning goodbye.

Two days passed. Claire came to visit, and we lay on the cloudbed in the afternoon and talked about our parents. In the evening I was eating a meal at the dining room table with Rita and the kids when the front door burst open and Javo came pounding in, ready to use the studio to make some posters.

'Gimme a rapidograph, and a pencil, and a ruler, will you, Nor?' he croaked. I got them for him, and began to feel bad-tempered. He refused food and thundered away to the studio. Rita and I gave each other a look. We put the kids to bed. I cleaned the living room, swept the floors, decided to stay home and let Rita go out on her own; collapsed in a chair; and remembered Javo saying in Sydney, 'You never take any interest in the work I do.' So, in the warm evening, I wandered along the street to see what he was doing in the studio.

The roller door was wide open, light streamed out on to the pavement. He was sitting at the table in the bare white concrete room, working neatly and cleverly at a drawing.

'You're good at it, aren't you?' I remarked, impressed.

'I'm a good copier.'

I stood beside him, watching.

'Hey, Nor – will you do us a favour?'

'Depends what it is.' We were smiling at each other.

'I think I left my packet of Marlboro at the house – get 'em for me, will you?'

'You lazy bastard!' I cried in amazement. 'Why don't you get 'em yourself?'

'Oh, get fucked!' he said, laughing too and tossing his head about. 'I'm *working*!'

'Well, what do you think *I've* been doing for the last two hours? Don't you call that work?'

'Yeah, I know it's work, but . . .'

133

I was already on my way out the door, conned once again by his laughter and his *damned hide*, actually heading for the Marlboro I was, until my foot hit the pavement outside, and at that second the feminist rage struck, and my intention changed to its precise opposite. I walked back to the house, very steadily past the living room where no doubt the small red object was lying, up the stairs and into my room. I lay on the bed and picked up *After Leaving Mr McKenzie* and read until I fell asleep.

Javo came into the house at four the next afternoon, having slept the day away in the studio. I went downstairs and stood around the kitchen while he helped himself to a meal. I even cooked him an egg. We talked: it was a close parody of the way we used to talk when we loved each other. But . . . we walked together over to Carlton, and by the time we reached the big roundabout we had ceased to *be* with each other: just striding along parallel paths, three feet apart, silent; him for real, me faking. When we got to the tower, he disappeared. And I left again, in haste to catch up with Jack and Gracie. I jumped into a cab and chased them down Russell Street to Jimmy's in the city. I ran in, eager for a sight of their familiarity. They were sitting at a table with Willy and Paddy, who had their backs to the door. I put my hands on their shoulders, and said,

'Oohoo!'

They were glad to see me. My heart inflated again to a comfortable buoyancy and I sat down with them to eat. When we left the restaurant we walked up Russell Street, strung across the pavement, Gracie riding on Jack's shoulders. I put my arm round Willy's waist and he laid his over my shoulder – o sweet companionableness! I felt his hard healthy body under my hand. No fears, no hopes. Simply what was there. Our boots beat the footpath in rhythm, and we walked back to Carlton in the cold spring night: air dark blue and sharp, a faint scent of things growing.

At the tower I borrowed the Falcon and headed for Peel Street, but the radio was playing the kind of music that made me want to turn right out Royal Parade and head for Sydney, or just along a fast clear road. I didn't want to go home, not because being alone there was distasteful to me, but because I wanted to share the fizzing inside my head. I drove down to Napier Street, thinking to see Jean's brown Queensland face and hear stories of travel. Nobody home; but I was not discouraged. On the way out the gate I passed Claire coming in, her cap of silky fair hair flopping round her face, flushed and chilly from the bike ride home in that clear spring night. She was laughing and sparkling at me in the darkness, dressed in a cape and boots like a young cavalier, arms forward to the handlebars. We greeted and parted and I drove home, content to be elated on my own.

Now, how can I ever sleep, in this exhilaration? The spring air comes cleanly through my window, I'm in love with the air and the city and Rita sleeping in her brass bed across the landing and the kids stacked in their bunks and the cat curled in Gracie's waist and Paddy's black hair and Willy's blond and Jack's pointed chin and my hair growing and the wrinkled skin on my writing fingers and my sister Cobby far away in another country.

Enough of you, Javo, and your death. I've had enough. Now, if only I can live that out. Enough. I will gather my strength.

> 'Doubt not.
> You gather friends around you
> As a hair clasp gathers the hair.'
>
> *I Ching: Enthusiasm*

There's hope for all of us, I swear.

In such a House of Dreams

On Gracie's sixth birthday I did not want to go to the circus. The others ran off to the car with shrieks of excitement. I lay disconsolately on my bed. It was a muggy day, dull and clouded. But in the late afternoon the sky cleared and my spirits did the same. The sun went down; the bath heater was roaring away downstairs, Nick was playing with the kids (thumps, screeches, laughter), and Bill came into my room after the circus and stroked my head and put his warm hand on my arm. It wasn't that I was lonely for Javo, but that my body was lonely.

'Stay with me, Bill.'

He did. When I slept next to him (he was as massive as a whale and twice as placid), I never dropped clear into the well, but rose and fell on the river currents.

For nights, then, I slept alone. I was so restless that it seemed I woke and turned over in despair every five minutes. I thought I must be going crazy. It was the loneliness, and the fantasies. Maudlin songs drove me to distraction. I had an adolescent longing to be absolutely enfolded by someone. The fantasies were out of control. They were indescribably delightful. The most trivial word or image would trigger off a bout of them. And every time, when I could no longer ignore their total lack of connection with, or meaning in, the *real world*, the bad moments followed, as reliably as the thump at the end of a coke flash.

Into the hollow left by Javo dropped an unexpected stone.

Nick took me with him to a gig. I got drunk and danced merrily all on my own. The band finished working and came down off the stage. Angela and I were horsing about amiably. People were arranging lifts home.

'What about you?' said Nick to Gerald. He looked up from where he was sitting at the table, leaning his dark, expressionless face on one fist, and said in a casual voice,

'I want to go home with Nora.'

I thought he was teasing me, and laughed. He shrugged and smiled: his face, propped motionless over his drink, was perfectly inscrutable. He drew back his long thin legs to let me pass.

'See you round, then,' he said, by way of farewell.

'Funny Gerald should have said that,' I remarked to Nick on

the way home. 'I always kind of liked him, actually.'

'Well, why didn't you go with him?' shouted Nick, the fast worker, laughing incredulously.

'Don't be dumb! He was only teasing me!'

'Listen, dummy, it would have taken him a real lot of nerve to say that to you.'

We laughed at the ludicrous irony of it.

Next day Nick said, 'I told Gerald what you said about last night. He said, "Yeah, I should have made it clear that I wasn't joking".'

Nick was lounging on Rita's bed with the curtains drawn, idly staring into space. I said,

'What do you reckon my chances are of – you know – racing him off?'

'I'd say pret-ty fuckin' good,' replies Mr Cool, one hand under his head, grinning wickedly. 'Why don't you let me be the go-between?'

'Shutup, shithead. You'd love that, wouldn't you.'

'I reckon. I already told him you said you liked him.'

'Did you, indeed. What did he say?'

'He said, "I bet she only told you so *you'd* tell *me*".'

We were rolling with laughter on the bed.

'What's wrong with *that*? I said, trying to calm down.

'Nothing! Nothing. He asked me where you lived, but I – '

' – But you'd forgotten the address. Oh, you useless shit!'

'And then he said, "Why doesn't she just come round here and hop into bed with me?" '

I couldn't keep up this adolescent game. It always ended up showing its fundamental brutality, and I found myself suddenly depressed, and frightened by the gap between a remark like that and my fantasies, which were of *love*.

Idiotic.

I dreamed again and again of houses, always big airy open houses, always beside the sea, wind flowing freely through the rooms, people pleasantly disposed or working quietly, and miles and miles of ocean out every window. In such a house of dreams I spoke with Gerald, this unknown figure: though our heads were close together, his voice was indistinct, hard to hear, like a bad telephone connection.

I woke up and my room was full of sunny wind, red curtain flying and the noise of the market battering away out there past the Ah Chang Trading Company.

Nick and Javo were in my room.

'Lend us your rapidograph, will you, Nora?' asked Nick.

I said, to tease Javo, 'Well, it's kind of special, because Javo gave it to me for a present, but now it's OK for you to use it, because I don't love him any more.'

'Good on ya!' cried Javo with a laugh. He meant it. I did not mean it. But at that moment I realised I had better *start* meaning it. Any kind of love for him was no longer appropriate, if I wanted to stay in one piece. The day before, he and I had been eating lunch at Jimmy's, enjoying ourselves until he brought up the endless subject of our relationship.

'Since my old man left,' he said, 'and my old lady tried to make up for it by smothering me with affection, I've always valued my friendships with men more than my relationships with women. Maybe that had something to do with what happened between you and me – I've always had plenty of female love, but not enough male.'

My face must have dropped, for he became all attention, fixing me with his blue eyes only a fraction whited out. I had a few bad minutes . . . and what man, I thought bitterly, would take what I've taken from you? . . . but we left the restaurant and in the sunny street my dismay jumped off my shoulders and simply flew away.

'Ah, come on, Javes,' I said in a burst of good feeling. 'I don't want to talk like this. Let's just be friends. Let me take your arm – can I take your arm?' I squeezed and prodded his skinny elbow, to tease him. He grinned, and said,

'Yeah. I like it.'

And we walked back to Peel Street in the best spirit we could manage, which was a rough companionableness. I must make that do.

Holy in the Orchard

At Tullamarine, waiting at the barrier for someone I'd never seen, Martin's elder brother Joss. T shirts, denim jackets, no, no, that's not right, but then I see him, couldn't be anyone but the owner of that soft voice on the telephone – small, he's small and he's wearing a jacket with ties instead of buttons, and a cap pulled down over his dry, untidy, bleached-out hair. He comes towards me where I stand uncertainly, holding Gracie's hand.

'I'm Joss.'

We shake hands. I never shake hands.

'I am not used to this flying,' he said. 'I can't handle planes and cars. I am used to driving bullock carts.' His voice was faintly tinged with American.

'You are so unlike Martin,' I said. 'You are not speedy. I suppose it's because you don't live in a big city.'

He laughed shortly. 'I've lived in much bigger cities than Martin ever has,' he retorted. It was the only egotistical remark I ever heard him make. I remembered Martin saying, 'He was burning cars in Paris in '68.'

I steered the big beat-up Falcon back down the freeway in the dark. The night air streamed in, vaguely sweetened with grassy scents. I glanced sideways at his hooked profile blurred by thoughtless hair. He was quite still. The desire to chatter left me. I was very, very tired. I was in a trance of fatigue. He sensed the looseness in the fabric usually drawn so tight, and without a word he came flooding in.

In our house he sat quietly at the table. The children moved unerringly to his side.

'Tell us about up in India,' begged Grace. 'Is there any cars?'

Up in India, up in India.

He drew for them. He told them stories of few words. They stood beside him with their mouths open.

After they had gone to bed, I made a fire in my room. He came in and we sat on the floor for a long time, not speaking,

139

hypnotised by the flames. He slept on the floor and I crept under my blankets on the bed. When the fire went out and it became cold, we woke up at the same moment.

'I'll go upstairs and get a blanket, or . . .' He got up.

'You could sleep in here,' I offered, afraid of being misinterpreted; all I wanted was for this peacefulness to continue. He took off his clothes: he bent over and I saw the weather-beaten skin of his belly: you are as old as I am. He got into my bed. We held each other, not speaking, and he sent out his beams of warmth.

In the morning when the children went to school, I was standing at the sink.

'I am going down to Hobart today,' he said. I turned to look at him. *Don't go away.* I didn't think but opened my mouth.

'Can we come with you?'

'Yes.'

I began to understand the dreams of houses near the sea. In Hobart, Gracie slept beside me in a comfortable room. The windows were shut against the cold night, but out there somewhere water was heaving gently against a shore, and a full moon was covered with cloud. I was in a state of fatigue so extreme, and so harmonious, that it had become ecstatic. No drugs. No sleep.

It was a morning with clouds. I sat on the bed. Gracie was painting. Joss came in with his clothes full of cold air from the beach. He turned around in the room and the air flew out of his clothes and went past my face.

'Joss, Joss, where's Joss?' says Gracie every three minutes.

'I was down on the beach,' he replies.

'Next time will you take me?'

'Yes.'

'Joss!'

'Yeah.'

'Joss! Are you gone again, Joss?'

She wants to be with him all the time. So do I.

When we got to Franklin on the bus it was dark and cold. We walked along the road, expecting to meet Charlie as he drove down from the orchard to pick us up. Gracie was riding on Joss's shoulders, wearing his cap. Again and again I felt her agitation. There was water somewhere to our left, its dampness rising in the silence.

'I want to go back to the pub,' Gracie kept saying, in a voice she strove to make conversational. At a bend in the road we realised we had come too far, and turned back. The light was yellow through the glass of the pub door, and Gracie sighed with relief, and Charlie was waiting in the bar.

We came in the dark to the house in the apple orchard. The three of us slept in the double bed. A big fire, a lamp, a candle.

'How are you doin'?' asks Joss. 'You are sighing a lot.'

'Am I? I've been thinking about Martin.'

The radio was on faintly in the next room. The pips went for the news, and we heard voices shouting.

'A rebellion, a revolution,' I said. By the time we reached the radio we could hear the hysterical sirens.

She missed, she missed.

A 45-year-old woman with one child raised a gun and fired at President Ford. The second go they'd had at him in California in seventeen days.

Rain like the small rain of Ireland. Across the lumpy fields you can see it thicken and move.

The way he conducted himself made my normal life seem raucous. And yet . . . What is it? I'm out of sync, here. No grip, clutch slipping. I'm not frightened. I know when he goes back to India I won't miss him. He gives me nothing, and yet at the same time everything. The way I usually talk has no purchase on the surface of his life, or on its surfacelessness. At the point where I realise this, the point at which frustration or annoyance would normally push me past such a situation, my mind quietly slips a cog and I float away.

It's all right.

The big clean pale logs hiss on the fire. I am the only one awake in the house. Grace has been asleep for hours in the front bedroom. Joss has fallen asleep, half curled up with his back to me, on the other side of the fireplace. Rain sprinkles softly. A small rabbit which was saved from the dogs this morning stirs in its brown cardboard box.

Joss has spectacular scars, on his arms and feet in particular. 'A scorpion bit me,' he explains, showing me a livid mauve scar three inches long on his left fore-arm. 'It was a trip.'

I look up sharply.

'A real pain trip,' he continues placidly, smiling at me with his brother's eyes: goldish-green, rimmed finely with a brown line. 'My hands were clenched, like this –' showing me bent, tight fingers.

What am I doing here?

He assumes, not asking me but discussing it in my presence, that Gracie and I will go with him on Thursday down to Dover. If any other man I know had made such an assumption, I would have been furious.

Why amn't I, with him?

I'm too spaced. I am tentative. I do not take initiatives.

When he talks about India, I don't understand what he says.

Sometimes he looks me in the eyes, intently, for such a long time that I have to look away.

He is still asleep.

I can never slow down to his placidness.

It was a morning.

I was lying on my back on a raft on the deep dam, dreaming of nothing while Joss and Gracie attempted to extract papyrus from the rushes on the verge. The sun was beaming down and I was in a state resembling sleep. The air was still, except for the sound of the stream rushing, further over. Suddenly there was a tremendous hissing and pushing in the air. I looked up with a start and saw a whirlwind come spiralling down from the gumtrees to the surface of the dam about fifteen feet from me. The water there boiled violently for a few seconds over a round area as big as a dinner table. The disturbance vanished as suddenly as it had come, the trees settled again, there was nothing left on the water but a line of bubbles.

'Did you see that?' I called to Joss.

'It was a spirit!' He was laughing on the bank.

I stood up on the raft and picked up the pole, because for no apparent reason I had begun to drift, slowly but decidedly, towards the patch of water where the willy willy had been. Then I thought, well, if it's a spirit as he says it's almost certainly a benevolent one, and there's no harm in drifting; so I lay down again and let my mind fly away, and the raft drifted exactly to the whirlwind place, and stopped, and I lay there in a kind of somnolent trance.

It seemed hours later when I came to, sat up, saw Gracie and Joss had disappeared, poled my raft back to shore, moored it to the tree, and reeled down the track in a dream. Back at the house Joss was cutting up vegetables.

'What about that whirlwind,' says I.

Says he, looking up like a grandfather from his carrots, 'If you'd known what to do with that whirlwind, you might have gone into another world. It was a doorway. It was specially for you, that one.'

When he makes these cosmic remarks, I get a double response: firstly, a stillness, in which I accept the comment along with a steady look he gives me; and simultaneously but somehow secondarily, a flash of scepticism, expressed purely in a visual image: Willy's face and his mocking smile.

Sitting in the kitchen, I remember I had arranged to go out with Paddy tonight. A small fantasy slips across the screen: I send her a telegram saying 'Never coming back.' At this I give a snort of laughter. Joss hears me, smiles, asks,

'*Pourquoi ris-tu?*'

Not really a need to reply; nor a chance to, through Gracie's exuberance. I modify the message to 'Not coming back.'

The three of us and the rabbit slept in separate beds round the big fire. I dreamed, I forgot the dreams. Joss woke up in the morning and said,

'I dreamed that we went back to Auroville.'

'Who's we?'

'The three of us – you, me and Grace. And it had all been turned into an . . . electronic light show. There was a machine

for making sand-castles. And on the beach we three did tricks,
but no-one watched. They were all waiting in queues for their
turn at the sand-castle machine.'

If Gracie hadn't been there, I would have lain and dreamed
all day. She was restlessly energetic and, though Joss was her
focus, she wore out my patience.

I rang Rita and asked her to cancel my arrangement with
Paddy. Hearing her light, slightly breathy voice, I filled up
with warmth towards her.

'Something weird's happening,' I said, cradling the rabbit
under my cardigan.

'Yeah? What *is* it?'

'I don't know yet.'

'But – is it good?'

'Oh yes! It's terrific. I feel really good.'

'Javo,' she said, 'was really upset.'

'Yeah? Because I went away?' Runs of laughter kept burst-
ing out of me. She laughed too.

'That's part of it. Also, of course, he doesn't like Joss
because he's into that religion which he reckons is "fascist".'

' "Fascist", is it?' I was shaking with laughter. Maybe it is! I
don't know anything about it. I don't know anything about
anything.

'Mark thinks – I was round at Easey Street the day you
left – and Mark said, "Javo has a very tenacious personality".
He thinks Javo is still . . . really rapt in you – which is quite
obvious. Javo is down in Hobart too, you know.'

'*What*! He's in *Hobart*!' I was dissolving with internal
laughter. A sudden memory: being up in the mountains and
fantasising whenever the phone rang that it would be Javo, that
he would say in his grating voice,

'Nor, it's me. Come back.'

If he's in Hobart he must be coming down something
terrible. Poor Javo. I remember his face at Easey Street, the
day I left Melbourne: he came to the door pulling up his
jumper to scratch himself, revealing a pale swollen stomach
creased from sleep; his face also puffy, the colour of putty,
eyes staring with dope and fatigue; his voice, though, soft out
of that battered face. As I turned away:

'See you . . . Nora.' He ventured my name. I accepted.

We went up a hill with Charlie and the tractor to get some wood. Gracie and I wandered off on our own and began to build a hut. The timber lying about was inadequate to her design, and when I sat down she whinged and shed crocodile tears.

'You don't love me,' she whimpered, looking at me sideways to see how I was taking it.

My anger dissipated before it formed and I sat there on the damp hillside, staring with a dull peacefulness out over the valley. I takes a long time, longer than I've got, to clean out the city head, and longer still when you've brought most of your emotional environment with you.

I got up before dawn and walked through the wet grass up to the dam and beyond into the orchard. I saw the sun rise over a thick mass of mist that stretched like a sword up the valley of the Huon river. The only thing to do was to chant OM, and I did, staring dizzily into the sunny mist, until the air was humming with my breathing.

Night, now.

The rabbit insinuates itself between my thigh and the bed. Grace asleep again, Joss reading an out-dated *Rolling Stone* by the light of a candle and a kerosene lamp.

I would like to say, hey, sleep with me over on this side of the fire.

Why? Because I love being near you. Underneath all the complications introduced by my addiction to words, there is one quite certain thing:

Joss, I like being near you.

Give me some of your peculiar warmth and stillness.

When we part, there will be no ragged ends left hanging.

I came into the house from a walk in the wet grass. He was sitting at the table, quietly smoking. I sat down opposite him. He looked up, straight into my eyes as he does, and smiled at me. At that moment, we were both a hundred years old and we had known each other for ever.

145

We went back to Hobart on a bus, an hour's drive on a sunny, still morning, along the Huon river: fruit trees coming into blossom, the river trimmed in places with rows of thin poplars reflected still as stalks in the calm water. We turned a corner and came upon a pear tree in full bloom, rich white with a shadowy tinge of pink at its heart. My breath stopped. His hands went up in an involuntary gesture: greeting and prayer.

And that's how it was.

He drove us to the ferry. He took my arms, smiled right into my eyes, said,

'See you in a while. I'll almost certainly be coming back through Melbourne, but if by some chance I don't ... remember, any time I can help you, by the power which is diverted through me ...'

I did not trouble myself to wonder what this power might be, or where it came from. I just went on smiling, and nodding my head. He turned and walked away.

On the ferry Gracie miraculously became her ordinary, cheerful self: instead of whining and clinging to me, as she had done at the orchard, she trotted off to the railing and spent the whole journey chattering to herself and staring at the water. I supposed she was confused by the gap between what I normally expect of her – independence and some kind of stoicism – and what Joss had offered her – complete openness to his time, and willingness to serve her.

We got off the bus in Melbourne at six o'clock on a Saturday evening. Cars waving blue and white streamers cruised down Victoria Street as we walked up it carrying our two string bags.

'What is it?' asked Gracie, bewildered.

I stared about me in confusion, still slow from the orchard.

'Yew fuckin' bewdy!' bellowed a drunk in a T shirt, leaning out of a passing car and pointing at my blue and white striped jumper.

'They are people who believe in *football*,' said Gracie with disdain. 'And you have got on one of those – what is it? – *Richmond jumpers*.'

If I am not careful, my reservoir of quiet will be punctured here, it will leak or squirt out, and I'll lose it.

At home I took the pictures down from my wall. I slept well, and dreamed a lot, of urban delirium, lying quietly in my familiar bed. I woke up to the sunshine and began to think about simplifying my life. I ought to take care, though, that I don't strip it of supports I need in order to live in the city. I can drop a lot of things – possessions, like the clothes I never wear – but in the city the thread that holds it all together is not easy to find.

Willy teased me, as I knew he would.

'Been converted, have you?' he needled, grinning at me from behind his twinkling spectacles as I drove up Johnston Street in the rain. I laughed and picked up his hand. He jumped at the unexpected touch.

'Come on, Willy. Let's go up the bush and grow veggies.'

Coming home was difficult. Dispossessed, even by minor changes. Nick had virtually moved in and had bought tons of market food, quantities at which the frugal soul rebelled, poor quality food, bought because it was cheap. He bought like Javo: to prove he could beat the price structure, come out on top with more for less. The apples, bought only yesterday, were already going soft. I thought about the kitchen at the orchard, where the sun came in on three sides and we ate apples and cheese and made soup out of lentils. Nick would tease me too, if I talked about it. I was afraid of the first moment of rage at the children, of the unnecessary masses of food Nick and Rita would fling on to the table, of the noise and our crowded living room, of what I'd have to do to protect myself.

Too Ripped

Already I was spreading myself too thin. I spent another coke night, almost till dawn, in my bed with Bill. We talked about things I had never talked about before: what it means to be alive in 1975, what change is and might be, how we see ourselves fitting in (or not) to this society, what the next step is or might be. We talked about these desolate things. We couldn't have slept longer than an hour and a half; the dawn came and we got up and attended to the children.

Javo came in from the studio, already stoned at eight o'clock in the morning. He saw Bill in the kitchen wearing my dressing-gown. He laughed.

'Great dressing gown, isn't it!'

He and Bill grinned at each other, two giants in the small room.

Javo actually made the kids' lunches. Rita and I raised our eyebrows behind his back at this display of agreeableness, too surprised to comment. He was doing the thing one does when one is a bit jealous but wanting to show that it's all right. We spent the day together, wandering about the city, into the state library and out again, walking with our arms round each other, talking gently and laughing. We came back to the house and lay on the bed, and fucked together, looking into each other's faces.

And the next morning he stole the last five dollars from our food kitty. It couldn't have been anyone but him. I stood in the kitchen with the empty jar in my hand, staring at Rita in silence.

'Come on,' she said. 'Let's get him.'

We rode over to the tower and found him on the landing.

'What about it, Javo?' said Rita. 'What about the five bucks? We know it was you.' She was out of breath from the ride; on her face was a strange smile of anger.

Javo dropped his face, also grinning but with embarrassment. 'OK. I took it.'

I had expected a denial. I was almost speechless. He sat down on the bench, face turned away, hands dangling between his knees, like a child waiting to be punished. I could not get my breath.

'You give me the shits,' I stammered, sick with anger. '*You give me the shits*.'

He said nothing. We turned and thumped down the stairs. Too much victory too quick. We didn't know what to do with it.

An hour later I was in Lesley's Ham and Beef Shop with Bill. The door flew open and Javo burst in, very stoned, ugly with it. He was fumbling feverishly in his jeans pocket. I thought he hadn't seen me and, my anger having dissipated in the intervening hour, I said,

'Pssst! Hey, Javo!'

Instead of answering, he pulled a handful of notes and coins out of his pocket and flung them on the marble counter, at the same time turning on his heel and croaking over his shoulder,

'What really happened was – I *took* the money to get a *pie*, and I *forgot* to put the *change* back.' The glass door banged behind him.

'Pretty expensive pie,' observed Bill mildly, seeing that the scattered money did not amount to more than about three dollars eighty. I gathered it up, feeling as if I had been given a hard push.

Gracie went to Perth on the train with Eve and Claire and the Roaster. The Roaster kissed me goodbye like old times. I felt sad when I said goodbye to Grace. I looked at her smooth-skinned, beautiful little face, and would have liked to . . . keep her forever, or something.

The rain did not stop. I stayed in bed till midday. I ate too much for my needs and felt disgusted with myself.

I would like to love and yet not to love.

Maybe it's all semantics.

Where are you, Grace? putting your face against the glass. Rita went back to bed with Nick, and Juliet was on the loose. I cooked her an omelette which she didn't like; still, it was bright yellow and I looked at it.

Chris rang to speak to Nick.

'He's asleep,' I said. 'Will I wake him?'

'No. Just tell him – the man didn't show; but if he does, I'll call again. It's a score.'

'OK,' I said, and hung up, annoyed that Nick could insinuate even scoring into our household. I went upstairs and put my head round Rita's bedroom door. There they lay in the black sheets, smoking and watching TV with the curtains drawn.

'Nick,' says I. 'Chris rang. The man didn't show, but if he does, she'll call back.'

He looked up at me and made a face which indicated, 'Dunno what *that* could mean.' The injured innocence of junkies.

I came flying into the house at nine o'clock at night, panting from the bike ride. In the corner of the room I saw Gerald, a photo through a fish-eye lens, long legs sticking out of the armchair, glass of scotch in his thin hand. He reminded me of some large wading-bird, wary, stiff, and graceless.

'Hullo!' I froze in midstep.

He smiled at me uncomfortably. 'Hullo. I've been wondering about you.'

'I've been out of town.'

'Yes. Rita told me you were in Tasmania. I was hoping you would come back.'

'I nearly didn't,' I said with a laugh. I pulled off my gloves. He twirled the glass in his fingers, their tips flattened from playing guitar.

'Want some of your own scotch?' He was looking at me with a funny sideways smile.

'Javo's mum gave it to me. I don't usually live like this.'

There was a stillness in the room. Wary. He was not a person to take lightly.

'Do you want to come upstairs? It's cold. I'll make a fire in my room.'

He loafed across the end of my bed while I broke up the sticks and lit the fire. Clever, cool fellow. I darned my jumper and listened to him talk. Seeing him now in my own house, out of the glamorous drunken smoky air of rock and roll, I felt dimly disappointed. There was some shadow in his face, a strangeness across the narrow cheek-bones, a self-conscious-ness about the wide thin mouth, that might have sounded a warning had loneliness not echoed more loudly in my ears. At some ungodly hour I said,

'I'd like to go to sleep now. Do you want to sleep here?'

'OK,' he said cheerfully, and in a matter-of-fact way took off his clothes and got in beside me. Immediately I felt physically at ease with him: skins touched unsignificantly, without sexual intent. I felt curious, and friendly towards him.

In the morning, when he was leaving, he hesitated in the small hallway, one hand on the door knob:

'See you soon?'

'OK. You know where I live.'

For a second, in his oddly closed, dark face, his brown eyes turned soft. He took hold of me with one long arm and hugged me, right against the front of his body, but gently. I fell back, surprised, and touched.

But I let him railroad me. A week later I was sitting with Bill in the tower kitchen where I had arranged to meet Gerald to go out for a meal. I accidentally got more stoned than I could handle. I was very tired. Gerald rushed in.

'Come with me,' he said, hustling me towards the door. 'I'd forgotten I had to go to this meeting. It will be just people sitting round smoking dope and talking.'

Bill raised his eyebrows, expecting me to refuse the rush. But I feebly replied, 'OK,' and followed him down the hall.

Halfway down the stairs he added,

'The meeting is in Caulfield. We're getting a lift with Philip.'

Caulfield! The other side of the river. By the time we got to the bottom of the stairs I knew I was doing something stupid, but some lethargy was paralysing me, and I got into the car unprotesting, with five other people and two dogs. The door closed behind me and I knew it was too late to escape. I started to hallucinate with the dope: Philip, sunk in the collar of his sheepskin coat and holding a well-bred dog on his lap, was the Prince of Wales at Windsor, and the old FX we were travelling in had become a Rolls-Royce with a long, elegant bonnet. Struck dumb, I let myself slip down into panic. There was no way for me to comport myself, because I had no reason to be there: I had come as an appendage to a man.

The living room of the house we went to had one light, harsh, high up in the centre of the ceiling. I sat at a table. One of the women had a small child on her lap. I stared at it eagerly, as if

151

it might save me. Someone handed me a joint, which gave me five minutes' unexpected physical pleasure: going to be all right: but in my fright I smoked too much and stampeded myself further into the panic. I knew Gerald had noticed I was battling, and I felt his anxiety not as comfort but as further reason to be frightened. My head clattered with fear. I was out of control. I experienced irrational dislike of everyone in the room. Their voices grated on me. Some thin thread of reason which I clung to did not lead me to safety, but into self-punishing thoughts: why can't I be with people outside my normal social group? Can I only be comfortable with people who communicate in that clever shorthand we all use? Why don't I give these people a chance?

Through this fog of panic I noticed that Philip had been out of the room for ten minutes. I had to gather myself to the sticking-place to stand up and walk out, picking my way between dozing dogs and people's feet: I stumbled out into a hallway, could not find the light-switch, but followed the sound of Philip very softly playing a guitar. He was in the bedroom. He smiled at me. I blundered over to the bed and took off my shoes and crept under the eiderdown. The thin wiry little sound of his guitar continued beside me, and the panic subsided.

'I'm so ripped!' I sighed helplessly.

He grinned at me over his shoulder. 'Too ripped.'

And pretty soon I fell asleep.

What seemed like two minutes later, Gerald was touching my shoulder. 'Time to go home.' I thought it was a sadistic joke. But when I looked at my watch it was nearly two hours since I had passed out.

On the way back to Carlton we did not have to stop once: every traffic light turned green for us.

When I got back to Peel Street, Paddy was there in the living room, sitting in front of the fire warming her hands round a cup of tea. I stumbled in, drunk with relief.

'What's the matter with *you*?' she asked as I fell into a chair.

'Oh Jesus, I've got to start giving the dope a miss,' I groaned. 'I've just had *the* most horrendous evening.'

I told her what had happened. She listened quietly with her

thoughtful, deceptively dreamy half-smile, her eyes remaining fixed on the fire.

'Why'd you go, in the first place?'

'I knew I was mad to go, but I was so stoned, and I just let him drag me out the door.'

'Did you tell him how you'd been feeling?'

'Yeah – on the way home.'

'What did he say?'

'Oh, he hung his head, and said, "I suppose I was just trying to drag you into my sexist fantasy – I wanted to show you off to my friends".'

'Jesus, *he* must be a bit wet behind the ears.' She pulled down the corners of her mouth. 'But at least he saw what he was doing.'

'But wouldn't you think *I'd* see what *I* was doing?'

'Don't worry!' she said, starting to grin. 'You're not the only one. The other night I went out with this guy – we were in *my car*, and he actually put it on me to let *him* drive.'

'You're kidding.'

'No! He just didn't like to be in a situation where I was in control.'

'What did *you* say?'

'Well, I let him. I sort of wanted to see how far he would go. He started by making some casual remark about Volkswagens, how he always forgot to put them into top gear; and then he drove off round the *Boulevard*, to show what a great driver he was.' Paddy raised her disdainful eyebrows, still half-smiling. 'He was driving at an *immense* speed in third gear, and I pointed out, quite politely really, that it *might* be a good idea to change into top. 'Oh!' he said, 'fourth in a VW is really an *overdrive*.' Well, he *could* be right, I suppose, but . . . he wanted to *drive handsomely* – you know – *scarf flying*. Even my buying the ice-creams later was not quite right. And yet the thing was – he was putting himself across as *one of us* – into politics, teaching at Preston and being radical about *that*, living in Fitzroy' – she made an ironic grimace.

'None of that means anything,' I said gloomily.

'Y-e-es . . . well . . . one wonders sometimes, doesn't one . . .'

'*I* wonder sometimes if we ought to be giving *men* a miss.'

She laughed. 'Oh, *I* don't know.'

'But to be perfectly honest, I've got no plans to do that.'

'Neither have I.'

On the contrary, two mornings later I was crawling round Gerald's ankles outside the kitchen door, letting down his jeans.

'If anyone from the women's centre saw me doing this,' I said, 'my reputation would be shot to pieces.'

He clicked his tongue in pleased exasperation. 'I don't even think it's necessary. They were all right before.'

'They *weren't*. You look a dag with your pants flapping round your calves. Don't you want to be cool?'

'What does it matter?'

'Well,' I mumbled out of the corner of my mouth past the row of pins, 'ultimately, of course, it doesn't; but the world being as it is, one may as well strive for a little elegance of line, don't you think?'

'No, not really. But go ahead.'

'Go on, admit it. You love it.'

He laughed.

'Turn round a bit – not too far! Back a bit.'

He shuffled round in his boat-shaped Adidas runners.

'And you need some new shoes.'

'Lay off, will you? These are *OK*.'

'I don't want to walk down the *street* with a dag like you!' I grunted crossly, and thought involuntarily of Javo, who never gave a moment's conscious thought to his clothes but carried off the most appalling, smelly rags with casual flair. Comparing again. Vain and silly. But I went on folding and pinning, and turning him around.

Joss rang from Hobart.

'This is *Joss*,' he said in his slow voice, offering me the gift. I wanted it, but had lost the grace to accept.

I streamed drunk and stoned in at my bedroom door, Gerald one step behind me, at four o'clock in the morning: the air in my room was dense with Joss's unexpected presence. Blown it, blown it. I retreated in panic, took the wrong option, made a mess of it. I lost my chance. My city skin had closed up tight again, like stretched canvas. I was unable.

The telephone rang and rang, next day, with business calls for Nick who was out trying to score. Joss sat, puzzled, at his corner of the table, the ugly no-neck cat on his knee.

'Please. Will you come and walk in the park with me?' I begged, almost in tears.

'Yes.'

We walked, arms about each other, round the damp gardens.

'You're much stronger than I am,' he said with a laugh. 'I'd have cracked up by now ... but you're in touch with so many good people!'

I couldn't speak. My life looked to me like a stupid tread-mill. I wanted to say, you've taught me to love differently, you have changed everything, this madness has only swamped me for a day, or two; let me try again at your extraordinary peacefulness; wait for me; teach me the lesson again.

But he went away to Sydney two days earlier than he had meant to, driven away by my jangling. I wept over it.

A Fate She had believed Implacable

The phone rang one morning.

'Nora? This is Angela. Can you do me a biggish sort of favour today?'

'I guess. What is it?'

'Can you drive me to the birth control clinic over the river? I'm going to have a try at an IUD, and I'll need to be delivered and picked up later, 'cause I won't be able to drive. Would that be possible?'

'It would.'

'I'll be over at ten.'

Angela had been home only two days from her mother's funeral: a sudden death from cancer. She talked about it as we sped along in Gerald's car, up the hill on the sunny morning.

'Willy wouldn't come up to New South Wales with me,' she said, her great brown eyes filling with tears as she spoke. 'He said it was something I'd have to handle by myself. I s'pose he was right . . .'

She looked out the window and let the tears run down her cheeks. Angela wanted from her relationship with Willy something he would not, could not give: something romantic, exclusive, complete; and Willy's determined constancy in loving both Angela and Paddy, while living with neither, was no less painful to her for being ideologically impeccable. She absorbed and endured an infinity of small rebuffs. I silently envied the ease of her tears, the way she lived with her heart bravely on her sleeve, no levelling out of the violence of everything but full blast and shameless.

'Was it awful up there?'

'Pretty awful. But I've been reading *A Very Easy Death*, about Simone de Beauvoir's mother dying of cancer – it's just brilliant. It really helped me.'

She wiped her eyes on her cuff, sat thinking for a moment, and then brought off one of her characteristic lightning-fast recoveries. She turned back to me. 'I've been wondering,' she said, that stubborn note of irrepressible laughter sounding again in her voice, 'just what you are doing with Gerald?'

'What do you mean, exactly?' I asked cautiously.

'Well – Nora – he's so *weird*!'

'Weird, you reckon?'

'Yeah! You have scenes with really *weird blokes*. Javo – and now Gerald! I *ask* you!'

She was looking at me with mock sternness, gloved hands folded on her lap, her head with its fine feathery flat-top cut cocked towards me on an admonitory angle. A wicked smile trembled at the corners of her mouth; I couldn't help laughing, and when I started, she threw back her head and let out one of her peals of delight, her gold tooth flashing. There was something completely irresistible in her laughter.

156

'Weird!' I repeated, half to myself. She was grinning at me expectantly, tapping her hands to the music that was always running in her head. 'You monster, Angela', I thought in exasperation, 'you are a monster and I just love you.'

'Well, all men are as weird as hell, if you ask me,' I retorted, still laughing in spite of myself.

'Yeah – all men except Willy,' she said, and pantomimed a loving sigh.

'*Willy*?' I shrieked. 'Are you *kidding*? He's the weirdest of the whole fuckin' *lot*!'

We were roaring with laughter.

'But there's something funny going on,' she added, suddenly sobering up, 'between him and Rita. You just watch.' She nodded ominously.

'Fair dinkum? First *I've* heard of it.'

'Well, she wouldn't be *telling* anyone – she's such a fuckin' sneak.' She pursed her lips and darted me a sidelong look. I was shocked, and showed it, though I simply couldn't help laughing at her outrageousness.

'Angela! How can you *say* that?'

'I've seen the way she comes on to him – I just can't *stand* it. You know – what really shits me is how you spend years working on yourself to get rid of all that stupid eyelash-fluttering and giggling, and then just when you think you're getting somewhere, you find out that guys still *like* women who do that sort of thing. I watch 'em fall for it, every time.'

I frowned uncomfortably, caught between being Rita's friend and admitting the undeniable core of truth in Angela's objection.

'I guess she does come on like that sometimes – '

'*Sometimes*! That's the way she *operates*, with men!'

'Oh, that's a bit rough, Ange.'

'Well, what about the way she dresses – those see-through shirts and high-heeled sandals?'

I thought of Angela's small store-room full of almost-discarded clothes, which once she'd worn in a normal day's march but were now brought out only for singing gigs and for her more repressed friends to dress up in on acid trips: crippling ankle-strapped towering shoes sprayed silver, lowcut satin dresses with shoestring straps, baubly jewellery, feather boas. I looked at her now, dressed in overalls and blue boots – no matter how plainly she might dress, she had some eccentric spark which, even in the interests of ideological purity, she could not quite snuff out.

'You're not exactly a frump yourself, mate, are you?' I ventured, struck with timidity.

'But at least I fuckin' *try!*'

We pulled up outside the clinic. Angela gathered her bag and coat together and reached for the door handle. For the first time I noticed how pale she was.

'You're not scared, Ange, are you?'

'Course I am, dummy. I'm terrified of pain.' She tried to smile. I scrambled out of the car, thinking, 'She needs me, she actually *needs* me.'

'But it's not going to *hurt*, is it? I didn't feel a thing when I had mine put in.'

'You've had a *child*, Nora. And *probably* a couple of *abortions*' – she elbowed me in the ribs with a touch of her old bravado. 'All that helps to stretch the cervix, you know.' She drew herself up: something manifcent about Angela and her gynaecological expertise, most of it laden with pessimism and doom. I felt small and a bit shrivelled next to her. She was like a ship in full sail as she advanced up the steps and through the glass doors to the reception desk. But she seized my arm and hissed to me,

'Nora, you will come back for me, won't you? They're going to give me a general – I might be a bit dopey.'

'Of course I will.' I dared to reach up and kiss her wan cheek. Too preoccupied to notice, she was ushered away by a nurse. I ran off to the car.

Two hours later I pushed open the door again and stood at the foot of the stairs looking up at Angela who was coming down very shakily on the arm of the nurse. Her face was quite white. She saw me and gave a tremulous smile. Seeing her thus reduced, prey to the unpredictableness of her female organs, I felt for her nothing more complicated than total allegiance, love for one of my kind.

I helped her to the car and drove her home. She was quite

quiet, arms folded over her belly, waiting for the first twinge of pain. When none came, she was surprised, as if at an undeserved release from a fate she had believed implacable. I installed her in her bed in the empty house and made her a cup of tea.

'Bring the phone up here, will you Nora?' she called. 'I couldn't stagger down the stairs again, and the others won't be home till dinnertime.'

She settled down among the pillows with the latest *Rolling Stone*, still white-faced but almost cheerful.

'Maybe this time I've found a contraceptive I can live with,' she said. 'Or maybe I haven't.'

I laughed. 'Give it a chance, Angela. Well – I'll see you soon, I guess.'

'Thanks, Nora!' she sang out after me. 'You've been terrific.'

'For you, anything. You're welcome.'

Between her bed and the door I spotted a small photo propped against the mirror: a performance photo, all black but for one glittering lower corner: I peered closer and saw Willy's shining head among his cymbals, sticks raised, eyes closed in that mysterious musical transport – is that how he looks when he fucks? face hard with concentration and yet at the same time utterly melting? No wonder she loves him. I passed by quickly and thumped down the steep, narrow stairs.

Fall in Their Own Good Time

Nick rang up.

'Is Gerald there?'

'No, he didn't stay here last night,' I said. 'Where are you?'

'At his place. He is supposed to be meeting me here.'

'I don't know where he could be.'

I didn't know anything about the parts of his life that I was not in. We existed outside his daily round, though well inside the domestic part of mine. I liked it that way, but I wasn't sure that he did. I wondered what he wanted. I mean, what did he wish for. It seemed a bleak life, sometimes. I could only guess.

'I never get jealous,' he said, and I believed him. Sometimes I wished to fade through his inscrutable skin and see what there was inside him.

'I'd like to crack you,' I said.

'The only way that could happen would be if I burst into tears,' he replied, not wanting it to happen.

What was this urge? I could have left him closed. But the sneaking little wish was always there, to worm my way past him and into him and make him split open and cease to guard himself. I did not like it: it was for the conquest.

He said, one day, that he felt himself to be softening, a process which he liked. Driving in the red truck, while the town filled up with warm rain, he remarked,

'I've never said I loved anyone, except you, and the kids.'

When he did open out, in his particular way, I was always too surprised to speak. Once, in the middle of the night, lying beside me with his arms round me, he asked,

'Do you feel loved?'

In my astonishment, I said, 'Yes,' but in such a tone that he may have felt dismissed.

Often in the evenings when the house was still he would play his guitar and I would lie in bed reading: strangely peaceful interludes in a cranky relationship. Once, I felt the waves of sleep coming, and put the book down.

'Don't stop playing,' I said. 'I love hearing it when I'm falling asleep.'

And then I *was* asleep.

When he came to bed he put his arms round me and said,

'You give me whole lots of confidence, you know.'

'Whaddayamean?' I mumbled out of my pillow.

'I never thought anyone would like falling asleep while I was playing.'

Gerald stayed with me two nights. I was ill-tempered and snapped at him.

'There's a limit,' he remarked, 'to the amount of time I can spend in your house without becoming a threat.'

So I slept alone in my low bed. Juliet fell asleep downstairs, and Rita went out visiting, to try and stop her heart from aching after the careless heels of Nick.

I dreamed I was trying on my mother's clothes: everything was either too big for me or not attractive enough. I woke to another dull, warmish, rainy morning. I remembered how many mornings I had spent on my own in that house, when we first moved in and Javo was in jail in Thailand. I liked it: but became dried out with loneliness.

I went out with Rita, drinking brandy alexanders at the Southern Cross, eating at Jimmy's, visiting Easey Street. I saw Javo there: smiled at each other. He looked white and unbuttoned, his hair standing on end. At home again I sat up in my bed, feet sore from walking. I was wondering if Gerald would come around. How many times have I lain in my bed waiting for footsteps or the sound of a car? Too many.

No more.

Maybe.

I was sound asleep when he came down our side lane and pushed at the locked front door. I was on my feet and down the stairs before he had time to go round the back. Glad to see him back from his gig, lugging his huge flat case and grinning at me in the rainy doorway.

I was lying with my back into his curve, when he began to hug me, and stroke me, and to kiss my neck and ear. As any human being would, I turned to face him.

'Are you really horny?' he suddenly asked. What a word!

Caught unawares, I made a surprised joke,

'I dunno – want me to consult my metre?' We laughed, up close with our arms round each other.

'It's just that I'm *not*, particularly,' he said.

I felt as if I'd shrunk, instantaneously, to the size of a pea. I must have gone stiff, or made some move, because he said with half a laugh, as if at his own bluntness,

'Well, that certainly put a stop to *that*! Some nice things were happening.'

'It's all right,' I said, wanting to say, 'It's *not* all right, you bloody great oaf', but obeying some unwritten law, blood-deep, too deep to be fished up at that moment to the light of rational scrutiny.

'Do you know what?' he remarked conversationally after a small pause, as if nothing untoward had happened; 'I think Willy and Angela actually still fuck.'

He *can't* be that cool.

I had an irresistible urge to punch and pummel Gerald; sometimes I hurt him and he yelled, with more annoyance than anger. In a shop, between the shelves, he teasingly bent my arm up my back, keeping it carefully this side of real pain. I laughed as if at a clever mimicry.

Javo, trying to be helpful or to ingratiate himself, went to the school to pick up Juliet without asking Rita first. The teacher refused to hand her over; he came into our house cursing, filthy, stained with paint and pin-eyed.

Juliet told me,

'When Javo came into our classroom, he had red stuff all over his hands, and the other kids thought he'd killed someone.'

He went into Rita's room to watch TV. When I thought of going in there, I knew he would move over on her bed to make room, and I'd lie alongside him, and it would seem natural for him to put his arm under me, and I'd lean against his shoulder, and it would all seem as if nothing had ever happened to wreck everything.

So I stayed where I was.

I slept so still that the bed was undisturbed. When I got up I just had to tuck it in. Rita was not in the house. She must have stayed at Nick's. She would *not* give up on that man. It looked crazy to me, wanting to run herself again and again into the wall of his indifference. Juliet cried when she found Rita's bed empty in the morning, but she was easily comforted.

162

'Why don't you and Gerald sleep together these days?' she asked when she came in in the morning.

'We do,' I replied, 'but we like to take a break from each other every now and then.'

I was missing Grace.

Rita came home. I sat, disgruntled, on my bed ploughing through the last eighth of *War and Peace* which I already knew I would never finish. The rain came down, and came down. I got dressed and thought of walking across the market to the bookshops, but looked out at the rain and lost heart.

I stood in the kitchen drinking a cup of tea with Rita. I was all curdled with irritation at her. She wanted to tell me what had happened with Nick the night before.

'He promised me he'd go a week without having a hit,' she said, 'but when I got there he was stoned.'

'Rita – that crusading stuff is *not on*! The junk's *his* problem – *you* can't get him off it.'

'It's not just the smack, though,' she said. 'He says I never trusted him.'

'You had no reason to,' I retorted. My voice sounded curt. I didn't care. I wanted to push the point home, force her to see what she was doing to herself.

'It was so sad, Nora! He says it tortures him, the way I torture myself.'

'You are certainly a tiger for punishment,' I said. 'I just couldn't believe it when you didn't come home last night. You go on and on bashing your head against the wall.'

Oh Nora. Butter would not melt in your mouth.

Rita crouched there on Gracie's Minnie Mouse chair, staring at the floor. Which comes first, her masochism or my sadism? I want to force her, shake her, give her the righteous blows which people deal out to hysterics. I put my tea down and stumped up the stairs to my room.

I came down an hour later and found her sitting on the stairs, bag on shoulder, pants rolled up for the bike, head in hands, sobbing. I knelt on the step below her and put my arms round her and rocked her. She accepted comfort.

'I can't work when I'm like this,' she wept. 'I go into the studio and I just keep knocking things over.'

163

No work, no love from where she wants it.

It was my thirty-third birthday. I was sick. Thick head, lungs full of yellow stuff, eyes only half-seeing. I was bleeding, and aching, and bleeding, and aching. When I lay down and tried to go to sleep, it got worse in my head.

The rain had stopped, the air was clear and very dark blue. I took two codiphen in the hope that the aching in my face and neck might lessen enough to let me sleep, but I was wide awake, on my birthday, in the silent house, head full of mucus and ideas. In a room by yourself, at that hour of night, you can beam your mind out on the ether. I felt berserk, mind on the surge. For a second at a time I could hallucinate the sound of waves breaking outside our house. I wondered what time of the day I was born.

In the daylight I lay stupefied. Javo thumped up the stairs and into my room. I took one look at him and felt a great rush of love and sadness: he looked wrecked, filthy, dressed in ragged jeans. Through two horizontal tears in the front of the jeans I could see his thighs, their white skin. His hair was matted, his right eye was all red and swollen with styes, he scratched constantly. I wanted to pierce his bravado, ask him for the truth, but these days his ego was invested in keeping that brave smokescreen well in place. I felt like crying.

He sat at my table and read the new *Digger*. I lay under the blankets, breathing through my mouth and watching him. He had a glass of coca cola beside him: when he picked it up and tilted his head back to drink, I saw his throat, that vulnerable and seldom-exposed part of his body. At Freycinet, the day we walked out of the bush at Coles Bay and stuffed ourselves with lollies and soft drinks, I had seen him in the same way, guzzling eagerly, head back in that same position, showing his throat and the flat underside of his bony jaw. A kind of weak sadness oozed out of my thoughts and I turned over on my side and began to read. I fell towards sleep, stopped myself for a second to wonder if it was safe, remembered it was Javo in the room whose presence if nothing else I could trust, and let myself slip away. I couldn't have slept more than a few minutes. He had finished the newspaper, and was getting his things together to leave. I woke up and looked at him. He smiled at me in the way I remembered, without defensiveness, standing next to my bed looming up to the ceiling. I put out my hand and touched his leg. He took my hand, and we smiled at each other and I said,

'Are you all right, Javes?'

'What?'

'Are you – is everything all right?'

'Yep – yeah! I'm OK.'

'See you soon.'

'Yeah – see you, Nor.'

And crashed off down the stairs and out the front door.

Gerald came, in the evening.

'Want to go for a drive?' he said. 'It might do you good to get out of the house.'

I got up and struggled into my clothes.

'One thing, though,' I said, 'can I have a window open? I feel as if I'll suffocate, otherwise.'

'But my *neck* will get cold.'

'Wear a *scarf*.'

He tossed the keys at me and said, half angry, half joking,

'Here – take the keys and go for a drive by yourself.'

I was pulling my jumper over my head. It fell in saggy folds and I stood still, unable to gauge his tone. He threw me a sideways glance. No-one spoke. I went over and lay on the unmade bed, kicked off my shoes and curled up in a ball. I could hear my own noisy, sick breathing. I wished I could dematerialise, simply cease to be there. I didn't care what he did. I just felt *awful*.

We drove down the bay. I thought for the first ten minutes that I was going to be sick, or faint. I couldn't get used to the motion of the car and my ears were dead. My head was stuffed with cottonwool. But under everything describable, there was something else wrong with me – not depressed, just *bad*.

'You ought to go to the doctor,' said Gerald, looking at me with the mixture of resentment and concern people feel when they begin to realise you are not malingering.

It was a terrible night.

I fell asleep at 11.30, dozed while Gerald quietly played his guitar, heard him get in beside me, remembered nothing else until a sudden wakening in the dark, turning in time to see him fully dressed sliding out the door. Going! where? to the dunny? I put my head back on the pillow and must have fallen asleep again: next thing I knew, he was getting back into bed. I woke up and turned over.

'Are you all right?'

'No . . . not really.'

'What's wrong? Where have you been?'

'I feel terrible. There is some awful lump inside me. I've been downstairs. I was lying on the floor crying.'

Crying! He told me once he never cried. Wide awake now. I took hold of his shoulders, held him very hard and listened to small sounds he made, gasps almost of relief.

'But! What's wrong? What can I do for you?'

'Oh, this is what I need,' he whispered, head back on the pillow, submitting to hard hugs and cradling. My heart filled up with a puzzled love for him, and my head stayed quite steady, thinking,

'This is going to be harder than I thought: but I can do it.'

'Come on, talk, talk,' I urged.

'Well – I was – lying down there thinking – Why are you sick? And why do you go on bleating about Gracie coming home – when *I* need something from you?'

Small shock waves, at the injustice of what he is asking, while I still held and rocked him, wanting to soothe. Does he want a mother? Can I be that to him? Ought I to be? I began to sense myself as something very balanced and steady, and him as a dark mass yawing wildly and out of control. Got to let him pass through and round me, keep my centre, not let his disorder pull me askew.

It seemed we lay for some time with our arms round each other. He got calmer.

'Let me move a bit.' He shifted his body. I turned over and fitted my back into his curve. It was more peaceful.

'I thought about you a lot today,' I said, 'when I was reading.

I thought about fucking with you.'

'I masturbated three times last night,' he said.

'Did you? What were you thinking about?'

'About this girl who was at our gig on Saturday night.'

'Yeah? What happened?'

'She was sitting at the table with us, paying us a lot of attention. And when we'd finished playing, she invited us to this party. By the time we got there it was nearly over, people were picking up bottles and cleaning up . . . there were lots of rooms, and I couldn't see her anywhere. And when we were leaving I went looking for Philip to get a lift home. I found him in a room I hadn't been in. I went in and said, 'Can I get a lift with you?' – and then I saw the girl, she'd been in there all along.

'So I went and sat down with her, and talked, but before I could work out if anything was likely to happen, Philip came over and said, 'Are we going, then?'

'So nothing did happen.

'I went home, and masturbated, and went to sleep, and woke up, and masturbated, and went to sleep – and there was one more time that I wasn't sure about . . . I was all in a flutter.'

All the time he was talking my heart was turning over. I stared in the almost-dark at the corner of the bookshelf where my black jacket hung. I remembered him saying once, with just enough self-mockery to make it true, 'I want to be a rock and roll star'. I saw myself in a house, alone and still and old enough to be alone and still, while he rotated like a rhythmic planet, somewhere in the world outside.

'How do you think it makes me feel, hearing you tell that story?' I asked, very carefully.

'In terms of jealousy, you mean?'

'Something like that – jealousy, or whatever.'

'I don't think you need to be jealous. Because it was just a groupie thing – she was all, you know, dressed up – silver boots, tight top, dark red lips – and it's not that I regret it not happening.'

'You don't?'

'I didn't even start to get to *know* her. And I don't think she ever would have lost that smile. Why . . . how *does* it make you feel?'

'Awful. Sort of left out.'

He hugged me. 'If I hadn't got to know *you*, I'd regret it a real lot,' he said.

I said nothing. He went on,

'Does it worry you that I might get more sexually excited by people like her than by you?'

'Of course it does.' (Remembering him saying, 'Do you feel horny? Because *I don't*.' Bang, the door slammed in my face.)

'But,' he said, 'I think our fucking is really good. Even if . . . technically . . . we don't . . . the feeling is still there, and that's what it's all about, I reckon. Don't you?'

'Yeah.' (His face always turned aside, away from my eyes; how rarely what I do can make him gasp, cry out, lose himself.)

'You talk a lot,' he said, 'about other people you've fucked with as being more compatible with you.' Long-ago people.

'Oh, I . . .' I give a groan, unable to dredge up words. *Oh Javo, how your face would turn tender, how you would say my name softly, how I would come just watching the sweetness flow into your face.*

He hugs me again, I'm comforted by his body all down my back. I get out of bed and take off my nightdress, thinking partly of fucking, partly of the foolishness of our skins not touching through all the layers of my sickness. I turn my front to him, we lie along each other close and comfortable.

'Oooh, I must go to sleep,' he says. His tone is tinged with warning. I move aside from him, into the cooler space.

'Did you think we would fuck?' he asks.

'I guess I thought we might.'

'I am too miserable to fuck. I can only fuck when I'm happy.'

'That's all right.' My back is turned to him again. I'm lonely out there on the edge of the bed; but I'm sick, sick, sick, everything I think or say is made drab through my sickness.

'I can't get over,' I say, hearing again that careful note in my voice, 'the way you turn off.'

'What do you mean?'

'One minute you're asking me for love, and the next you are pushing me away, get away, arms' length.'

A pause.

'I get scared,' he says, 'when someone wants to fuck me and I don't want to.'

We do fall asleep; and wake at the same moment to a room full of sun, eight o'clock in the morning and I have been dreaming:

I am in a kitchen. Its walls are peeling drastically. I take a knife, insert its blade behind a peeling section, and turn it as if to strip off the layer; it loosens easily, but I see that the area which will fall is very large, that it will make a mess on the floor which I will have to clean up, and that I don't know whether the condition of the wall underneath it is good enough to be exposed. I change my mind, remove the knife and put it back on the bench. I decide to let the peeling sections fall off in their own good time.

'I think,' I said to Gerald, 'it would be a good idea if we didn't see each other till the end of the week.'

Instantly he backed off, withdrew, turned a black face away from me.

'That's a bit rough,' he said. 'When you're sick you want to have me round – but as soon as you start to get well you say you don't want to see me.'

'Oh, that's so *unfair*!' A man, a man. He doesn't let the feelings show but snaps up that steel screen of *reason*.

He clammed up on me, slammed shut. His face was tight and accusing.

'It would be better,' I suggested, 'if you said, "That makes me feel bad", instead of putting up a reason why I'm wrong.'

We battled it out. It was like having my foot in the door and him pushing it shut. He let it open a small crack, then a crack more, and I reached round it and grabbed his hand; and he let me touch him but kept his face turned away.

'All right,' he said. 'I made a mistake – *don't let's go any further into it.*'

I let it drop, but I thought, listen mate, one day we'll go so far into it that you won't *want* to turn back. And I'll shove you off the cliff and you'll fly away.

Tiny Puncture Holes

After seven days of illness I could still hardly breathe, and waves of weakness came over me whenever I stood up. I wished to be out in the windy sunshine, but I lay flat in my bed, staring at my red curtain flying against the white wall. In the afternoon Javo thundered in. Seeing me in my glory, he turned and bellowed down the stairs,

'Hey, Hank! Come up here!'

And Hank, either not stoned or not as stoned as Javo, comes in and sits on my chair smiling. Hank's face is so streaked with car grease that for a second I think he is wearing stage make-up. They start talking about some freaked-out non-junkie crim they know called Kenny.

'He's *right* off 'is brick,' declares Javo.

'He kept asking me for a hit,' says Hank, 'but I didn't *have* any. I kept *telling* him, "Mate, I haven't *got* any!" ' Spreads his hands and laughs, showing his broken teeth.

'Yeah,' opines the king of beasts, loafing back against my wall with his great boots on my bedspread, red styes gleaming on his eyelid, hair matted like straw or rope – 'I reckon junk'd be that guy's saving grace. I really reckon it's just what he needs. It'd calm him right down.'

My jaw drops. I steal a look at Hank and see him watching Javo sideways, smiling a small smile. Oblivious, Javo rants on, gesturing expansively, enjoying himself. Hank turns and catches my eye and we both burst out laughing. Javo is unabashed.

Hank leaves, Javo stays. We begin to talk.

'Who do you fuck with?' I enquire, folding my hands on my chest.

'No-one.'

'Do you miss it?'

'No – oh, sometimes.'

'I miss *you* sometimes,' I admit.

From this moment we are friends again. He smiles at me, hugs me clumsily. He nods off, comes back, apologises:

'I shouldn't come here when I'm this stoned.'

'That's OK,' I say, and lie back on my pillows, restfully regarding his battered face. I'll love that wrecked bastard forever, along with all the other people under whose influence I've had *my* hard shell cracked.

He leaves. On his way out he says, 'Give us a kiss, Nor.'

Willingly I put my mouth against his blackened junkie lips.

That night everyone was out but me.

Doing my washing in the rickety machine in the bathroom. While the machine toils and shrieks, I crouch on the Minnie Mouse chair outside the back door, looking quietly up at the half moon which rolls stubbornly in the narrow gap of sky between our house and the shop next door. The air is deep, deep blue, one star, I feel a hot day coming when this night is over. I'm full of restlessness. Not lonely, exactly – my head is racing with ideas. But it is that old treacherous feeling that real life is happening somewhere else, and I'm left out. The air stirs a little, Rita's newly planted herbs move their small leaves. I finish hanging out a dozen hankies from my flu, which is almost over; and I close the back door behind me and go upstairs.

In the morning, light and air wake me. I go outside and see the sky a thousand miles high, covered with a fine net of almost invisible cloud. My head begins to turn, it fills with unspoken words, I don't try to seize them but let them run unchecked. They seem to slip into my veins and my limbs and the capillaries of my skin. It is just convalescence, and the summer morning. 'The universe resounds with the joyful cry "I am!"'

I waited for Gracie, thinking of her intelligent, ready face, her wiry legs, and her secret, thumb-sucking smile. But I knew that, as soon as she came back, the house would be too small again and we would all go crazy.

It wasn't that I didn't *love* Rita and Juliet: on the contrary, I suffered from some painful emotion towards them, something to do with Rita's daily struggle to live, and the fact that I had been through this struggle myself with Gracie, years before: hating her because her existence marked the exact limits of my freedom; hating myself for hating her; loving her, all the while, gut-deep and inexpressibly; and beginning each day with the dogged shouldering of a burden too heavy for one person: the responsibility for the life of another human being. I had been rescued from this bind by Eve and Georgie and Clive, back in the old house: they had prised us apart patiently, lovingly tinkering and forcing. It takes more than one person to perform this most delicate operation, and, trapped there in the tiny, beautiful house with Rita and her battle, I knew I didn't have it in me. All I could think of was to escape. For weeks I thought treacherously of getting away: I lay in bed at night and racked my brains for an honourable solution.

When Gracie did arrive from Perth, she came down with measles within half a day. I was still weak from the flu, and stayed with her all day, lying beside her in my hot room, a blanket over the window to protect her sore eyes from the light, and tickled her traumatised skin with the corner of the newspaper. She recovered more quickly than I did. When I was still sick and weak, she played downstairs by herself, singing and drawing and reading aloud great tracts of *Baby and Child Care* by Doctor Spock. She came up occasionally to say hullo.

'Grace,' I said, 'you are good company when I'm sick.'

'I try my best,' she said with a stoical expression.

Eve and Georgie came to visit, the two of them radiating goodness and humour, and we lay on my bed in the warm night room, swigging capfuls of cointreau (my birthday present from Paddy) and laughing together about the follies of the world. They went out to their bikes. The three of us stood there in the narrow alleyway, a million miles of sky overhead and a moon shining somewhere nearby; Eve squeezed me with her thin, strong arms.

'Wish we were livin' together again, eh, Nor?' she sighed,

172

rolling her eyes. 'Life's a fuckin' struggle, ain't it!'

'You are not kidding, mate.'

Georgie kissed me goodbye. His teeth flashed in the dark. I watched them pedal away and I felt small and lonely for a few seconds. It was sexual loneliness, I supposed, but it was also the loneliness of remembering summer-night bicycle rides, rolling home to the big house with a full heart, sailing through floods of warm air, the tyres whirring on the bitumen, then over the gutter and into the park, and feeling the temperature drop under the big green leafy balloons.

Oh well. Times past.

Bored, still half-sick and dismal, I went wandering up and down Lygon Street, in and out of Readings and Professor Longhair's. I succumbed to a sudden urge to sit in front of one glass of strong alcohol. I walked into Jimmy Watson's (a businessman held the door open for me, with a faded smile) and ordered a glass of port. Ten cents. *Ten cents*! and I paid a dollar a hit for brandy alexanders at the Southern Cross and did not grudge the wild expenditure. I sat down at a small round brown table, unloaded my books, and drank the port rather fast, gazing blindly at the floor. Which, I knew from memory if no other way, was made of dark red tiles or bricks, very smooth and cool.

Disgruntled.

I felt as if I were being drained through very tiny puncture holes.

When I got home, Javo was wheeling his bike down our side alley towards the street. I hugged him as he stood there, grinning, holding the bike, one trouser leg tucked into his thick dark blue sock.

'Gotta go, Nor,' he croaked. 'I left you a note. Wanna go out and eat tomorrow night?'

'I sure do.'

He pedalled off and I ran upstairs.

'Dear Nora, things are hot and sticky – preoccupied with this welt I've got in the guts. How come you never said to me I was a self-engrossed slob? Anyway it's turn away and laugh some more. Listening to Taj Mahal thinking of last summer funny how things were lying on Georgie's bed shying away it's just a matter of try a bit harder eh Nor, a little no a lot more courage on my part – so easy to talk – me with my big mouth and big foot they fit each other like a glove.'

I went into Myers to buy myself a pair of bathers. I began to see my body as an object, and an unsatisfactory one at that. The fluorescent lights in the fitting room emphasised the looseness of my skin; the elastic of the bikini pressed unattractively into my flesh which would probably never be really firm again. In my heart I started to grieve over my body. In the next cubicle I heard a woman saying to the saleswoman,

'No – not that one; all the stretch marks show.'

I remembered hearing another woman, on another day, saying to another saleswoman,

'I can't seem to lose weight any more, since I turned forty.'

She spoke with humorous regret in her voice, appealing to the womanly sympathies of the shop assistant, but underneath it I heard the fear and sadness that I felt myself, today, in small measure.

Javo arrived on time, white-eyed but friendly. He had a bottle of methadone in his jacket pocket. We walked into town in the stifling dry air. The cool change came racing up Bourke Street behind us, out of a dirty yellow sky. We ate a meal, pushed our way through Friday night crowds, came back to Peel Street to watch *Shoulder to Shoulder* on TV, lying comfortably on Rita's bed. Javo left to go to the supper show, and I dozed off under the eiderdown.

Very early in the morning Rita came home from Carlton and into my room where I was lying half-awake. She stroked my treacherous head for an hour while we gossiped companionably; told me stories of what had been going on without me east of Lygon Street.

'What's happening with Gerald?' she asked, pushing her fingers through my hair.

'Everything's sort of OK. He's been sleeping at his place a bit lately – also he's fucking with someone over that side of the river.'

'The bastard! Is he really?'

I laughed and shrugged. 'I don't care. It's all right with me.'

She gave me a sharp look: she didn't believe me: she thought I was acting cool. For that moment she experienced on my behalf, in her generous heart, all the rage and hurt feelings she imagined I ought to feel.

'I'd better go to sleep now,' I said. 'I'm still so damned weak.'

'OK, Nor.' She was smiling again. She kissed me goodnight on my cheek, like a mother or a sister. At the door she stopped, standing against the cracked frame in her black T shirt and white airtex knickers.

'You know,' she said, 'Nick used to say, 'Why do you wear those terrible pants? My *mother* wears those! Why don't you wear those little *sexy* ones?'

I laughed. 'Once, back at Delbridge Street, I was hanging *my* knickers on the line, and Nick said, "I love those white pants".'

We exchanged knowing looks.

'Oh, men!' she said. 'They are so fucked up! And yet we keep on hanging round them.'

'Well – goodnight, Rita.'

She gave me the salute and disappeared.

A moth had blundered in at my window and was beating itself to death against the lampshade.

'Nora. Come in here.'

I went across the landing to Rita's room. She was standing at the fireplace. In one hand was the lid of the many-sided Chinese jar that always stood on her mantelpiece with a picture of Chairman Mao leaning against it.

'When was Javo last here?'

'Last night after tea. Why?'

'Because – there was eighty dollars in here at lunchtime yesterday. It was the rent for the studio. And it's gone.'

'Gone,' I repeated stupidly.

'Javo.'

'Javo, you reckon?'

'Who else?'

She clicked the lid back into place, and twisted her mouth in a grimace of disgust. I felt sick.

'He won't get away with this one,' she said. 'I'm going over there now.'

'I'll stay here with the kids.'

She got on her bike and rode away. I remembered uncomfortably what she'd said when we first decided to try living together: 'There's only one thing bothering me, and that's your junkie mates.' Well, she'd found her own junkie mates by now; but what had I started? An hour later I heard the bike clatter against the wall and she stamped in, pulling off her jacket.

'What'd he say?'

'Oh, I know it was him, the fucking bastard. I went straight to Easey Street – he'd just left there, Chris said she'd sold him a cap for forty dollars. So I went to his house and put it on him. He *denied* it. He was so stoned he could hardly see me.'

She stared at me, biting her lips, her eyes full of furious tears.

'Let me have a go, Rita. Maybe he'll talk to me.'

I walked in at his kitchen door and found him slumped in an armchair watching television.

'We know it was you, Javo.' I had to yell over the gunshots and thundering hooves. He stared up at me dully, chewing the insides of his cheeks. A frown formed slowly on his dirty face.

'I don't fuckin' care what youse think,' he shouted, voice thick with dope. 'I never touched the fuckin' money! Every time something disappears you try and pin it on me.' His hands dangled between his thighs.

'Mark says you're going down to Hobart.' I could hardly hear myself.

'Yeah. I'm gonna get a job. And get off dope.' Defiant stare: go on, call my bluff. I put one hand on the television set to steady my shaking, and bent over, putting my face near his.

'*Well, don't you come near me again*,' I hissed. 'You've done it this time, mate.'

I pushed past Hank on my way out the door.

'How'd *you* get on?' asked Rita when I got home. She was grinning by this time, raising one eyebrow with that ironic resignation which was going to be the saving of her.

'Hopeless.' I dumped my bag on the chair and looked at her helplessly, my hands hanging at my sides.

'Well, get a load of this.' She jerked her thumb at the table. Next to the vase of flowers lay the *meat cleaver*.

'I don't get it.'

'Remember, it disappeared about six weeks ago? Well, I went along to the studio just now to pull Javo's bed apart, and I found it between the two mattresses.'

We stood looking at each other.

'What do you suppose he's scared of?' she whispered.

'I don't know.'

We put our arms round each other.

'The poor fucking bastard,' said Rita.

And though I didn't know it at the time, Javo was already forgiven.

Attitudes of Struggle and Flight

Whether Rita would forgive me so readily was by no means certain. It was a betrayal, of sorts, when I found the big house in Rowe Street, rounded up as many of the old householders as I could muster, and made one of those insane leaps of faith, brushing aside undeniable truths for the sake of a clean break.

'Are you worried about our living in the same house?' asked Gerald.

'Not exactly *worried*,' I said, still suffering from a bout of mindless optimism. 'But I want you to understand, though – I've done this before, and it was disastrous. I don't want us to move into this house as a couple – in fact the very thought of it gives me the horrors.'

Gerald raised his eyebrows. 'That's a bit strong, isn't it?'

We laughed.

'No, mate! I mean it. It's nothing to do with personalities. I just can't *do* it any more.'

'Well – we'll have our own rooms – I guess that will establish us separately.'

As if to warn of intention were enough! The forms are too strong to be simply talked away. But in I leaped, feet first, eyes shut.

'Do you feel guilty about leaving Rita and Juliet behind when you move?' asked Gerald.

'Do you think I have anything to feel guilty about?' I asked, trying to control my tone.

'Oh . . . I don't know . . .' he said in his maddeningly casual voice. 'If you can do it and not feel guilty about it, that's really good. I've never done it, that's all.'

'Done *what*?'

'Walked out on someone who needed me.'

A great rush of distress and its protective accompaniment, anger, filled me.

'But I'm not *married* to her. If she needs me, then that means I can never leave her. Isn't that true?'

Pause.

'Yeah . . . I suppose it is.'

I groaned and put my head in my hands, more out of weariness than anything else. But he seemed to take it for anger. He got off the bed and said,

'Where's the car key?'

He searched my room while I sat at my table staring out the window. Seeing me sitting glumly there, he said in a mocking tone,

'Oh! Snooty, snooty!'

I looked up in surprise. 'I'm *not* snooty – really I'm not!'

He looked over his shoulder at me on his way out the door. He had a sceptical smile on his face; he said nothing and disappeared down the stairs.

'Oh, shit.' I put my head on the table, exasperated and sad, wondering why we bothered to keep going together when it seemed so passionless, and difficult. I grabbed my bag and ran downstairs, caught up with him on my bike as he was about to start the car.

'It's not snootiness,' I said, upset again as I looked at his closed, dark face. 'I was miserable. Why not have another look?'

His eyes turned soft. He put his hand on my arm through the car window, and nodded, saying nothing.

When at last I did break my guilty silence, Rita stood in my doorway, trying to smile.

'Nora – why didn't you give me the choice of coming with you?'

I was sitting at the table, scribbling on a piece of paper. I drove the point of the pencil into the pitted table surface, unable to look at her.

'I can't handle your relationship with Juliet – I don't seem to be able to help you with it, and I can't bear it the way it is.'

'I know. I thought that's what it was.'

I glanced up and saw her cheeks flushed with unhappiness, her eyes lowered.

'I have been going crazy here,' I muttered, ashamed of my meagre loyalty. She walked out of the room without another word. I sat on, thinking miserably of my willingness to commit myself domestically to a man who was still all but closed to me, while Rita, who had never held back, would be left behind. I thought all this, and yet I went ahead.

At eleven o'clock that night Chris walked in with some coke. I woke up and we talked a bit.

'I hear Javo ripped you off,' she remarked as I fumbled in my bag for the price of the deal.

'It was Rita, actually. He took eighty bucks off her mantel-piece – the rent for her studio where he's been crashing for months, the fucking rat.'

179

'Well, he's gone to Hobart. He left this afternoon.'

'Good riddance.' We exchanged a flick of the eyebrows. 'Well . . . is the coke any good, mate?'

By way of reply she showed me her arms, which were horrible: a row of manically neat, evenly spaced tracks all down the veins in her fore-arms, the crooks of her elbows bruised and swollen, her hands dotted with the marks of that greed. She was hollow-faced with coke-paranoia:

'The cops know all about me,' she declared, resigned and final. 'They'll do a series of big busts before Christmas to get their paperwork cleaned up. I can't stay,' she went on, half getting up off the bed where she was sitting in her ragged lace blouse and long green velvet coat. 'I don't know where Mark is – I'm scared he's run away.'

'*Run away*?'

'Yeah – taken Nina and gone to Tasmania. He said to me the other day that he'd go, and take her with him, if I didn't stop dealing. I have to deal to get my shit – and people come round all the time, which makes it really hard for him to get off. He *wants* to get off – he's so strong-willed.'

'But surely he wouldn't have gone,' I said, trying to think of him standing at the airline ticket counter, Nina on his hip, his thin fingers on the shining counter and his messy fair hair green in the fluorescence.

'He might've. He might've gone to his sister's – or somewhere else, where I couldn't find him.'

She got up suddenly, took a step towards the bedroom door, paused with her hand on the door and her face blank, then flashed me a nod and a vacant smile, and disappeared in one fast movement.

I put the cap away, too tired to contemplate using it, and fell asleep. At two in the morning Gerald came in from his gig and I backed up to his long curve and we fell asleep again together. At six a.m. Chris walked into my room. I woke up completely and instantly. She knelt on the end of my bed (Gerald slept on) and whispered,

'Have you used all that coke?'

'I haven't used any of it,' I replied, sitting up and putting my hands to her cheeks, a familiarity I probably would not have dared if I hadn't just leapt out of a dream. 'Why – do you want some?'

We laughed. I scrambled out of bed, trying not to disturb Gerald's deserving slumber, and we went down the stairs, me with the cap in my hand. The kids were just beginning to stir in their room next to the front door.

'Do you want me to hit you up?' she offered as we passed through the hall and into the living room.

'No thanks,' I said, feeling no pull towards the proposition, but no revulsion from it either.

'Do you ever hit up?'

'I've never hit up anything.' I gave her the cap and we sat down at the table.

With her bony, experienced fingers she shook out half its contents and fixed herself a large hit. Her outfit was elegantly wrapped in a small piece of chamois leather.

'Will you hold my arm?'

I remembered the night I worked on the junk movie, when she asked me to hold her arm for her: but then I was scared, and revolted; and she herself was nervous, wanting me to stay by her in case she had too much. No such fears now, nine months later. She rolled up her sleeve in her quick, matter-of-fact way, showing her thin, thin arm, spiked all over and pale from lack of sun. I took hold of her upper arm, which I could almost encircle with one hand, and squeezed it firmly. Up came the vein. I looked at her wonderfully beautiful face, boned like a princess, stripped of the flesh of normal women. Her eyes were concentrated on the action of her hand, which held the fit poised like some artist's tool, hesitating over the vein as if to catch it unawares before it could roll away and betray her. In went that fine needle, gentle steady pressure; she jacked it expertly, no blood, probed a little, tried again – ah yes, the tiny thread of red ran back into the glass tube and her intent expression relaxed a fraction. Pushed the stuff into herself with an unwavering hand.

'Thanks, Nora,' she said, and I let go, wondering if I had really felt the pressure of her heart's force shove the small burden up her arm under my thumbs.

She put the fit down on my living room table and sat back in

181

the chair, eyes closed, face trembling infinitesimally. I
watched her, not needing to hide my curiosity. She opened her
eyes and smiled at me under the wavy henna'd hair, thick
silver ear-rings hanging at her jawbones under her finely
shaped ears.

'It's still happening, the flash,' she said quietly. 'It's real
good coke.'

Her eyes closed again. Silence. I sat watching her intently.

'I think I might've had a bit too much,' she remarked. But
she was completely confident and I wasn't afraid, though I saw
a quick picture of her blue face dying and my attempts to
revive her. We sat in a peculiar companionship. And I felt the
flickering of a contact high start in my chest: the heart ticked
faster, the breath came clearer and colder, the hands and
stomach began to tremble with a nameless excitement.
Which passed.

She made the effort to talk with me. We discussed our
children. Mark, she said with a self-mocking shrug, had of
course not run away, but had merely gone to a movie. She told
me how Rita had come to visit them and had cleaned up the
kitchen.

'I'd have done it myself,' she said, 'but I'd just had a hit and
I kept thinking, "In a minute I'll get up and *do* it," but
somehow I just kept lying there, and then Rita came in and did
it for me.'

Twenty minutes later she said,

'Hey – will you let me use the rest of that coke, and I'll get
you another one this morning?'

'OK,' I said. I went upstairs and got it from its hiding place
where I'd replaced it after her first hit. Gerald was still asleep.
I could have a quick snort, I thought, looking at his long bent
body under my blanket, but I'd rather wait till he wakes up
and share it with him. So I took it down to the kitchen and
handed it over. She made a cocktail with some immense rocks
she had hidden somewhere in her voluminous torn clothing. I
watched her intricate preparations, leaning against the sink in
my silk nightie and red T shirt.

'Lots of junkies don't realise,' she said as she worked, 'that
coke loses its strength if you leave it in hot places. And they

say "Coke doesn't do anything for me". The fridge is a good place for it.'

'Yeah?' I say, listening to the dope lore. 'It's a cold drug, all right. It always makes the inside of my head feel like it's full of cold air.'

While she worked at it, I went out to the bathroom and got into the shower. I was covered in shampoo when she came in for me to hold her arm again. I held out my hands, trying to keep the shower water from running off them on to her clothes and her butchered arm. As she felt for the vein, and I stood there somewhere between patience and boredom, I saw a small face appear, between shielding hands, outside the bathroom window: Juliet, in her cotton nightie, peering in at this mysterious ritual.

'Shit, Nora, I'm sorry,' said Chris. She paused a second in her probing and looked up at me.

'It's cool. I'll explain it to her late,' I said. She caught the rolling vein, dealt with it, and went back into the house. I came inside dripping and found her curled up under her velvet coat on Juliet's top bunk, grinning sleepily at me.

'Are you all right?'

'Yeah. I'm fine. Just having a little lie down. I'm satisfied now.'

I went upstairs to get dressed. Gerald opened his eyes and looked at me. I wondered what he thought I'd been doing: not only the flash, but a tinge of her paranoia had reached me.

'She hit the whole lot up,' I reported, for the first time feeling incredulous at the sheer quantity of my dope she'd used.

'*What*? The whole *lot*?' he echoed. 'I don't care – about the coke – but shit, how much *money* must she need! Jesus!' He stared at me. 'How long have you been up?'

'Since six.'

'I didn't even know you were gone.'

He rolled over and pulled a pillow over his head.

Rita went away for the weekend, and for a day I drove an old Rommel-grey Volkswagen ute between our new house and

Eve's old one up in Northcote. It was hot and sunny and I was wearing a singlet and overalls. I watched my arms, very brown and marked with bruises and sunspots, working the flat steering wheel. I felt sweaty, hard and confident. We worked like dogs, we were cheerful and full of energy. At each new arrival at the house, the doors of which were wide open to the sunny wind, a sort of dance was performed: in and out we moved, the six of us, silently in our rubber shoes on the polished floors, carrying and not carrying, smiling and not smiling as we passed each other in the airy corridors. Gracie was to be seen walking quietly in and out of the immense rooms, thumb in mouth, feeling the space.

The Roaster had a double bed.

'Hey, Grace,' he said on the first night. 'Do you want to sleep with me tonight?'

'Yeah!'

'Hang on, Gracie!' says I. 'Are all your nits gone?'

'*Nits*?' cries the Roaster, with an instinctive gesture of rejection. 'For-*get* about tonight!' However, as it happened, the nits had been routed, and the children did sleep together. I came by in the middle of the night and found them cast across the bed in attitudes of struggle and flight.

'March, march, shoulder to shoulder,' sang Gracie out on the verandah, but it was election day and Labor was going to get done like a dinner. The rain stopped and I went mooching about in the Flea Market. Rita streamed in, Juliet at her heels; she greeted me affectionately. I wandered off towards the street door of that stone-floored, barn-like place. Willy, up unusually early, strode round the corner.

'Hullo Willy,' I said, carefully keeping the irony out of my voice. 'What are you up to?'

'I was looking for Rita, actually,' replied the erstwhile object of my fantasies, looking over my shoulder into the dim barn as he spoke. 'She said she wanted to go for a cup of coffee.'

'She's back there,' I said, jerking my thumb behind me. My insides went curdly with envy, thinking of the way she turned up her face, charming, her skin smooth and polished. Sometimes I was afraid of becoming man-like, of losing softness.

And sometimes, still, I longed for Javo, just for a sight of his violently blue eyes. Maybe I always needed to love someone weaker than myself, in exactly the right degree. Maybe that was why I had already forgotten his outrages.

I dreamed: I came home and found my room had been ransacked. Papers were scattered all about. I was devastated. I was standing there looking at the torn cover of a book when Javo walked into the room. He had been in Tasmania and was off dope (understood, not spoken); he looked clean, clear-eyed, clear-skinned, sun-tanned, full of health.

'Javo! Did you do this?'

'Yeah.'

'Why? Why did you do it?'

'I just threw the stuff in the rubbish bin.'

I burst into tears. It was real grief-weeping: I sobbed and sobbed. He hugged me against his chest (clean shirt, smelling good) and held me very tightly, as if to love or comfort. I just stood and wept.

I woke up remembering the sobbing. To sob like that was a pleasure and a relief, as if finding out that I was still emotionally alive. I had no such passion in my waking life.

I rang Javo in Hobart. When I heard his voice (he croaked, 'Hullo? – oh, good day, Nor!') my heart turned over a couple of times and beat harder than usual.

'I have been off dope for a week,' he announced.

'How do you spend your time?'

'I spend a lot of time on my own. And I'm drinking a lot.'

'Yeah? Going to the casino?'

'Nah. Just hangin' out. Me and a woman called Jane.'

To my astonishment I felt a pang of something like *jealousy*.

'Maybe I'll come to Hobart and visit you. Maybe some time in January, when Cobby comes home from America.'

'Is Cobby coming back? Too much! Yeah, come down, Nor.

185

That would be great. I get a bit lonely.'

'How are you feeling?'

'Oh – pretty shithouse. I can't sleep at night.'

We laughed: those endless, terrible nights when he groaned and thrashed in my bed.

We said goodbye.

The jealousy, upon being scrutinised, metamorphosed into a sadness I could not shake off for a day. My heart ached whenever I thought of him. But then, somehow, the pain stopped, and I went about my business.

On Christmas Eve we had a party. I stood with Willy, leaning against the half-open window in the big kitchen.

'What is happening between you and Rita?' I asked.

'Well . . .' he replied, looking into his glass. '. . . nothing, really, because I know that if I fucked with her it would freak Angela out one hundred per cent, completely and totally. And I know only too well the reason why I've got the urge to do it – I'd be acting straight out of my conditioning.'

I thought of Rita turning her face up to him, sparkling for him as she could for a man; she shone for *me*, though, loved me loyally in the overcrowded house where we all went crazy. Poor Rita. Poor Angela, who should have seen that Rita was no threat to her, ultimately; who raged against Rita's '*empty-headedness*,' as she called it, and suffered tortures when she couldn't keep both Rita and Willy well within her gaze.

So, Willy continued,

'The reason why I had to put a stop to what looked like happening between me and *you* was largely Angela's jealousy – the objective contradictions I was having to confront there – but it was also because Gracie rejected my approaches. She really hated my guts.'

'I've always noticed,' I pointed out, swallowing a pea-sized lump of irritation, 'that she gets on best with people who make no approach to her at all, but just let her come to *them*.'

'Yeah, well, I guess so; but I have to have my approaches confirmed. I want – what I *really* want,' he said, rolling his eyes behind his spectacles, baring his teeth, beginning to parody himself, 'is *total affirmation!*'

'You mean one hundred per cent of the time?'

'Yeah! I want someone to confirm me completely and forever! I want a SLAVE! So that's *my* biggest contradiction!'

We were both laughing.

'Wouldn't five minutes of total affirmation, every now and then, do? Come down here whenever you like – I'll affirm you in short bursts.'

He drank. I glanced round the room, nervously thinking that Angela would not be enjoying the sight of our conversation. Indeed, there she was in a cane chair near the fridge, hands in pockets, legs thrust out in front of her, cropped head to one side against the back of the chair, eyes rolled a little in the same direction, face still and long with what looked like boredom inadequately concealed. Still, I pressed on.

'I was really thrown by what happened between us. I know no-one can understand why I kept on with Javo, and I'm not going to explain that now – but it all happened while he was away in Thailand, and I was lonely and freaking out of my brain, and *missing* him. And you kept coming on to me sexually – '

'I know I did! I know!'

' – But what threw me was the way that, whenever I made any response, you just went BLAT – stonewalled me.'

'I *know*. But I told you the reason, that day.'

'You mean in the car?' (The clean washing between us, smelling sweetly of hot cotton and childhood.)

'Yeah.'

'You call that an explanation? I was really hurt by what you said.'

'I know you were.' Laughs. 'I was embarrassed.'

'So you should have been.'

Long pause. He drank, I looked at my reflection in the dark, clean window, strange bare face above a small bowl out of which I had been eating fruit salad.

'Well, I hope we get it together eventually,' I said with a sigh.

'The day comes ever closer,' he said, quite seriously.

Me, I had my doubts.

187

It was Christmas and Gracie went with Jack. I tried to find clothes which would serve as a disguise when I visited my grandmother, but nothing could soften the impact of my haircut.

'You in the Hare Krishna?' asked a friend of my brother-in-law's, rudely staring. I looked at him and he took a swig of his scotch.

My uncle, or 'the big boss' as his sister called him with not quite enough irony, filled my grandmother's house with his ruling class confidence. I watched him from inside my peculiar head. I thought of him in boardrooms: very expensive clothes, Italian shoes; big loud laugh, the expansiveness of being able to buy the whole world. His wife, whom I had always liked and whom he called 'Duchess', was also there, smiling her own benign version of that ineffable certainty. My father, behind her back, called her a 'bottle blonde'. Her clothes were of stiff white cotton with huge black patterns, worn tight over her solid, overfed, packed flesh. A long string of pearls hung down to her waist. Her perfume and her sureness filled the small passageway where she paused a second at the sight of my shorn, small head and faded clothes, remembered who I was, and smiled again without a break in her stream.

'Hul-lo, Nora!' she drawled in her breathy voice, laying her scented, firm cheek momentarily against mine. A small rush of voluptuous pleasure in her fullness stopped me in my tracks: as a child I had felt like swooning when she talked; I used to breathe her in.

I sank into a cool, fat armchair and watched my uncle, big-headed, top-heavy, seal-like, leaning with one hand against the mantelpiece, drink in the other hand as if he had been born holding it, making the family laugh with his rolling voice and irrepressible surges of humour, effortless and absolutely in his element. I watched him and thought,

'You are the enemy, mate. What am I going to do?'

We ate wonderful food, turkey stuffed with chestnuts, oh, the fruits of the earth but I don't want them here, though I take them, from the hands of Mammon himself. I thought of Joss eating millet, I tried to imagine a feast in his meagre life, I remembered his joy which cost him only complete capitulation to some force I did not understand: love, or an immense inevitability of things.

We came out into the hot, bright sunshine and saw my uncle's silver-blue Rolls parked at the kerb.

'Look,' said my youngest sister. 'A Royal Children's Hospital entry sticker.'

'Hmmph!' I muttered, half to my father who was walking beside me. 'Just another privilege of the ruling class.'

'All right!' said my father, half-laughing, half-protesting. 'That's enough.' But he knew.

After the huge meal I would have helped clean up, but there was a dishwashing machine and no immediately visible kitchen system, so I stood about helplessly, unable to make myself useful. By four o'clock the men had all fallen asleep in their chairs and the children were fiddling fractiously with their toys. I got on my bike and rode off through Kew Junction, up the hill, along past the gardens of Raheen and the Catholic properties and the pine-scented dry ground of the edge of the golf course, over the hump to where Studley Park Road opened out in front of me: half a mile of steady, inexorable downhill run. I let go and flew down it in ecstasy, head thrown back, mouth open, feet at quarter to three, my bag of Christmas presents bumping against my back. The wind pushed at my front, the mudguards rattled so fiercely I thought the machine would fly apart. Down and round the wide metal curve, over the river almost invisible among humped trees, on my left the convent low down on its mediaeval banks, ancient trees shadowing its courts; and on to Johnston Street, slowing down from flight and back to legwork along the narrow road between the rows of closed factories.

Chlorine and Rock & Roll

Full summer in the city: chlorine and rock and roll. Burnt brown on the concrete; washed clean, shampooed and dried; sitting at the kitchen table looking out through the bead fly curtain at the sky. Nights at the Kingston: dressed like an Alabama hooker in secondhand white satin, I take the money at the door and drink scotch brought to me by Paddy: I look at her glossy hair pinned back over her ears, I like her, and when the place is full we dance together, shouldering in for a spot on the packed floor. Oh, so drunk! which I do not realise until the music stops and Philip begins to count the money in my bag and the crowd thins out and I am sitting in an abandoned posture with my legs apart, hot and sweaty and completely happy.

In the dunny I ask a passing girl,

'I'm afraid I might've bled all over the back of my dress – have I?'

'No!' she answers cheerfully. 'I was a bit worried *I* might've, too, but I haven't.'

'It is just the sweat,' I say, and we part.

Cobby came home from America: Cobby, whose wit, as Javo used to say, was 'as dry as an eight-day-old bone'.

I headed out the freeway again, into the huge grey sky over Tullamarine. At seven o'clock I was hanging out in the departure lounge; at 7.12 the doors opened and I was watching for her blonde head. Out she came all dressed in baggy black like a Viet Cong. She dropped her wicker bag in the middle of the gateway and we flung ourselves at each other and both began to cry and laugh, and I moved the bag so people could pass, and we hugged again and again; I forgot other people were there, we were saying 'Oh, oh!' and hugging each other like anything.

We went up to the Golden Nugget bar. I left her in the middle of the crowded room with a small island of baggage

while I went to the bar and ordered. I glanced back at her and
she pantomimed a wave – bent her knees and grinned with a
closed mouth and waved one hand in a circle in front of her
face – I burst out laughing, foolish at the bar in my flowery
dress and funny haircut, holding a purse in one hand and two
dollar bills in the other.

We picked up her beat-up, collapsing suitcase tied together
with rope, and packed her things into the car and drove home.
I mimicked her American voice: 'uh huh', 'do you have . . .?'
and 'far-out!' At the house we ate a meal the men had cooked.
Cobby 'took a shower'.

'You know what they don't have over there?' she yelled
through the louvre windows. 'Methylated spirits.'

'Don't they call it "rubbing alcohol"?' said Gerald.

'Is that what it is?' she said vaguely, her mind already on
something else.

On New Year's Eve Angela streamed drunkenly into our
kitchen.

'Well, it's finally happened,' she announced.

The ring of faces turned up to her where she stood poised
dramatically on the step, one foot up, one down, hands out to
balance.

'What?'

'They've started fucking.'

Everybody knew who she meant: Willy and Rita.

She hoisted herself on to the high bench, took a deep breath,
and poured out a great flood of forbidden feelings, making us
shriek with guilty laughter. We surprised ourselves by the
simplicity and violence of our identification with *her* in this
most ancient of situations, the one we had theorised endlessly
about for the past four years: until Eve made her statement,
leaning back against the bench with her arms folded:

'Yep – there's one thing you just *don't do*, and that's take
away another woman's man.'

I stared at her.

'*Eve*! What are you *saying*?'

She looked defensive and cross.

'Well – you know what I mean.'

'But – if you think *that*, what've we been agonising about all this time? All that stuff about breaking out of monogamy? Jesus, Eve!'

Angela, too miserable to care about theory, took another swig from her glass of beer.

'I told him I wouldn't fuck with him again while he was seeing her.' She turned her eyes sideways to me with a child-like, tearful smile. 'But . . . I'm scared he might . . . *rape* me,' she whispered hopefully. 'He's really strong, you know.'

I started to laugh in spite of myself, thinking of Willy, the most unlikely rapist north of the Yarra. She was laughing too, or almost. I wrapped my arms round her.

'Oh, *Ange*. You're *nuts!*'

'*Anyway –* ' recovering herself with a sniff and a shrug; 'so I said to him, "Go ahead and get it out of your system, but you needn't think I'm gonna share you with *her –* it's just a matter of pride – just *get out*," I told him, "and don't come back till you've finished".'

She started to cry, rubbing the tears off her beautiful, clear-skinned face, sitting up there on the bench dangling her roxy pink shoes down against the cupboard door.

'Oooh, I hate her, I hate her!' she sobbed, drumming her heels with such abandon that we hardly knew whether to laugh or cry; and I thought about Rita and the way she turned her face up and fluttered and shone; how she hid her own private fear and wretchedness; how she gave herself generously, without reserve, loved too loyally, without criticism; and how we all thrashed about swapping and changing partners – like a very complicated dance to which the steps had not yet been choreographed, all of us trying to move gracefully in spite of our ignorance, because though the men we knew often left plenty to be desired, at least in their company we had a little respite from the grosser indignities.

On New Year's Day Cobby and I did some acid and everyone drove down to St Kilda to the Boardwalk gig. I sat in the front of the ute with Gracie on my knee, my stomach riding airily on the movement of the big car. An assortment of roxy types in baseball caps and sun visors, and yellow-faced junkies un-flattered by the clear sunlight, swarmed loosely round the old concrete stands. If you got too close to the buildings the smell of piss became overpowering: the smell of every concrete dressing shed on every civilised beach in Australia. But it was a day of rock and roll; Angela stood beside the mixer grinning proudly at Willy oblivious behind his drums; and down at the water's edge the lesbians and the unaligned women and the kids danced on the hard sand in a steady, warm wind that came ploughing in off the bay, oh, the looseness of the spine! and moving in the streaming salty air.

In the evening, when everything had quietened down, I worked with Gerald on the back yard, planting lawn seed. He was pulling the roller across the yard and I was standing on the back porch watching. I saw his thin, hard arms.

'Hey,' I said suddenly, 'let's get into bed and *fuck*.'

'What?' He looked up, smiling. I said it again.

'OK. Let's do that.'

We finished the grass and came into my room. He lay on my bed and I wandered round the room putting clothes away. The doorbell rang. He went to open.

'It might be Clive with the acid!' I yelled.

'No, it's not Clive with the acid,' came back Gerald's voice from the hall.

'It's Philip with a paper bag,' called Philip, and they walked past my door to the kitchen. I went out and sat with them at the kitchen table.

'Do you want to go up to your room and play some stuff?' said Philip.

'Sure,' said Gerald, and without a word to me they got up and clomped along the passage to Gerald's room.

Oh well. Back to the purdah.

I went over the Peel Street and found Rita tidying her room. Her face lit up sharply when she saw me. Quick as a flash she hit me with the news.

'Guess who Javo is hanging out with in Hobart?'

'Oh . . . I guess it's probably . . .' I began, but she cut across me to announce:

'Sylvia, Mark's sister.' She wasn't looking at me, but was sorting through some papers on the table.

'Oh yeah? Can't say I'm surprised.'

I remembered the one time I had met Sylvia, last summer in her small kitchen; how I wandered through her house while she and Javo awkwardly talked, and came upon a huge photo of him, gaunt and smacked out in some show he'd done, pinned to her bedroom wall.

I imagined him in her house, in her bed, waking up grumbling to the shouts of her children. I felt that small leakage of pain, which dissipated itself immediately.

'I'm just going over to the tower to talk to Angela,' said Rita, pulling a comical face of apprehension.

'What are you going to say?' I asked, quite curious.

'Oh, I don't even know why I'm going. I'm really scared of her. I just want to say that I don't think she ought to blow it with Willy just because of what's happened. They've got something really good together.'

'Do you think anything more is likely to happen between you and Willy?'

'Oh . . . yeah, probably.'

Over Angela's dead body, I thought privately, noticing how in Rita's presence I forgot the image of her as nothing but a scatter-brained twit which Angela had been unscrupulously promoting in her accounts of the situation. I drove her over to the tower and felt like hugging her when she got out of the car, but dared only give her a small tousle to the hair.

Gerald and I walked over to Rathdowne Street to borrow Georgie's bike, on a sunny afternoon. The front door was opened by Lillian, also there on a visit. At the unexpected sight of her, I instantly felt she was too close to me: I wanted to take several steps backwards, instead of which, under the influence of social impetus, I stepped forward and into the house, feeling my eyes drop and constantly go past her, as if to escape the intensity of her notice. I was afraid she would touch me, and my flesh shrank at the prospect; of course, she did no such thing, but merely smiled at me from inside her mop of salty, untidy hair and said, 'Hullo, Nora,' allowing me to be courteous.

'Do you know Gerald? This is Lillian,' I mumbled. They inspected each other with frank interest. I remembered Gerald saying once, 'I think she's stunningly beautiful.' I watched her toss him the challenge, almost a ritual gesture: she flipped her hair back over her bare brown shoulder and glanced at him sidelong, with half a laugh, doing something indescribable with her mouth – *just like in the movies*.

'Here we go – and you'll fall for it, too, you great fucking dunce,' I thought savagely. In some peculiar mixture of relief, pain and self-disgust, I slipped off into Georgie's room and sat in his big, overstuffed armchair and listened to Steely Dan, my arms along the rests of the battered chair and my spine against its back. Ugh, Nora, you dog-in-the-manger. Not in love with Gerald, never have been, don't want to be, but so afraid of loneliness that the very cells simulate the chemical reactions of jealousy, in some primal instinct to grasp and hold against all comers.

After what I thought was a decent interval I got up and went into the kitchen, where Gerald was sitting at the table with Lillian, being charming.

'Hey, Nora!' said Georgie, presiding at the head of the table behind a huge chocolate cake, knife in hand. I looked at his big, beaky face and bleached hair and felt better. 'Reckon you can handle a slice of my magnum opus?'

'I'll give it a try,' I replied, hiding my misanthropy under a rocky smile.

'What a nice house you live in, Georgie!' said Lillian, resting her pointed chin in her hands. I felt a stab of some unidentifiable pain, something to do with Georgie and three years in that old brown house on the corner of Delbridge Street and our having lost it; and resentment of Lillian's presence, almost too deep for the rational mind.

Georgie handed me a piece of cake and I felt the sweetness of the icing hit a hole in one of my back teeth.

'Do you want to get the bikes and split?' I said to Gerald.

He was looking up at me from his chair. I fantasised him saying, '. . . oh, you go, I might stay here for a while,' and me hiding my mortification and saying, 'OK, see you later.'

'OK.' He stood up and we said goodbye. Georgie walked to the front door with us. He put his big hand on my shoulder.

'What's up, Nor?'

'Oh – nothing I can feel good about admitting,' I said with a shrug. 'It's Lillian. There's so much old bad stuff between us, I find it really hard to be in the same room with her. Sorry! Sometimes I'm just an old grouch.'

He grabbed my neck and gave it a gentle squeeze, clicking his tongue and shaking his head. 'You're OK, mate. If *you're* not, I dunno who is.'

I glanced up and saw Gerald shrug his shoulders and raise his eyebrows, as if to say, 'What's all the fuss about?' Georgie just grinned at him, still holding my neck in his warm hand.

A letter, painfully printed on blue paper, came from Javo in Hobart.

'I am making a solid blow against my past. I want to come back but I won't. I am thinking a bit, falling in love with strangers – new ones every day – getting better at being me again.'

I folded up the letter and stashed it away. In the heart very little happened.

In the middle of a night I woke out of a thick and bottomless sleep. Silent house, alone in my bed. I must have fallen asleep early in the evening. I went out to the dunny and found the sky, clear and hot for two days now, had covered itself with cloud. The air was still and cool. I had no idea of the time. I stood between the new grass and the vegetable garden, in the dim air. What a strange night. I was afloat in it all by myself. I held my breath. *Something was gathering itself to happen, not now, but very soon.* I shook my head and the premonition flew away without a sound.

I went down the passage to Gerald's room. His door was

propped open with a chair. For a second I thought perhaps he wasn't there, was somewhere else; but I wandered in, in the dark, and saw him doubled up under the blanket. I knelt on the bed, put my hand on his hip, and said,

'Can I get in with you?'

'Yes! Of course,' he replied, speaking as sleeping people sometimes do in a perfectly ordinary voice. 'Have you had a bad dream?'

'No. I just woke up and couldn't go back to sleep.'

He put his arm round me, and I backed up against him for warmth. I thought, the ecstasy and the tortures waste too much time. Maybe I should settle for this.

I dreamed: I went to China, in a bus, with a lot of other people. What I saw there – happy people, full of energy and life – made me weep with joy.

Left with a Gritty Residue

The next evening we went down to Southside Six to dance to Gerald's band. Grace was determined that I was not going to have a good time.

'You've already had a *hundred* drinks,' she said as I came back to the table with my second scotch and ice. 'You're going to get *drunk*. I don't *want* you to!'

I watched Gerald playing, and started again to understand the romantic lust that rock and roll musicians provoke. I looked at his strong arms and the way his face tightened and relaxed in concentration, working in sympathy with his hands. I was dancing with my head down, concentrating myself on letting my spine go loose. Once I glanced up and he grinned at me, hesitantly, as people do when they are not quite sure whether they are being looked at or not. I smiled back and his funny curved face split in half.

Back on our side of the river, Gracie wanted a souvlaki. I took her to the Twins in Lygon Street and we stood there among the drunken, stoned, glassy-eyed late-night crowd silently waiting for food. My ears were still ringing from the music. The vats of fat hissed. The lights were harsh and people there, customers and cooks alike, looked dirty, tired, washed out, old, pushed past the limits of fatigue.

Gracie said into my ear,

'I'm tired, but I can't lie down in here.'

She went and squatted in a corner by the fridge, sucking her thumb and staring blankly.

A boot, a leg, a body, a head burst through the plastic fly curtain. It was Javo. He saw me and stopped in mid-flight, arms still flung out from the force of his entrance. We stood three feet apart. We smiled the same ancient, wary smile.

'Sssst. Hey, Javo,' I said, very softly. He said nothing, but continued to smile. Hank slid in behind him, blond hair glowing in the hard light.

'Good day, Nora!' he said. He jerked his thumb at Javo. 'Look who's back.'

Javo dropped his arms to his sides.

'When did you get back?'

'Two hours ago.' In his voice I heard the harsh grate of the dope: but even the cold neon could not leach out of his skin its new colour. He was alive again.

He lay down across the foot of my bed and I lay the length of it. He stroked my leg and we talked idly, with many pauses.

'I am only here for a week,' he said. 'I've got a part in a movie.'

I was wondering whether Gerald had gone off into his own room, when I slipped off to sleep and was woken, probably only seconds later, by the shock of Javo's hand on my back.

'Do you want to sleep here with me?' I said, looking at his brown face and shiny hair.

'Yeah.'

He took off his clothes and I watched him out of my dozing eyes: brown skin, hard body, healthier than I'd ever seen him.

He came over to the bed and got in, and turned off the lamp, and our bodies moved towards each other as they had moved a hundred times before. His skin felt burning, a fever from the first hit of smack in six weeks. Our arms went round each other and I heard him whisper my name, 'Oh, Nora!' and again my heart turned to water. I picked out in the dimness the bony lantern of his head and his eyes and teeth gleaming with that fierce smile, I came joyfully with no hesitation: but then the fact of his being stoned made itself apparent, for he did not come, and his body went on trembling and burning, cock hard and face turning again and again to my mouth in the dark, long after my energy had been exhausted and I wanted to fall away and go to sleep. At last I said,

'I have to rest – I'm too tired to fuck any more,' and we shifted apart and fell into a restless sleep, tossing half the night. His skin seemed so hot and dry that whenever we touched, in our restless movements, I woke up and felt him burning me with his arm or hand or side: I'd wake and he'd wake too and I'd feel eagerness run off him like a charge, and I'd mumble some helpless word and slip back into the same thin, uneasy sleep, right on the edge of the bed.

Very early in the morning I felt him get up out of the bed and go out of the room. I woke up, sat up; he came back in, dressed. He sat down on the side of the bed and said,

'I'm gonna split now, Nor.'

'OK,' I said, thinking that I'd never seen him up and dressed before me, *ever*, in all the time I'd known him.

'See you at the baths later, if it's swimming weather.'

'It's going to be,' I said, glancing out my window past the brick wall to the strip of dry, lightening sky. He leaned down and kissed me goodbye. I heard the front door close and slipped away into sleep at last, properly, for an hour or so. When I woke up again I crept into Gerald's bed and hugged him and felt an immense relief – done it! Fucked in the house with someone else, liked it, managed to get through the night, parted friends, found myself still open to being with Gerald (though I felt the odd flicker of apprehension at the thought of his doing the same thing – tit for tat).

'I almost wished,' said Gerald with a twisted grin, 'that I

199

could have heard a few groans or sighs, just so I'd be sure it was . . .'

'. . . Not a matter of suffering for nothing?'

'Something like that. The only thing I was dreading, really, was the morning – coming out and seeing him – but he's already gone, so that's not a problem.'

'I guess he's gone to score. But also, you know . . . when he can be, he is a kind person.'

The next evening Javo and I went to Jimmy's for dinner. He made me gasp with tales of his bourgeois friends in Hobart: days on beaches, nights in the casino, falling in love with married women with rich and jealous husbands.

'Geez, Javo, you look so well, I can't get over it.'

'I am. Must be almost exactly a year since I was in St V's with septicaemia – remember?'

'Do I what! You were off your brick. You pulled the drip out of your arm and nicked off. I was *spewing*.'

'You know when you came to visit me that night, with Martin? It was a pretty . . . cool visit. I wanted to say a lot of things to you, but I couldn't, not while Martin was there.'

My heart ached a little, in retrospect, at my briskness towards him that night.

He went to the theatre and I went home. He came in later when I was lying on my bed reading.

'Nor, is it cool if I crash in your lounge room?' he said. 'They're having a big coke binge at Easey Street and I can't keep away from it if I hang out there.'

Surprised again at his resolution.

'Of course.' And he slept in there and I slept in my room and Gerald slept in his, and there we all were.

In the daylight I was careful to concern myself largely with my own affairs. I was quite detached from him, or from my own feelings about him, and I thought it would never be the same again: as if I had unconsciously, over the six weeks of his absence, come to terms with the ways in which we would never be able to be harmonious. But occasionally I got caught out by his violently blue eyes, and the way he riveted me with them sometimes. The old fantasies were still hanging about . . . but I let 'em boil away for a bit until I was left with a gritty residue, which could be rolled up in balls and stored in the bottom of my pocket.

He left our house at ten in the morning to have a turkish bath in St Kilda, and didn't come back. By seven in the evening I was lying on my bed wondering if I ought to go and fetch him.

'Do you think I should?' I asked Eve.

'I reckon whole groups of people can take the load of helping someone get off dope,' she said.

'Tell him he hasn't worn out his welcome,' said Cobby.

Grace and I took the car and followed his trail from one junkie household to another. At Neill Street something mysterious was happening in the bathroom: when Micky came out he was a shade too polite for comfort. Javo had just left. I went back to Easey Street: no Javo. As a last chance I drove over to Napier Street. Gracie in the back seat asked,

'Nora, will you tell me some stories about people dying?'

'Why?'

'Because I like those stories.'

'I'll tell you some later.'

'OK.'

At Napier Street I saw through the overgrown vegetation Javo's pink T shirt and rough head, his back turned towards the gate. I parked the car. By the time I'd got Gracie out and crossed the road and entered the garden, he had climbed up the nectarine tree with Hank: I could see his face smiling down at me from among the leaves, and yes, his eyes were pale, the china blue whited out again, and I pretended not to see and talked brightly about having come to ask him round for tea.

'Thanks, Nor,' he said, balancing his feet in broken sandals on the crumbly grey branches, 'but I've gotta see a bloke about this movie, and pick up my jeans.'

'Pick up your jeans?'

'Oh – you know – the free ones you get for the movie. But thanks anyway.' He smiled and smiled, veiling himself behind the leaves.

'That's OK,' I hear my normal, sensible voice say. 'I'll see you later, then.'

'Yeah – see you, Nor.'

'See you,' said Hank, standing an improvised ladder against the fence, and said Jean, crouching under the Hills Hoist poking in the dry lumpy soil with a trowel. Gracie and I got back in the car. We ate half a nectarine each, very big and sweet.

'Is he stoned?' she asked me, chewing over my shoulder as I put the car in gear.

'Yep.'

'Why?'

'Oh, I dunno. I guess he feels better that way.'

'Do you feel sad?'

'Yep.'

'I wonder if he will ever stop being a junkie?'

We pondered this in silence, rolling home down the Napier Street hill. Home from seeking him out, I felt quite bad, and sad, my heart and stomach mixing themselves up together. At dinnertime I couldn't stand the noise, which was increased by the presence of the whole Rathdowne Street household.

Gerald was unhappy.

'It's not your relationship with Javo I mind,' he said. 'I just feel so neglected.'

I tried to reassure him, in his bed after midnight; but my words were hollow, banging around in that empty chamber of my head in which I waited treacherously for the thump of Javo's familiar step; and, as sometimes happens during late-night talks of this kind, I was dismayed to find myself continually almost overwhelmed by great floods of sleep. I battled to stay awake, but at last through a fog I dimly heard him say,

'. . . Don't you think that's true?'

'I'm sorry,' I said, ashamed of myself. 'I just can't help falling asleep. I didn't hear what you said.'

'OK,' he said, patiently enough but turning his back. 'It's all right.'

I said over my shoulder, 'Goodnight'; we turned to kiss, and suddenly we were in each other's arms, rushed through with that surge of desire that comes sometimes at the hopeless point of any argument.

Flapping like a Bloody Bandage

At the baths I lay back on my elbows on a towel, Rita on one side of me and Claire on the other. We surveyed the antics of the children and gossiped benevolently, straw hats pulled down over our eyes.

'You look like the three wise women,' remarked Gerald on his way past.

Claire let him get out of earshot and asked me,

'How is it with Javo back at your place?'

'Oh, OK. A bit weird. But good.'

'Geez he makes me laugh. Yesterday Gracie wanted to light his cigarette for him – but he said in that croaky voice' – she mimicked him – ' "Come off it, mate – you'd take a week!" I think he's *great*!'

Something about Claire always made me work hard in conversation. I riffled through my recent reading for titbits to relate to her, and told her some things I'd read about Dorothy Parker in Lillian Hellman's autobiography. She kept letting her head fall back in paroxysms of silent laughter.

Gracie came to ask me for some money. She leaned right over me in her sopping bikini, and put her face almost against mine to speak. I gave her the money and she trotted off with the Roaster.

'She's beautiful, isn't she,' said Claire. 'She's got a mist around her eyes.'

After the baths, Paddy showed up at my place. I washed myself and put on a clean cotton dress and we went to the Southern Cross. Paddy looked like someone in a war film. I stared and stared at her thin, elegant face with its thick flop of black hair pushed to one side of her forehead. We laughed so much that it made a scandal in the quiet bar.

At six in the summer morning the wind got up and woke me by banging a window and blowing something off the kitchen table.

203

I crawled out of thick sleep and stumbled out to the dunny. The air moved from the north and the sky was clear. All our swimming things were hanging on the old church pew in the back yard. The wind rustled in the bamboo leaves over the next-doors' brick fence, and in the sky I saw a faint streak of pink, low down in the no-colour of six o'clock. I began to pick up the towels and fling them back over my shoulder, standing barefoot in the tanbark which was still soaked from the kids' evening games with the hose. As the dry, stiff cotton flicked past my cheek, I heard the bead curtain rattle. Javo was standing there, tired and hunched, dirty, his hair on end. I looked at him, my arms full of dry towels. He gave me half a smile. Blue eyes burning.

'Do you want a cup of coffee?' I said.

'Yes. Please. Mate.'

When I took Gracie to school that morning she screamed and wept in the yard, and clung to me. I tore myself away, and staggered home in tears of guilt and misery, back into our kitchen where Gerald and Eve and Javo were sitting at the table smoking and drinking coffee. I saw myself in a great rush of impotent rage seize the back of a chair, with someone's bathers hanging on it, and hurl it half out the open back door. It missed the glass. The bead fly curtain clattered loudly. No-one said anything. I sat on the bench with my head in my hands. Eve came and stood beside me and took my head against her hip and stroked me. Everyone helped me. Within minutes I was prancing round, the tears barely dry on my cheeks, doing imitations of my own discomfiture, and we were all laughing. Meanwhile, Gracie was squatting in her classroom, bored into a trance, singing 'Baa baa black shee' ', while she might have been reading whole books or learning to dance or drawing her beautiful 'lady's'.

Javo that morning was in his mooching mood. He wandered round the house with a closed face, the bib of his overalls unbuttoned and hanging down. After the postie came and did not bring his dole cheque, he packed up his possessions in his calico bag, put on his denim jacket, and made as if to leave. I met him on the step of the kitchen.

'You off?'

'Yeah.' He tried to smile. Still a deep sleep-crease down one side of his face. Where had he slept? I didn't ask, for fear of knowing.

'Give us a hug, you mingy bastard.'

He laughed, and put his arms round me. I was still on the step, so that his face was in my shoulder and my arms around his neck. We hugged each other very hard. I felt sad and puzzled, but tried not to show it, and stepped back to let him pass. Out he went, banging the front door behind him. I cast my eye round the kitchen to see if he'd taken everything with him: he had, except his old brown journal, which had been on the bench behind the table. Gone! I couldn't find the spirit to do anything except lie on my bed under my dressing-gown and try to read myself to sleep.

I dreamed:

The beginning a confusion. The first clear event was Javo leaving the place where I was, and next, the arrival of Hank with the news that he was dead, killed in a motorbike accident. I was frantic, at first with disbelief, then, as the news was somehow substantiated, with terrible pain and grief. I couldn't go to Gerald for comfort, not because it would be hurtful to him, but because he would not be able to understand how someone from that *group of desperadoes* could provoke that much love in a person like me. Hank was there again, and I turned to him and flung myself on him: suddenly we were in a driverless car, being propelled along a country road. We were lying in the back seat and I was on top of him and we were fucking; but I was also weeping most bitterly, sobbing my heart out, knowing that Hank was understanding this appalling grief I was feeling; and somehow the weeping and the fucking were mixed up together in a powerful sensation of ecstasy and pain, pain, pain.

But the shock waves of this awful ecstasy receded, leaving me in a kitchen, standing behind Jean who was peeling vegetables over the sink with her back to me. I put my arms round her from behind and hugged her and said,

'Jean – I've been fucking with Hank – I hope you'll

understand.'

'Yes, I do – it's OK,' she said, without turning round. The rush of grief started again and I walked blindly round the kitchen, blundering into the table and putting my hands desperately upon its flat surface. I could barely speak, but stammered,

'Has anyone told his *mother*?'

'Yes,' said Jean, still with her back turned to me. 'Chris has told her.'

The telephone rang and I dragged myself out of gluey sleep and staggered off the bed. It took me an hour to fight my way out of that dream. Cobby came home.

'I can't find my sunglasses,' she said. 'I've got a sneaking suspicion that Javo might've stolen them.'

'What makes you think that?'

'It just all fits together. Yesterday he looked at that old red scarf I was wearing and said how much he liked it. Last time I saw the glasses, they were with the scarf and the Berger paints cap. Today the cap's here but the glasses and the scarf are gone, and Javo has gone too, taking his bag. What can I think?'

My heart simply wriggled with horror. I didn't know how to confront the suggestion. I didn't know why he'd gone, but he'd gone. So we rode our bikes round to Napier Street, me with the tatters of the dream still flapping round my head like a bloody bandage. Claire was watering the garden. In the kitchen we found Jean and Hank cheerfully cooking themselves a meal.

'Has Javo been here?' I asked.

'Yeah, he was here,' said Hank, 'but he's gone round to Easey Street, to hang out there.'

I told them about the dream, and we all laughed, because I dared not tell them about that grief. When I got to the part about fucking with Hank, he mimed a little parody of pleasure, clattering his feet on the floor and racing with his arms. There were weird overtones of the dream itself in the telling: Jean was standing at the sink with her back to me, working; but she turned her face to me and laughed as I talked, her sturdy little body firmly planted, feet apart, laughing and working. Claire came in just as I was saying,

'And Hank and I were in the back of this car, fucking . . .'

She glanced at me in amazement and I said hastily,

'It's a dream I had when I was asleep this arvo.'

'You *dreamed* you were *asleep*?' she said, bewildered.

'*No*! I was *asleep* and I had a *dream*!'

'Oh!'

'Have you actually *seen* Javo today?' I asked. 'He's *not* dead, is he?'

'No, he's not dead,' said Hank. 'He's not even stoned.'

I knew he wouldn't have mentioned that unless it were true. We rode home. Half an hour later Javo walked into my room, clear-eyed and smiling, carrying his calico bag over his shoulder.

'Boy, am I glad to see *you*!' I cried. I told him about the dream. He sat sideways on my chair, listening with half a smile flickering across his face as I knelt up on the bed, pantomiming out the story.

'So,' I concluded, 'I went to Napier Street to see if you were still alive.'

He laughed.

'I freaked out this morning when you left,' I said. 'No – that's sloppy talk – I didn't "freak out". I was upset, because I thought you'd gone for good, and you hadn't said anything. I was torturing myself with stuff like "I haven't done enough, he's gone out to get stoned, it's all over, what more could I have done?" '

Again he laughed. 'Why did you think I'd gone for good?'

'You were in such a strange mood this morning, mooching round, not talking or anything.'

'I was just vacant.'

'Oh – by the way – you haven't got Cobby's sunglasses, have you? She can't find them.'

'No.' He looked directly at me, slightly puzzled by the question. I remembered his hysterical denials the day before he left for Hobart. All my doubts flew away.

207

No Logic

I knew I wouldn't have to go searching for acid. It arrived with Clive in time for the second Boardwalk show. I was tripping again by myself. The sun was thundering down on my back as I sat under my torn hat on the scrubby grass, peering out at the world. I watched Selena walk slowly down to the water with Juliet trotting along beside her. Selena was wearing a large blue hat and a white lawn skirt to her feet. As she walked, the wind swayed the skirt in wide, deliberate sweeps around her strong ankles. She placed her feet in a leisurely but definite rhythm. When she reached the water she hitched up her skirt and tucked it into the legs of her knickers, exactly as we used to do when we were children. I gazed and gazed. I noticed that tears were running down my cheeks.

Later in the day the wind swung round to the south and came tearing up the slope from the sea. Sand whipped in our faces. The children in the water panicked, thinking it was a storm: Gracie, sandy and dripping, flung herself on my lap, gibbering and snivelling. Javo came up to me. I looked up to greet him and saw his red-brown Indian face and faded blue overalls and fierce blue eyes against the metal clouds which were gathering. I gaped up at him, struck dumb by the beauty of his colours.

There must have been speed in the acid, because I couldn't go to sleep till long after midnight. I talked with Gerald on the front verandah for a long time after everyone else had gone to bed. I lay in the hammock and the rain started and dripped on me in my cotton dressing gown. Gerald was kind. He said,

'Why don't you *ask* Javo what he'd like you to do – if he *wants* you to help him stay off dope?'

'I will.'

But I didn't.

It seemed, then, that I could do nothing with Gerald but hurt him. I slept with him in his bed, under the open window through which the new cool wind streamed, raising with difficulty the heavy silver curtains; but I went straight to sleep, and did not want to fuck in the morning either. He was hurt, and offended. I felt nothing but a rising tide of anger. When I spoke, my voice sounded harsh, though I did not want it to be.

'It is all one-sided at the moment,' he said. 'It's coming from you, your fear of me.'

'Nothing is ever one-sided,' I wearily replied. I tried to summon up a memory of how I used to argue for my life against the cold face of someone I was in love with. I couldn't remember. There is no logic in feelings. *No logic.* I said,

'Maybe this is something you just have to go through. I have, and I didn't like it either.'

'You're probably right. I don't suppose I've had to go through much, in my life. But please understand – I'd give anything not to be putting you through all this.'

We were lying on his bed. All the while as I talked I was glad of the warmth of his front against my back. I liked the feeling of the fine dry hairs on his arm.

'I don't suppose,' he remarked gloomily, 'we'll ever fuck again.'

'Oh, that's just *silly*,' I snapped in a rush of irritation at his dogged pessimism. 'How can you think that?'

'Because the only way we can ever approach each other again in a relaxed enough way to fuck is if I stop hunting you and you stop stepping back. And I can't see how that can ever happen.'

'Time helps, you know,' I said, noticing a tartness in my voice.

Just as our whole household was marching out the front door on its way to a birthday party at Rathdowne Street, the sand for the children's sand pit arrived. They didn't want to go. I said I would stay home for the first half of the party; Eve promised to be back by 5.30 to take over. Javo, on his way out the door with the others, heard what we said and turned back.

'I'll stay with you, Nor,' he said.

The kids stopped whingeing about having to go out, and ran into the back yard to play. I lay on my bed and began to read. After a little while Javo came in and lay down beside me. I put the book down and we talked, companionably at ease. I stroked his forearm, and the inside of his elbow, thinking vaguely of the hardened veins where the needle had gone in too many times. Kids were tearing up and down the hallway outside my room. We rolled towards each other and kissed with tongues. I could feel him give a great shudder, all up and down his body, his eyes tightly closed: I thought he had already come. But I put my hand on him and felt his cock still hard.

'Let's go up to Cobby's room and fuck where the kids won't find us,' I said.

For a moment I was afraid he would say no: he looked at me steadily for several seconds, and then he smiled and started to get up off the bed. We scurried upstairs and undressed quickly and crept into Cobby's unmade bed in its ship-like alcove, and got our skins together with a sigh. What was it about him? Whenever he touched my cunt, my clitoris seemed to be in the exact spot where he first came in contact with my flesh: I was ready for him before we started, as if hastening all my processes to be there for him. I took his cock and put it inside me, and looked down at his wrecked and beautiful face, how it melted and turned gentle and even the blue eyes blurred, up that close. I seemed to start coming almost immediately; he saw it and smiled with joy, and we came together effortlessly, smiling and smiling into each other's faces. We lay together without speaking for a little while, half-laughing with happiness and astonishment.

I sprang out of bed straight away, to get ready for the arrival of the rest of the household, and indeed they walked in the door at the moment my foot hit the bottom stair. Nobody knew about it except Cobby; she laughed and frowned and glanced sideways.

At the party Javo got drunk in a corner and danced by himself. I ate too much and played vampires with the children and tried to engage Philip in conversation. By the time the chocolate cheese cake had been eaten and the homemade brandy alexanders drunk out of vegemite jars, everyone was in the next room dancing and I did it too, grinning at all the same old delightful faces. Cobby and I decided to walk home. I gave the sign and the raised eyebrow to Javo, who was wedged in his corner dancing and smiling and closing and opening his eyes; but he shook his head as if to say, I'll stay a while. We grinned and waved through the small thicket of dancers, and Cobby and I left, and wandered drunkenly home.

'I need another drink,' she said, dawdling at the gate.

'Let's take Gerald's car and whiz in to the Southern Cross?'

'I'll ask him.' She emerged from his room with the keys. 'He wants the car back in twenty minutes. Reckon we can make it?'

'Can we what!'

In the bar we set up a line of drinks, two each, guzzled them, licked out the glasses, and ran out on to the plaza, disgusted but satisfied. On our way home along Rathdowne Street we flew past the party. Outside the house stood Angela flagging us down, and beside her a white-faced, bedraggled Javo with his overalls bib hanging down: he was leaning on Angela's shoulder and appeared barely able to stand.

'Javo is a sick boy,' she said as we pulled up. 'Can he come home with you?'

'Of course.'

She kissed his cheek – Angela the junkie-hater kissed Javo's cheek! We loaded him in and Cobby drove as smoothly as she could. He leaned on me as far as my room, and collapsed on my bed. I got him a bucket and a towel, and painstakingly untied his complicated arrangement of sandal strings. I dragged his overall off his long legs and leaned over him. As I watched, a paroxysm of vomiting caught him unawares: he was lying on his back, and a few drops of the watery yellow vomit flew into the air and splashed on to my cheek. I turned him over so he hung over the bucket, and he spewed weakly. I felt no revulsion about anything that was happening.

When the spasm was over I laid him back on the pillow and dried his face with the towel.

'Sorry, Nor,' he whispered. 'Guess the dope has fucked my liver.'

'Don't be sorry. People have had to do this for me dozens of times.'

'Thanks.' He smiled at me from under his drooping eyelids. I noticed tears creeping out, and a small sob or two.

211

'Why are you crying, Javes?' I asked in dismay, trying to hug him gently.

'I'm just – so – happy!' he whispered. I almost laughed out loud, full of my own happiness, and remembering the times I'd cried drunkenly, years ago, in the luxury of excess. He held on to me with bony arms sticking out of his two T shirts, one blue, one pink.

'I've been thinking,' he said with difficulty, 'neither of us will ever be one-out while the other one's alive!'

I sat in the curve of his body and held his dirty hand.

'And also . . .' he went on, 'before I got drunk, I was thinking – everyone should have a fuck like that before they go to a party.'

I was holding his hand, nodding and smiling.

'I'm going out to the kitchen,' I said after a while. 'If you need me, call out.'

'You don't *have* to be so good to me, Nor,' he said, still hanging on to my hand. I just looked at him and we both grinned, almost laughing.

When I came back, he'd fallen asleep. He slept all night in my bed on his own, and I slept with Gerald and made him miserable with what he saw as my indifference. I did not tell him I had been fucking with Javo.

I was driving in the car with Gerald.

'Last night,' he said, 'I asked Selena if she wanted to come home with me. But she said, "No, I think I'd rather just go home to bed".'

'Oh, yeah? How did you feel about that?'

'Rejected.'

We were driving round the Swanston Street roundabout where the two big clean gums grow.

'It doesn't matter, though, does it?' I remarked, suddenly filled with a certainty that fucking occupied far too important a place in all our lives. He didn't agree, that it didn't matter.

'You don't seem to suffer from loneliness, do you?' he said, as we passed a corner of the university. I was staring in some acid memory at the cars parked under the shade of a concrete

212

structure, probably the bottom of a lecture theatre.

'No – I don't get enough of it – solitude, that is.'

'Well, then, it's easy for you to say it doesn't matter. You don't have that longing to get *close* to someone.'

I supposed I was speaking out of some immense, unexamined privilege. I began to feel myself in a position of power arrived at, inadvertently, through an absence of deep or passionate feeling. I remembered someone asking me, years before, 'Has there ever been a time in your life when you haven't been loved?' I answered no. But Gerald would not make that answer.

'There are,' I said, 'quite a few people I'd like to ask to fuck with me, but I don't, because I'm afraid of being rejected.'

'*You*!' he exclaimed, not believing me.

'Of course!' I looked at my battered feet in their battered sandals, and thought about Philip, and Willy. 'I am afraid of people thinking I'm ugly.'

'Wow, that's good to know,' he said. 'Well – good in one way – I've been thinking you're so cool, and I'm so uncool.'

Once again I felt that steady flood of certainty: 'It just doesn't *matter*, though.'

'How can that be true?'

'Well – with Selena – you're both still walking round.'

We looked at each other. I laughed, and he almost did.

Nothing to Give, or Say

But.

Caught out by acid three times stronger and longer than I'd expected.

Caught out by very small, very sharp thrusts from the knife of Javo's not reappearing, the night we all went out to dance. He left the pub with a woman I didn't know. I was drunk enough not to let on to myself that those very small, very sharp pains were beginning . . . like a labour come to surprise me. I knew I would have to work hard at letting him be born.

Tripping at the baths. *The meaning of life* constantly flicked away from me, eluded the corner of my eye as I turned to pounce on it in the precise condition of my cells at the very second at which I looked at the curved, bright corner of the children's pool. Gone! Missed it! I turned back to watch hundreds of children swarming shrimp- and sardine-like through the chemical water, and let myself be tossed and buffeted again by the turbulence of the day's air.

Rita was lying on her stomach under her large Virginia Woolf straw hat. She glanced up at me and her face looked pale and blotched with trouble.

'What's wrong?' I asked, all acid innocence.

'Oh, everything's been getting me down lately,' she said; her features seemed to be dissolving before my eyes, as if she were struggling to contain them in their customary form. Not sure how far I could trust my intuitions (wouldn't I ever learn to go along with them?), I lay down and said nothing. In the afternoon we were sitting on the bench surveying the bubs' pool, she under her floppy brim, I under the stiff peak of the Berger paints cap. I asked, again ingenuously unaware of the reaction my questions might provoke,

'How are things with Willy?'

She kept looking straight ahead.

'I never see him,' she replied. I said nothing, looking sideways at her. She took a breath, gasped, sat forward as if to hide her face, said, 'I'm going to cry . . .' and let her face crumble. I put my arms round her shoulders (her very soft brown skin) and she sobbed for a few moments, stammering out words about how Willy criticised her clothes and her demeanour, how she felt the weight of community disapproval on her. 'Do you know what Jack asked me the other day?' she said, recovering her equilibrium as she talked. 'He said, "How's your reconstruction program going?" ' She gave a painful laugh. 'It's not that I mind being criticised. It's just that it's done in such a hard way.'

Too much righteousness, not enough love.

I got home from the baths and found Philip crouching on the road beside the window of Gerald's car, as if Gerald were about to drive away, which indeed he was. I walked up to them and noticed in a flash Philip's teeth stained from smoking, Gerald's white clothes, and two sticks of incense burning in the dashboard. This seemed to me quite mysterious.

'Are you going somewhere?'

He looked up at me, faced closed and dark. 'Yes. For a drive, and possibly to a beach.'

I put my hand on his arm (tripper's privilege) and said, 'Incense! Carlos Santana.' I hadn't meant to tease too hard, but perhaps I did, for he put the car into gear and drove off with a nod. Philip and I were left standing on the road outside the house. Philip, as he always did, stood still, hesitant and slightly non-plussed.

'Want a cup of tea?' I asked, hoping he would come in.

'Yeah.'

'What are you doing?'

'Just that pre-gig thing: driving round to people's places.'

'To get some?' I suggested, looking at him from under my cap peak. He looked back quite steadily for a second, then laughed and nodded. I surprised myself by saying something I didn't know I was going to say: 'Well, suck away,' I said, putting my arms out in a giving gesture; 'I've got plenty, today.'

At the Kingston that night, Lillian was inexplicably there when I walked in. She was sitting quietly at a table by herself, very brown and smooth and long in the legs, her thick hair round her shoulders in a wavy mass. We nodded to each other. I was still tripping faintly. I sat down with Gerald at a table. He looked strange to me: his face was browner and the whites of his eyes showed all round the irises. I didn't like the way he looked at me. I said,

'Did you have a good afternoon?'

'Yep.'

'Where did you go?'

'Down to Arthur's Seat. Went on the chairlift.'

He was leaving off pronouns.

'Did you go by yourself?'

'No.'

'Who were you with?'

'Lillian.'

I understood the incense and the white clothes. My heart opened and closed like an anemone.

'What did *you* do?' he asked politely.

'Oh . . . mucked around at home.'

I danced, I sat, I drank orange juice. Rita put her arm across my shoulder, sometimes held my hand.

Gerald drove Lillian and me home. We dropped her first and then headed for our place.

'I hope I didn't blow it for you by coming home with you and Lillian,' I remarked from where I was lying across the back seat. 'Bit of a drag, me hanging round like a bad smell when a bloke's trying to get it on.'

He turned round and said to me, 'I'd really like to get it on with *you*.'

'Oh!' I said, taken aback. The familiar juice of fear trickled through my blood. I turned my head and stared blankly through the back window, desperately trying to put together a satisfactory answer. 'Well, I guess we will, sooner or later.'

'I mean *now*,' he insisted. He glanced back at me between the high front seats. I was afraid.

'I only want to *crash*, right now. I'm absolutely fucked.'

We had turned into the far end of our street. He was silent. I could see the tension in his cheek and neck.

'What's the matter?' I asked foolishly.

'FRUS-TRA-TION!' he bellowed in a harsh, loud voice, thumping the empty seat beside him with his fist. At that moment we were passing another car: he pushed his foot down hard and we were rushing along in third gear on the wrong side of the road. I was sick with fear. I thought, 'He is doing that thing men do, he's rushing to destruction, he's got me here, he's power-mad, I can't do anything.' I took a breath to call his name. I said, 'Ger . . .' and knew there was no point. I lay back on the seat. He passed the other car and got into the left lane, crossed the tramtracks in St George's Road, and stopped in front of our house.

Trapped in the back seat, stifled by closed windows and the high head-rests of the front seats, I half sat and half lay, looking at my feet, while he tried again to argue me round to the way things once were. For fifteen minutes we shouted at each other in barely controlled fury. A silence fell. I could hardly breathe. I said, in a small quiet voice,

'Gerald, I have to get out of this car *right now*.'

'All right.'

He opened the driver's door and got out and I folded the seat forward and scrambled past him. He sat down again, his legs out the door, hands between thighs, head hanging on one side, eyes downcast: his limbs, disposed in that way, made him look like a large, tired grasshopper. I realised that my reserves were empty. I had nothing to give, or say. I walked into the house.

In my bed, which I saw as a final refuge from the world but which to him was the centre of the battlefield, I took a dirty pink T shirt of Javo's under the sheet with me, to let the smell of him comfort me. I lay there with it shamefully under my stomach, flat on my face, two-dimensional like a thing steam-rolled. Gerald came into the room.

'I've calmed down,' he said. 'You're right.'

I wished he'd go away and let me die quietly into sleep. He sat down beside me on the bed. His movements seemed self-consciously casual. 'Do you want a hug, or anything?' I froze up inside and lay very still.

'If you feel like it,' I said, 'but all I can do is just lie here.'

He began to stroke me, and to touch the side of my neck and face, in a way I dared not submit to, lest it become sexual. I lay there in a crazy panic of revulsion, half-turned away from him, disliking the smell of his breath, wishing I could dematerialise. I escaped by slowing down my breathing and pretending to be asleep. He stroked on. He said,

'Hey – has Javo come back yet?'

Javo had not been back for two nights and two days; and the pains were small and sharp. I didn't answer. He let a moment or two pass.

'Are you asleep?'

I didn't answer. He stopped stroking me, lay beside me, non-

plussed, then got up off the bed and walked out of the room. I
spread out into the cool corners of the bed. Just before I went
to sleep I was half troubled by a rhythmical sound like a tap
dripping in the alley outside my window. I even got up to
check the bathroom taps, but they were all tightly turned off.
Puzzled, I got back into bed. The sound continued. It dawned
on me that it was the beating of my own blood.

I was lying on my bed reading when I heard Gerald come into
the house and speak to Cobby. My door was closed. I went on
reading. Scraps of the conversation filtered through to me.

'. . . Going somewhere?' asked Cobby, in her dry, drawling
voice.

'Yeah . . . Wilson's Prom . . . three days . . . Lillian.'

A big ragged hole opened up in my stomach. The words on
the page became black scratchy marks. I wondered, still on my
back among the cushions with the book upright on my chest, if
he would come and say goodbye to me. (Why should he?) I
heard his footsteps in the hall stop outside my door, and a
piece of paper was pushed under the door. He walked away. I
got up quietly, picked up the note and read it.

'Dear Nora, I'm going to Wilson's Prom with Lillian, and
expect to be back Wednesday night (but you never know).
Happy days to you and yours. Love, Gerald.'

I felt a shot of bleak anger which I did not trust. I sat on the
bed; I thought, I should go out and speak to him before he
goes. I got up and walked barefoot to his room (big bare un-
welcoming space). He was standing there in white, just-washed
trousers and a black velour jumper over which we once had a
stupid fight, and sunglasses. I saw his favourite blanket folded
neatly on a chair.

'You'll be cold,' I remarked primly. 'Is that all you're going
to sleep in?'

'I've put my whole *bed* in,' he said, standing there with his
hands hanging down. Then I saw that his mattress was gone.

'Where'll you put it?' I asked, curious to know how this tight
fellow would envisage setting up a camp, and seeing quick
visions of the crude (and thus, to me then, superior) camps I

had taken part in.

'On the floor of the tent.' The *floor*?

'Haven't you been camping before?' I asked rudely.

'Yes. Lots of times.'

We were face to face in the doorway. It was the moment to relent and hug. I did not touch him. I stepped back. He picked up a bag and I went out the front door and got into the hammock. The wind was streaming from the southwest, as turbulent as yesterday's but colder. I lay there in my flowery dress with my feet up high, and contemplated a sick feeling which was growing in my stomach. Why couldn't I let him go and wish him well? Why did I always need a man to be concerned with, whether well or ill? Why was I afraid to be alone, as Cobby was? Why did I involuntarily pick out Lillian's least attractive characteristics, to comfort myself? I fantasised ludicrously about the two of them driving along, their large limbs disposed inside that neat, tight little car. I wondered how he would characterise me when they talked. I imagined his account of my rudeness as he was leaving, and her pulling a face as if to dismiss or sympathise.

I was actually suffering low-level *pain*.

The wind kept rushing through the meagre leaves of a small gum tree in our narrow front garden. Gerald opened the wire door and shouldered his way out, carrying a bag, a pillow and his guitar. When I saw the guitar I almost laughed out loud at a small, vicious fantasy of the two of them sitting over a camp fire, him playing well and her strumming away crudely; a more pleasant picture followed, of him kindly teaching her.

He didn't come nearer to me than he needed to in going down the steps; nor did I heave myself out of the hammock. I said,

'See you.'

So did he. He got into the car, but by that time I'd ceased to look at him and the car started and departed somewhere behind my left shoulder. I kept staring at the gum leaves. The last I saw of him was his arm lying along the top of the open car window as the car passed on the other side of the triangular, treeless park across the road from our house. See you. I hoped it would storm and drip rain for a week. I thought of them fucking on his mattress on the floor of the tent, and I did not wish them well.

I am not a kind person.

I waited, on and off, for the heavy steps of Javo to come to my door. I knew they would probably not come for several days, and that I would become used to sleeping alone without guilt or desire. I thought that, with Javo, I understood how it was possible to love the most positive and good parts of a person and to co-exist with the rest. I missed him, very much, and tried to imagine what he was feeling and thinking.

I was not very happy.

I woke in the morning and found Gracie sleeping beside me in my bed. I stumbled out through the kitchen on my way to the dunny, and wondered if Javo might have come back in the night. I felt certain that the bed in the living room would be empty, but I looked anyway, and found that it was full of his long body, his dark tousled head sticking up out of the blanket in which he was rolled. Surprised, I stood still in the doorway looking at that head. Unspectacular, gentle happiness ran smoothly through my whole body. I closed the door very quietly so that the noise of our household at breakfast would not wake him.

But when I got to the baths that morning, the old aching feeling came back to plague me. Javo was there, but was concentrating all his friendly attention upon Jean and Hank, and I felt left out and lonely. I didn't stay long. I rode home in the extreme, dry heat, puzzled and sore; picked up Gracie from school and went back to the baths. I was at pains to hide my unhappiness; I was at pains not to ask him where he had been for those nights, but he told me anyway. We were sitting on the edge of the pool at the shallow end, squinting in the glare, water drying on our shoulders.

'Wow, it's been a weird weekend, Nor,' he said.

'Yeah? What's been happening?' *Very nonchalant.*

'I went home with Sue on Friday night – I suppose I sort of

expected that – she cornered me.' He laughed, abashed; I glanced at him and saw his awkwardness, which started it up again, ache, ache, the old ache, like music in the blood.

'And on Saturday night I was round at Napier Street. There was only Claire home, we watched TV. And then when I got up to leave she came to the door with me, and she said, "Would you like to stay?" '

Hearing him was like watching a film.

'So I did.'

I suffered under my cap. Not suffering I couldnt bear, but suffering none the less. He was smiling as he told me, and I smiled too, hoping it was not a grimace. Oh no, it wasnt the stabs of pain, but what you could call the subterranean home-sick blues. I refrained from comment, dangling my legs in the water, keeping the peak of my cap between my eyes and his face. I was careful, careful.

When it was time to go I did not ask him to come to my place. I picked up my belongings and said casually,

Which way are you going?'

Your way,'he said, shoving his towel into his bag.

He walked and I rode slowly along beside him with Grace on the back of my bike. When we got home we found the house full of people, kids mostly, with more expected for dinner. I felt claustrophobic and angry. I said to Javo,

'Do you want to go and have a drink? I'd really like to get out of here.'

'OK,' he said agreeably. We set out for the tramstop. On the bench at the corner of St George's Road I started trying to explain myself.

'I'm afraid of doing to you what Gerald is doing to me.'

'*What*? Don't be silly. You just don't *do* it. We trust each other too much for something like that to happen.' He kept grinning at me. The tram came, we got on it. Old, comfortable situation: going into town with Javo to fill our stomachs at my expense.

Back in my room, I walked straight in.

'Is it all right if I sleep in here?' he asked politely, standing at the bookcase.

'Of course! I was just going to ask you.'

'Good!'

We stretched out on the bed in the hot room full of dry, still air. We lay good-humoured and naked, stroking each other's skin. He heaved his arm to go under my neck and I smelled his good, sharp smell. I remembered the pink T shirt and blushed to myself.

'Hey, Javes. The other night I was so freaked that I used your T shirt as a sucker rag. I slept with it all night.'

He threw back his head and laughed, incredulous. I stopped feeling foolish. I watched his face, so familiar to me and loved.

'I'm having such a good time these days,' he said happily. 'I like my body more and more. I'm not afraid of fucking.'

Thinking of Claire, I felt at the same moment the aching start again and the beginnings of a small stream of happiness. The aching was for the realisation that, months ago, the dope had not terminated our relationship, but interrupted and changed it; the happiness was for the mother in me, watching him gather himself and take off.

'If it hadn't been for you, in that time after I got back from Bangkok,' he said, 'I'd be dead by now.'

We laughed and talked the night away.

'Who do you fuck with, Nor?' he asked me.

At three or so we went to sleep. He was still sleeping when I woke from a dream in which a group of people, including me and Rita and Willy, went to live in a redbrick house on the outskirts of Camperdown. I wept and wept about some sadness I could not remember, and Willy held me tightly in his arms, standing at the window, to comfort me.

Javo slept on, and I took the kids to school and went about my morning's business. At lunchtime I went to the baths, taking Gracie with me, early from school. Javo was there, holding court at the deep end where children may not go. I stayed at the shallow end with Gracie. He saw me, eventually, and swam and waded over to me, his brown face grinning against that electric blue water.

'I've got a room,' he announced, as we stood thigh-deep in the water, leaning against the side of the pool, arms along the lumpy silver railing.

'Where?'

'At Neill Street.'

'That's good.'

We stood for minutes in silence.

I said, 'I'm glad you've got a place, but I'll miss you.' I didn't look at him. We stared away from each other. Long moments passed.

'Yeah ... well, I need a place to work. I've got a show to do.'

Eager to agree, I hastened, 'You could never work at our place – I know.'

A pause. Gracie came dog-paddling up to me. 'Watch me! Watch me!' I watched, and in the corner of my eye his long dark body launched itself out into the water and he swam away.

Turkey, cold turkey.

I'll Do Anything You Ask

But two days later he came into our kitchen in the morning while I was ironing my blue and white spotted dress. He wanted me to put his dole cheque through my bank account. In the bank he sat on a chair waiting for the teller to call my name. I leaned on the shelf beside him.

'Hey Nor,' he said, 'have you got forty cents change to lend me for the tram?'

I looked in my purse and found the money. I held it out to him: he put out his hand, palm upwards, his face turned away towards the street. I dropped the coins into his hand and he made no acknowledgement. My insides performed a little dance of anger and sadness. No, no, said my resolution, the small voice of reason, he asked and you gave. You didn't have to give, and he didn't have to be grateful. Giving is not bartering. I handed him the ten dollar bills.

While the teller fiddled with my passbook, Javo wandered out on to the street. He tapped on the window and mouthed,

'Here comes my tram. See you.'

I nodded and waved. We were smiling at each other, our faces less than a foot apart, but there was a sheet of plate glass between us. I watched him walk away in his pink T shirt and overalls. I turned back to the counter, picked up my passbook, and walked out to meet Eve, sitting straddled on her bike waiting for me, half-stunned from a valium she had taken to help her stop smoking.

We pedalled off towards the city, to the art gallery. We walked around arm in arm.

'What'll we look at?' I asked.

'Oh, I dunno,' she replied. 'You just lead me round and show me things.'

So I did. I showed her my secret picture, *The French Window*, two women sitting at a circular table having a cup of tea; beside them a long window opens to let in a strip of bright garden, the hard lovely light of summer; in the middle of the lawn sticks up a polished brass tap, and on the verandah you can see half a deck chair.

'That's you,' remarked Eve.

I said, 'That's *us*.'

Sometimes I wished old age would hasten upon me.

In the street in Carlton I met Angela.

'Where's that junkie ex-lover of yours?' she asked, looking distracted. She was carrying a large exercise book.

'I don't know.'

'Well, you're more likely to see him than I am. Here's his call for the movie.' She scribbled the information on a piece of paper in her extravagant, unformed handwriting. I took it reluctantly, not knowing how to make it clear to her that I didn't expect to see him again before the time she wanted him. I rode away with Eve. We took the good, fast run along Rathdowne Street, playing at racing and rolling neck and neck, and parted at the corner of Richardson Street. As soon as we separated, the old ache sneaked back again. I came home to the empty house and rang Angela. I told her I didn't know where Javo was and would prefer not to have to go looking for him. She took the task away from me, and immediately the ache stopped.

I lay on my bed reading for most of the afternoon. I fell asleep. I woke up at 3.20 precisely and in that neutral moment between full sleep and full awareness my mind involuntarily conjured up a series of images: Javo and Claire standing facing each other, reaching out their arms and stepping forward and embracing each other tightly, her face pressed hard against his chest. The rapidity and vividness of these uncalled-for visions astonished me; and so did the fact that they did not bring back the ache. I lay there listening to the quiet falling of warm rain in the alley outside my window. Gracie pushed open my door and came in dripping and smiling, with a bag full of 'work' from school and her reader *Ronno the Clown*.

Half an hour later I heard Eve call out,

'Want a cup of tea, Gerald?'

I got up in my red underpants and wandered out to the kitchen. 'Is Gerald back?'

Eve nodded and pointed to the room with the TV in it. I pushed open the door and saw his long legs in stained white trousers sticking out from the couch. I was delighted to see him and went to hug him. Gracie sucked her thumb and watched us greet each other.

We drove to the Southern Cross for a drink and an escape from the house. He told me about his trip to the Prom with Lillian. I was very tense and defensive, and talked between clenched teeth about Lillian and what she could do with her opinions of my personality; but then I calmed down and told Gerald everything I could about Javo and the way I was feeling about him. He was attentive and kind, and listened patiently.

'And on top of everything else,' I said, getting into my stride and beginning to orate, 'I've got this thing in my ear which I think might be a *pimple*. Will you have a look later and tell me what it is?'

'I'll do anything you ask,' he replied.

I looked up sharply, thinking he was getting at me, but he was smiling at me with an open face; there was a layer of laughter behind everything he said. I relaxed.

I woke up before anyone else in the house. A dull, heavy morning, weighed down with yesterday's rain. I got up, shoved my feet into my sandals, walked quietly out to the kitchen, and noticed that the living room door was shut: this usually meant that Javo was asleep inside. My heart didn't even turn over. It ticked away as it should. I picked my way across our bomb-site of a back yard, past the gnawed, holey broccoli which Gerald swore would survive the cabbage moths, and into the dunny. For the time being, I'd lost the ache. I sat on the dunny, gazing bucolically out at the side wall of the garage, the bricks under the back wheels of the half-mended van, and the low wet thick sky. Small, non-specific visions of Claire and Javo in each other's arms flickered in the corners wherever I looked, but nothing registered on the pain metre. I was alive to the knowledge that they may have begun to love each other, that was all.

(*Gracie*: 'Three boys chased me in the yard and said they loved me. So' – demonstrating vicious punches to the solar plexus – 'I bashed them all up.')

Javo was not in the living room.

I took the kids to school and my washing to the laundromat. When I came home I got in the shower.

'Javaroo was here,' called Eve.

'Oh, yeah?' I was scrubbing my face and hair and talking to her through the louvre windows. 'Where'd he go?'

'To the dole office.'

'Did he shift his stuff out?' I jerked my head towards the living room. We grinned wryly at each other. Valium'd, she stood arms akimbo, one hand pointing the hose into a yellow plastic bucket.

'Nup. I think he was more like shifting it back in.' I laughed. She shrugged.

'I was thinking I'd get him to move it out. It makes it harder for me, the way he comes and goes.'

She nodded.

'But at the same time, I guess I don't want to let him see how much . . . *pain* . . . he can cause me.' The word came effortfully off my lips; afraid of exaggerating, of sounding melodramatic. Eve gazed at me, eyes dull with the drug but with a spark miles behind of knowing what I was talking about.

Gerald walked in the front door as I was on my way out with the shopping bag over my shoulder. Javo's calico bag was lying in the corner next to the front door. I gave it a casual poke with my foot.

'Bloody Javo,' I remarked without venom. 'Looks like he's still leaving his stuff lying round.'

Gerald instantly warmed to the subject. 'Yes! He came in this morning while you were out, and set up the ironing board, and stuff – I thought to myself, oh no! he's moving back in. I almost said something to him then.'

'What would you have said?'

'Oh, something about how you and I were having enough trouble living here with each other – and him being the third person was making it even *more* difficult, being here – and maybe he ought to go.'

I felt a rush of horror at the idea of him standing there and saying all that to Javo, like a husband protecting a wife who was battling with feelings too strong for her. I walked quickly away from him down the passage towards my room.

'Hey.' He said it uncertainly, on two notes, but with the un-ambiguous meaning: *stop*. I went on into my room. I stood in front of the mirror on the dressing table; I looked at myself helplessly. He followed me into the room.

'What do you think of that?' he asked.

'It's OK,' I replied in a neutral voice.

'But at least you could tell me what you *think* of it.' He was insisting. I picked up the eyedrops and squeezed them into my eyes, one after the other.

'It's up to you to say what you think. But . . . as long as you don't give the impression that what you say is the result of a conversation with *me*.' Ugh, the revulsion I felt at being spoken for, or at being thought to be spoken for.

'Oh, I wouldn't do *that*.'

I am not quite honest, not quite fair.

Dog Day

I sat in my room, weary and sore, feeling that familiar creeping sensation of being made use of by Javo ... how many times before? I wrote a card to tell him this: You are giving me a use, you can get your things out of my house, give a woman a break, mate. I rode my bike round to Napier Street where I supposed he might be. Claire's tape deck was playing loudly that Joni Mitchell song,

> 'And the song that he sang her
> to soothe her to sleep
> runs all through her circuits
> like a heartbeat ...'

which I had sung to myself early that hot morning a year ago after I'd worked all night on the junk movie and was walking home in white clothes across the crackling park towards my bed where I would find him waiting for me, a junkie, sick, needing me. I knocked on Claire's door, went in, saw his red and black shiny journal on the bed in the empty room. Unerring I went for it.

'In the bed of a new friend ...' and there it was, about how they were together, when they fucked. The last two lines were like a knife inserted neatly between my ribs:

' "Where am I?" I asked in my body.

"You're here," she said with her eyes.'

I deserve it, I deserve it, whined my guilt for snooping. I slipped the card I'd written into his book and sat down at the table to write a note to Claire. Four biros, one after another, refused to work for me. I sat there hopelessly staring out the window. Claire's dog ran in, recognised me and sprang on to my lap, and was followed into the room by Claire herself who was carrying a pink plastic bowl full of cut-up dog's meat. She saw me and stopped in the doorway with a look of uncertainty.

I said, 'Good day.'

'Hullo. How's things?'

'OK. A bit difficult.'

'I got your letter.'

'I got yours too. On the same day.' We gave the same painful laugh.

'We must have been thinking about each other at the same . . .'

I nodded. We were still looking at each other's eyes. I began to notice that a gigantic wall of some terrible emotion was swelling up inside me; it was being held back, barely, by a dull sense that this was not the place to let it go, lest I scare Claire out of her wits, give her cause to think that all of it was due to her new relationship with Javo, and make a scene which he might arrive to witness. Still, I sat there, dogged, mulish, unable to stand up and gracefully get myself out. I dropped my head on to my arms. There was a pause. Her hand touched the back of my hair, and began to stroke me tentatively. The dog crawled from my lap on to the table and offered her furry, trembling body for comfort. Claire stroked and stroked, and I grimly held back what I already knew was going to be a flood of tears if I let it. I butted my head against her thin hip, wanting to thank her for her gentleness. Finally I struggled to my feet.

'I'd better go. It'll be all right.'

My face must have looked terrible. She looked at me without speaking. Then she said, 'See you, Nora.' I nodded and ran out the door to my bike. Hank was at the gate, about to fix one of his endless cars. I managed to force out some normal-sounding words, and rode off down Napier Street.

I thought I would go and find a neutral bed in a neutral house and lie on it until the tears had finished: they'd already started to leak out and I could hardly see where I was going. No-one home at Bell Street, or at Brunswick Street, or at Percy Street. So I turned my bike round in St George's Road among the peak hour traffic and rode up to Rathdowne Street, which I had wanted to avoid for fear of running into Lillian. From the open front door I smelled a meal cooking. I dropped my bike and headed for the kitchen. Georgie was standing at the table, awkwardly pouring olive oil out of a baking dish into a yogurt jar. I saw his familiar fair head and big ungainly face turned towards me, and I thought,

'That's where I'm heading and I can only just make it that far.'

'Good day, Nor!' he said, looking shocked but ready for me. 'How are you doin'?'

'No good!' I wailed, knowing I was now in the place where I could let go. I ran up against his chest, he put his free arm round me, and out it came: tears simply poured off my face. He put down the dish and got both arms round me and I could at last let it rip.

'Come in my room, Nor,' he said, and led me back along the passageway into his front room with the blinds down against the traffic noise from Rathdowne Street. He brought me down next to him on the bed and held me tightly, and I wept and wept, amazed at the floods of tears that were leaking and running out of me. I turned over on to my back and began painfully to talk, while the tears ran and ran off the sides of my face, soaking the pillow, the way the water runs down the big glass panes at the gallery. Surely they couldn't keep coming, but they did, and I stammered out the story about Claire and Javo and the diary and Gerald and Lillian. He listened, clicking his tongue to show attentiveness and sympathy. All the while I talked, my eyes remained fixed on a cardboard box over his fireplace with big silver letters on it: F2, it read, thick enough to run a line with a textacolour between the black and the silver if one should wish to, in an idle moment.

Georgie went out to turn off the stove under what he was cooking. I was sitting up on the end of the bed, with tears still dripping off my chin, when Lillian came in. When she saw me her face changed. She hesitated for a second, then squatted down on the floor in front of me and put her arms round my shoulders. 'I can't stop crying,' I said, and went on letting the tears run. She made that 'oh, oh,' sound of wordless comfort which mothers utter. I thought, she is kind, how foolish of me to talk of hating her.

I'd been there an hour when I found I had stopped crying, and got up to go home. I was a bit afraid that Lillian might think I'd left because she'd come in, but I was so drained out and hollow that I couldn't make any further explanation. I looked at myself in the mirror and saw, to my surprise, that my eyes were neither red nor swollen. I got on my bike and rode home. I parked my bike on the verandah. Eve was calling the kids in for tea. Something in her glance and smile let me know that Javo was in the house. I came down the hall and there he was in my room, sitting at my table toiling over a note.

I looked at his big suntanned face and tousled hair. I came in and closed the door behind me, moved my bag off the low stool, and sat down. I could feel my cheeks hot, but I didn't care. I read his half-written note and took my courage in both hands and went at it like a bull at a gate.

He seemed upset, all his confusion thick in his face, angry at the tone I'd taken in the card I'd left for him at Claire's place.

'Giving you a use is the furthest thing from my mind!' he cried.

'It's – you don't need me like you needed me before. Now you only use my *things*.'

He stared at me.

'Remember that day in the bank? You just stuck out your *hand*, mate, and fuckin' took the *money*. You didn't even *look* at me.'

He smiled, shame-faced. 'I know. I'm insensitive sometimes. I do things like that because I'm guilty about always asking you for things.'

'But it's not just that you do things like that. It's other stuff too, that isn't your *fault*. Since you got off dope you're a different person. I guess I got used to you needing me to keep going . . . now I feel like I'm watching my kid grow up and take off – in a lot of ways it makes me really happy – do you understand what I'm saying? But it's so fucking painful! Sometimes I get the feeling you don't give a shit about me any more, now that you don't need me.'

'But Nor! How can you think that? Our relationship is *permanent*!'

I laughed. It almost felt like relief, a great rush of it.

'And Nor – what you read in the journal, about fucking with Claire –'

'Oh, it is *all right*!' I burst in. 'I really mean it – it is *all right* about you fucking with her!'

'No, it's not just that – but Nor, she fucks . . . with her

231

eyes shut.'

A pause.

'What does that mean?'

'It means –' he wrestled with the awkwardness of it –
'fucking just isn't so much *fun*.'

I thought in a flash of her reserved, full-mouthed face, how
beautiful she is and somehow pale and delicate; I thought of
his eyes gleaming with that fierce smile when I was coming;
and I understood in my bones that 'fun' was not what he
meant, that perhaps he wished to affirm to me that infinitely
deep and precise contact we made when we fucked, while not
belittling what he had found with Claire. My heart spread out
and escaped from its hard battlements.

'Maybe we ought to go out and get drunk, Nor,' he
suggested, lowering his tentative smile over his hands on
the table.

'Righto. Let's.'

We sat grinning at each other.

'I'd like to say I'd shout you, Nor,' he said; he stood up and
started going through his pockets. 'But I've only got about
five bucks.'

'That's OK. I've got enough for both of us.'

Out in the street the kids were playing kiss chasey. Gracie
ran up to say goodbye, in her long purple skirt. She was all
sweaty and tousled.

'Guess how many times the Roaster got caught!' she panted.
'About a *hundred*!'

I kissed her hot forehead and she ran off. Javo was waiting
for me between the tree and the fence. He dropped his arm
over my shoulder and the fear slithered off me and dropped
behind like a discarded skin.

We went to see *Dog Day Afternoon*. We laughed a lot and
exchanged glances. I couldn't get over how easy it had
become: instead of feeling like a half-drowned rat, bedraggled
and pathetic, as I'd expected, I found myself cheerful, quick to
laugh and talk, comfortable in his familiar company. We came
home on the tram.

In my room he was standing between my bed and the bookshelf on his very long legs. I looked up at him. I said,

'You could sleep in here if you liked. Or in the other room. I'd *like* you to sleep with me – but I just want to make it clear that it's cool if you don't. I wouldn't freak out if you didn't.'

Too many words; but he laughed, and said,

'I think I'll just go out and take a piss, Nor.'

He came back and undressed and got into bed beside me. He sniffed under his arm.

'Phew! I stink!'

We lay there side by side.

'I couldn't fuck, Nor,' he said.

'Neither could I.'

'I'm worn out, with all this.'

'Had enough shocks for one night, eh?'

'Yep. I'm really fucked.'

It crossed my mind: tomorrow night he'll probably be fucking with Claire again. This is the last time I'll sleep with him for a while: last chance. But I found I didn't care about anything else except the fact that we were lying together, skins bare, in a harmony we had had to fight to get through to. I put my arm round his back and my stomach against his bum: two spoons in a drawer.

'I wonder,' I remarked, thinking, in this exhaustion, of our parents, 'whether it's possible for people who get married and stay together for years to keep on liking fucking with each other.'

'I dunno. What do you reckon?'

'I doubt it. I was married for six years and I was sick of it by then.'

'Jessie's parents are still *in love* with each other; but I don't know if they fuck. I suppose they do,' he said.

'The longest time that fucking with one person stayed good, for me, was two and a half years.'

He laughed. 'We'll outlast the lot of 'em, Nor!' I lay there soaking up his warm skin. A long time later we fell asleep.

Gracie woke me at some unearthly hour and I staggered into her room and got into bed with her. She kicked mercilessly in her sleep, and I was too stunned with sleep myself to do anything about moving until the Roaster started yelling in some dream he was having. I decided not to go back to my own bed but to creep out to the living room where Javo used to sleep. I put an extra rug on the spare bed and sank into it, exhausted. It must have been nearly daylight when I was woken by someone crashing round in the kitchen. I knew it would be Gerald. I dragged myself out to the door and peered round it.

'What are you doing in *there*?' he asked in a slightly peeved tone. The last thing I needed was an argument. I blundered down to his room and crawled, stupefied, under his blankets. He hugged me till I fell asleep, comfortable but beyond anything else. It was 5.30 in the morning. At 7.30 the children woke up and the day began.

A Woman of My Age

Javo woke up hours after Cobby and I had rollicked round the market with the rucksacks and baskets. He was standing at the kitchen bench when I came in. We set off to the bank with his dole cheque. For a change he rode my bike and I walked along beside. At the bank, once again, the teller checked and double-checked my records: we were kept waiting for over ten minutes.

'They must think we look like crims,' I commented idly. 'This always happens here. I guess you do look a bit of a ratbag.'

'*Me*!' he cried with a laugh. 'It's *you*, mate, with that fuckin' crewcut you've got!'

We waited patiently for the money.

'When'll we go out to dinner, Nor?' said Javo.

'Whenever you like,' I said. 'But I'm going to Anglesea on Monday, so it'll have to be –'

I had meant to say 'sometime after that', but he jumped in and said,

'What about tomorrow night?'

'Yep, that'd be great,' I say with fine composure, beneath which I'm astounded at his pace. We agree on the restaurant. We walk out of the bank, folding our money and stashing it.

'Here comes my tram,' he shouts as it trundles out of the terminal. 'See you tomorrow night, about 7.30.'

'OK,' I say. He takes three steps towards the tramstop, then two back towards me, leans forward and thrusts out his lips for a kiss, eyes comically squeezed shut like a cartoon character. I get that run of insane laughter he provokes in me sometimes. I step forward and kiss him goodbye. He flashes me a grin and leaps off towards the middle of the road. I unchain my bike, wheel it around, cruise along on one pedal to the corner of Scotchmer Street, watch his gangly figure in blue denim stride across to the tram and disappear inside. See you, Javo. I am still smiling.

Gerald was sitting in the kitchen when I got home.

'I just had another weird night, that's all,' he explained. 'I have to get it through my thick skull that it might be a long time before you sleep with me again, and that you'll be sleeping with other people between now and then.'

I think of the warmth he gave me out of his body in the early hours of the morning, and get a small kick of pleasure at the thought of lying with him again in his hard, comfortable bed.

'How about we sleep together tonight, then?' I suggest.

We agree. He goes out. I hang out with the kids in the sunny kitchen, drawing and talking and listening to Skyhooks.

Later, while I was reading in my room, Hank came in and out of the house. I called out hullo when I heard his voice in the kitchen. He stuck his head round my door.

'Good day, Hank! How's it all going?'

'All the better for seein' you, Nor,' he gallantly replied, and went off grinning.

When I was serving up the dinner I tripped over Javo's calico bag and hurled it round the corner into the living room. I understood then why Hank had been around: all Javo's things had gone. Everything stopped, lurched, and started again with a regular beat.

'Javo has his film call tonight,' said Cobby.

I slept with Gerald, and surprised myself with the pleasure of it; but in the morning my disobedient mind was on the subject of Javo again, wondering if he would show up for dinner in the evening, wondering whether I was in any way a duty to him, if the excitement of touching new flesh and skin made our familiarity tiresome. But I was scoured out like an old saucepan, and the pain had gone, or become nothing to speak of.

The day was a hot one. At five o'clock I got home from the baths and found a note on my bed in Eve's writing:

'Nora – Javo called. He's at the beach – be here for dinner about 9-9.30.'

I said out loud to myself, 'I thought this might happen.' I put my bag down and went about the business of getting comfortable on a hot afternoon. Cobby came in and I showed her the note. We looked at each other in silence for a few seconds.

'Wanna come to the Kingston, then?' she said.

'Sure. I'm not going to sit round *waiting*.'

The anger took the pain away. See you round, *mate*.

Just the same, I threw the Ching. I got *Conflict*:

'Your only salvation lies in being so clear-headed and inwardly strong that you are ready to come to terms by meeting the opponent halfway ... You are sincere / and are being obstructed.'

Obstructed is right!

I went to the Kingston to hear Jo Jo Zep and danced till the floor was too packed for me to move, and then I danced on a chair. I went to a party, ate some sausage rolls with tomato sauce, drank a plastic glass of punch, came home, made myself a glass of Tia Maria and cream; fell into bed.

Javo, it appeared, had not been to my house. I guessed he was in love, for all his protestations to the contrary, and I was anaesthetised against this painful fact by the amount I'd drunk and the looseness of my bones from the dancing.

Next day I went to the baths again with the children and lay in the sun with Cobby's Berger paints cap on my head. It was a long, hot day. As it progressed, people we knew gathered in dribs and drabs at the kids' end of the pool, until we made up an encampment of thirty or forty people. At four o'clock I saw, from under the peak of my cap, Javo walk in. I turned my head away resolutely. I didn't know how I was going to behave towards him, and I didn't want to be the one to make the first move. I pretended not to have noticed him, and stepped into the water and sank in up to my neck.

'Hey, Nor.' I heard his voice. I looked round. He was sitting on the edge of the pool, behind me; he was wearing his bathers and had his sandals on; his feet were under water and he was wrestling with the ties of his sandals. I turned to face him.

'Good day.'

'I'm sorry about last night, Nor.'

'Oh yeah? What happened?' I asked, probably sounding cold. And feeling like a nailed-down box.

He looked at me with an odd, crooked smile.

'I've been racked with pain these last few days!' he said. I resisted the urge to make a crack about pain. I just looked at him, wondering if he was referring to an infected tooth he'd been complaining of for weeks, or some kind of emotional pain inflicted on him by the situation. I didn't know what expression crossed my face. I said,

'Have you?'

I looked at him a bit longer. I saw that his face had somehow darkened, lost its glow, become opaque again. I did not know the reason, and saw no way in which I might enquire after it. No more conversation seemed forthcoming, so I waded off. I felt unsatisfied.

Ten minutes later I encountered him again in the middle of the crowded pool. I called out to him. He turned round, up to his shoulders in the water.

'Look, Javo,' I said. 'I'd rather that . . . if you didn't feel like keeping an arrangement . . . it'd be better if you didn't make it in the first place.' I sounded so blunt. All I wanted to do was state my mind. His face clouded, he turned his head stiffly from side to side, as he did when he felt himself attacked.

'I *told* you,' he said angrily, 'there were other circumstances. We didn't get back from the beach until eleven o'clock – there were four other people whose wishes had to be taken into account.'

It rose to my lips to point out in a teacherish tone that if he'd

237

known he had to be back by seven, he shouldn't have gone (Hank had told me they hadn't even left Melbourne till five); but I heard myself arguing the unarguable, and disliked the prospect; so I turned and swam away before I had time to open my mouth. I climbed out of the water and wandered back to the crowd; get out, get out, came the sensible message, loud and clear. I packed up my things and slung my bag over my shoulder. I'd taken two steps when Lou put his hand on my arm and said,

'Hey, Nora! You're not leaving, are you?'

'Yep. I am not very comfortable here.'

'Come up the other end of the pool,' he said. 'I wanted to have a word with you.'

'OK.' I dumped my bag and sandals and walked up the hot concrete to the big steps. As we walked I gave him a quick account of what had been going on.

'But you're absolutely number one to Javo!' he protested. 'He's always saying that. And you are to me, too.'

Cold comfort.

'You've got to see it from his point of view,' Lou went on, predictably enough. 'He's got to see what it's like, living without you.'

Lou was right about that. I stared at a small, pale-green bobble which was hanging from his ear-ring and moved against his fine, unshaven jaw as he spoke. He seemed faintly agitated by what I'd been saying, and it struck me that he'd taken me aside in order to find out what my attitude was towards *him*. And this turned out to be the case.

'I've been wondering,' he hazarded, 'how you were feeling about spending some time with *me*.'

'Good!' I replied brightly. I thought, 'I must always seem maddeningly vague when he brings up this subject.' 'I'd like that,' I added encouragingly. He gave a small, uncertain smile, and slid his green eyes sideways to examine my face. Which was probably dead-pan.

'Of course,' he said, 'now we've moved over to Prahran, things will be a bit different.'

'But you'll be getting a phone, won't you?'

'Yeah.' I privately thought that not one of his household,

238

hippies that they were, would be efficient enough to get a telephone organised. Lou laid a bony arm across my shoulders and glanced sidelong at me again.

'Nora, you get sexier the older you get!' he declared, apparently meaning it. I burst out laughing. 'No – I know that sounds clumsy,' he protested, laughing too, 'but I mean it! It's true!'

I looked down at the sparkling, chemical-blue water with its herd of jostling bodies. I thought, yes, down here I am older and sexier and in some untouchable way freer than I am anywhere else. The summer was coming to an end and with it a unique and inexplicable sense of perfectness. I stood up and said,

'I have to split now, Lou. Got to go out at five o'clock. I guess I'll see you when I come back from Anglesea.'

'OK,' he said, still looking faintly dissatisfied as if there were something left unsaid. He went down the steps behind me. I went to kiss him goodbye but the peak of my cap knocked him gently on the forehead and kept our faces apart. He dived in and I walked back to the gypsy encampment at the shallow end. As I approached it, I saw Javo sitting disconsolately on the brick edge of the plantation, elbows on knees, face downturned, in a posture of weariness and disillusionment. Funny: my heart just simply softened, all the anger ran away. I went up to him and sat beside him on the hot bricks. He sensed straight away the ending of hostilities. He turned to me with a small smile and put his arm round me. At that moment I noticed Claire: she had removed herself from the big group and was lying on her towel on the top level of the concrete steps, reading under her straw hat. I understood without a word being spoken that everything would not be easy between them.

Javo said, 'I've had a terrible time today, Nor!'
We laughed.
'What happened?'
'It'd take too long to explain – hours.'
'Oh, come on.'
'Nah – I'll tell you about it next time we see each other.'
'It'll never happen. You'll promise to come round and then

'not show,' I said without venom. He shook his head. I gave up the pursuit of knowledge. We sat in silence for a moment. I got up and said,

'I'm going home. I'm going out later.'

'Who with?'

'Georgie.'

'Georgie the Pick, eh?' He smiled at me, crooked.

'Yep. That's the one.' I picked up my bag again. 'I'm going up to say hullo to Claire.' I sprang up the hot steps towards where she was lying on her own. She either didn't see me coming, or pretended not to. I was dancing from foot to foot on the burning concrete.

'Good day!' I said. She looked up. She was reading a book I had lent her a couple of days before she had started fucking with Javo: *A Woman of My Age* by Nina Bawden. She squinted at me in the sunlight.

'Oh – hullo.'

I burst out: 'Why don't you come and see me?'

She looked puzzled and slightly shocked. 'You mean – at your house?'

'Yeah. Come around and see me.'

I wanted to say, 'Why *haven't* you been to see me? We were friends before all this, weren't we? Why don't you come? Why haven't you come?' But I just looked at her face, wrinkled up against the sun, her tinted glasses down over the bridge of her nose, and waited for her reply.

'All right,' she said, still uncertain. I took the wheel:

'That's a good novel, isn't it.'

'Yes,' she said, probably relieved to be off contentious ground. 'Jack took it away before I could read it; when he brought it back to me he said, "You've got to read this – it's terrific".'

The concrete was too hot for me to stand still. I danced from foot to foot. 'Gotta go – can't stand the *heat*! See you later.'

'See you.'

I skipped down again. I went back to where Javo was sitting. 'I'll see you later, mate.'

He looked up at me, and surprised me by putting his hands on my bare skin, at the waist. He lifted up his face and we kissed goodbye. I walked away.

I picked my way between the reclining bodies of my friends.
As I passed Rita, she turned up to me and asked in a stage
whisper,

'*What'd he say?*'

I shivered with embarrassment.

'I don't want to talk about it. See you.'

I was comforted by Javo's gentleness; but I knew the
gentleness of the departing to the one left behind. Still plenty
of hard times coming.

Let It Be What It Is

I dragged myself off to Angelsea to try and get sane again. In
the car on the way down the highway we smoked a joint which
gave me a very bad twenty minutes, fear and sickness. I was
too afraid to speak. I saved myself by poking a hole in the top
of an orange and sucking the juice.

No-one talked much, in the ugly house. I had forgotten the
endless peaceful hours, unpunctuated by duty, of life without
children. Selena played her guitar quietly; I slept on my bed
all afternoon, and felt my hard shell start to soften.
Convalescence.

'It's happened so quickly this time!' said Selena. 'Usually it
takes me days to slow down.'

I went to the beach by myself in the late afternoon. I rolled
up my jeans and stood on the wet sand where the waves barely
reached. I stared at my brown feet. I just stood there. I only
stayed on the beach for about twenty minutes. Then I climbed
back up the ramp and walked very slowly back to the house.

The waves hissed all night.

I was balancing myself out nicely, there, in the quietness.
When the existence of Javo, and of Gerald, and of Gracie

crossed my mind, it had no edge or sharpness. It was merely a series of blurred, dull facts. Whenever I woke from dozing, I found the sky as grey, the surf noise as steady, the house as peaceful as they had been when I lay down hours before. I had no idea what the others were doing, nor what time it was. Selena began to shift things in the kitchen, preparing to cook a meal. I knew when she passed my door because I heard the brushing of her long skirt, the faintest clack of the silver bangles she wore. I picked up *Washington Square*. By the time I looked up from it, I had read half of it.

I had a bath. I looked at myself in the mirror. I thought that my body was carrying too much flesh. In the bath I lay looking at my brown skin with its white summer stripes. My belly looked soft. I wished for it to be hard, as it had once been. I heard as if in a trance the merry voices in the kitchen: the others were exchanging stories of long-ago school experiences.

I came and lay on the bed between courses of the meal: I wanted very eagerly to know whether Catherine Sloper would marry Morris Townsend. I was lying on my stomach, reading fast and absorbed, when Selena came in.

'Hey, Nora. Why don't you stay a bit longer?' She was holding a cigarette between her fingers. 'It's good here; and you need a rest.'

'I might stay,' I said, looking at her gentle face and the way her hair straggled at her round cheeks. 'I'll ring up Eve tomorrow.'

We smiled at each other and she went out of the room. I wondered if I seemed very unhappy. No-one was pressuring me. I was alone a lot, and not engaged in conversation. But when I looked in the mirror, I saw a preoccupied face, a worried head, a body out of sync with the mind. When I thought of staying on, small splinters of irrational fear prickled in my mind: Gracie will die, she will get sick and die without me. Also, disconnected fragments tumbled about: if I keep out of his way for longer than he is expecting, Javo will be surprised, and miss me. I remembered longing for his cracked voice, last winter when I went to my parents' house: 'It's me, Javo. Come back.'

I realised I had a stream of thoughts about him which ran for the most part below conscious level. I noticed jets spurting up from this stream: comparisons with other relationships I knew of which had weathered massive changes and shifts of balance; small crumbs of hope that he would find he missed the familiarity of my company, or that his gestures of comfort had meant more than a gentle goodbye. I grieved for these hopes, and their hopelessness.

I slept, and slept. When I was not asleep I was reading. I finished the book, and rather than lie there doing nothing but stare in front of me at the ugly fan-shaped light on the bare white wall, I instantly took up *To the Lighthouse* and plunged into it. I read half a page and put it down and stared at the light on the wall. In some indescribable way, staring at it was very peaceful. After a little while I went on reading, and soon I fell asleep. The others were out in the kitchen. Once I woke up to an extra loud burst of laughter. I lay in my blanket half-stunned, wondering how it was that I'd lost all my customary social urges. For a few moments I felt a small ache of loneliness. I wished for Claire to be with me as we had been before all this went wrong. I thought about her reticent, pale face. But she wasn't there and she wasn't coming, so I shifted in the bed and fell asleep again.

In the morning I rolled over and opened my eyes. Selena was a hump in the other bed; along the window sill she had laid her rings and ear-rings in a row. The sky was still cloudy, but the sun was fighting through that clear line at horizon level, laying a strip of light, uninterfered with, across the tops of the ti-tree scrub. Right across the low, determined ti-tree I could see a line of marram grass, vaguely shadowed within the curve of the dunes, and at its roots that cold, greyish-yellow sand, so familiar to my feet from my earliest childhood that in my imagination I felt it then – cold, cold, silken, both firm and yielding.

I walked on my own round the beach to the river mouth and along the road to the township. I looked curiously at my strong brown calves with their familiar scars, and newer marks from this year's summer. I tied my blue jumper round my waist and attached my sandals to its sleeves to leave my hands free. I walked along in the difficult sand, squinting under my cap peak. It was the first time I had felt cheerful in days. I sang to myself. I thought about the night Javo and Martin and Gracie and I had arrived at Disaster Bay. I picked my way across pointed rocks, hearing my own panting and exclamations as I toiled. I glanced down at my shoulders which the march flies were busily attacking, and which were covered with brown sunspots of various sizes. I walked steadily. I did not get tired.

In the town I rang Eve.

'I am going to stay one more night. Is that all right?'

'It sure is. Grace is terrific when you aren't here.' I would have liked to ask if anyone had seen Javo, but it didn't seem appropriate, and I hung up with my question unanswered.

On the beach I lay naked in the meagre sunlight with Selena, peering out comfortably under the peak of my cap, and talked about Javo. I laughed wholeheartedly about it for the first time.

That evening Cobby arrived in Claire's car. She brought no news of Javo. Finally I asked,

'Have you seen Javo?'

'No – or not to speak to, anyway.'

'Is he spending all his time at Claire's?'

'I guess so.'

A funny kind of pain, dull, not sharp, spread through my body as if by way of the bloodstreams. Doesn't matter, doesn't matter.

In the middle of the night I woke up and went outside to piss on the grass. The moon hung low in the sky above the quiet hedge. I squatted down at the corner of the house and let my piss run down the bare, grey earth in a trickle. I stood up, wiped myself with my hand, and rinsed my hand under the tap. I stood still, staring at the moon and feeling the soft air on my skin. Claire's car sat there behind me, a big silent bulk in the dark. I thought again of her and Javo, and instead of that pain came the thought,

'Well . . . so be it. Let it be what it is.'

I went back up the steps and crept under the woollen blanket.

In the morning the sky was clear. The sunlight lay on the scrubby grass in long, pinkish-gold strips. The absent-minded carolling of magpies dropped out of the pine trees half a mile away.

Time to go home.